Opening up a world of magic and adventure, *The Library of the Dead* by T. L. Huchu is the first book in the Edinburgh Nights series.

Ropa dropped out of school to become a ghostalker—and she now speaks to Edinburgh's dead, carrying messages to those they left behind. A girl's gotta earn a living, and it seems harmless enough. Until, that is, the dead begin to whisper that someone's bewitching children—leaving them husks, empty of joy and life. It's in Ropa's city, so she feels honor-bound to investigate. But what she learns will change her world.

   She'll dice with death (not part of her life plan), discovering an occult library and a taste for hidden magic. She'll also experience dark times. For Edinburgh hides a wealth of secrets, and Ropa's gonna hunt them all down.

BY T. L. HUCHU

Edinburgh Nights series
The Library of the Dead
Our Lady of Mysterious Ailments

T. L. Huchu

The
LIBRARY
of the
DEAD

Edinburgh Nights Book One

TOR

A TOM DOHERTY ASSOCIATES BOOK

NEW YORK

THE LIBRARY OF THE DEAD

Copyright © 2021 by T. L. Huchu

All rights reserved.

A Tor Book
Published by Tom Doherty Associates
120 Broadway
New York, NY 10271

www.tor-forge.com

Tor® is a registered trademark of Macmillan Publishing Group, LLC.

The Library of Congress has cataloged the first U.S. edition as follows:

Names: Huchu, T. L., author.
Title: The library of the dead / T. L. Huchu.
Description: First U.S. edition. | New York, NY : Tor, 2021. | Series:
    Edinburgh nights ; book one
Identifiers: LCCN 2020055857 (print) | LCCN 2020055858 (ebook) |
    ISBN 9781250767769 (hardcover) | ISBN 9781250767776 (ebook)
Subjects: CYAC: Supernatural—Fiction. | Ghosts—Fiction. | Magic—
    Fiction. | Fantasy. | Edinburgh (Scotland)—Fiction.
Classification: LCC PZ7.1.H766 Li 2021 (print) | LCC PZ7.1.H766 (ebook) |
    DDC [Fic]—dc23
LC record available at https://lccn.loc.gov/2020055857
LC ebook record available at https://lccn.loc.gov/2020055858

ISBN 978-1-250-76778-3 (trade paperback)

Our books may be purchased in bulk for promotional, educational, or business use. Please contact your local bookseller or the Macmillan Corporate and Premium Sales Department at 1-800-221-7945, extension 5442, or by email at MacmillanSpecialMarkets@macmillan.com.

First published in Great Britain by Tor, an imprint of Pan Macmillan

First Tor Paperback Edition: 2022

Printed in the United States of America

0 9 8 7 6 5 4

I.M.
JOSEPHINE HUCHU
1950 – 2017

I

I'm really not supposed to be doing this, but a girl's gotta get paid. So, here we go.

It's been a long day. Super long. Hiked up the B702, all the way up to Liberton, doing my deliveries, and swung back round the bypass, last stop Lanark Road in Juniper Green. I make that a fifteen-mile trip around Edinburgh, give or take a few. My quads ache and I've got chunks of hot lead for feet. Feels good to sit my butt on this sofa and veg for a mo.

'Would you like a cup of tea?' Mrs McGregor asks.

'Only if you're offering biscuits,' I say. Always squeeze 'em for more, and I'm famished like them Oxfam poster kids.

'How do you take it?' she says.

'White, five sugars and cream on top.'

Mrs McGregor raises her eyebrows, opens her mouth, thinks better of it and shuts it again. They need me.

'I'll help you, dear,' Mr McGregor says in a rich, gravelly voice. He gets up and the two of them head off to the kitchen.

I'm taking liberties 'cause them two are so minted it's enough to set off my allergies. Look at the size of this place. Even have to take off my coat, it's sweltering inside. This is one of them nineteenth-century stone cottages, so sturdy it could last another three hundred years. Built when land was aplenty, everything's on the same level, save for the loft conversion. The McGregors are really proud of this place; soon as I got here they were yakking on about it. Said, 'Did you know Thomas Carlyle and his young wife Jane Welsh stayed in this exact cottage after they got married?' I shook my head even though I'd read the wee blue plaque on the front gate. Now, I'm not one to judge, but if I got married, I'd want to honeymoon somewhere exotic, like Ireland or some such place, not flipping Juniper Green. Each to their own and all that. 'You do know who Thomas Carlyle is, right?' they'd said in unison. I pretended not to know and let them yak on. Must be something they do to whoever winds up on their doorstep.

I'm no buff or nothing, but I like history as much as the next lass, and so I do know Carlyle was a historian who wrote this and that back in the day. He was into heroes and great men, had something to say about how they influenced the course of human history. Always just men, never boys and girls, and seldom women. I didn't tell the McGregors that I found his wife Jane more interesting.

There's a framed print of Carlyle above the fireplace directly in front of me. He's an older dude, greying hair and well-kept beard. Rests his head tilted slightly left on his hand, index finger running up to his temple, thumb tucked under his jaw and the other three folded in. Posed to make him look like a thinker, brow lightly creased, but there's also a dreamy look in his eyes that's kinda endearing. I swear the old historian comes out like he's on a telephone to the future. Don't know if he had our shabby present in mind, though.

His was a time of voyages. A time of weird and wonderf
new things flowing in from the far-flung outposts of the
British Empire via the Port of Leith – now all we get is
flotsam washing back. They believed in progress in them
days, high-minded ideas and all that jazz. Now we can't even
look past tomorrow. The historian swallowed up by history
. . . ain't time a right bastard?

I sink back into the cushions on the couple's large sofa.
The room's stuck in some past era along with the Carlyles.
Light shade of terracotta paint on the walls, antique chest
serving as the coffee table, copper bucket with tongs by the
fireplace, and an old-style rocking chair in one corner. The
carpet under my feet looks Persian but could be from
anywhere. It's well worn; the threadbare look gives it that aged
feel this room's going for.

It's dark outside the massive windows. The light from this
room bathes the hedges outside in an ominous shade. The
sound of the McGregors pottering in the kitchen drifts out to
me. Mrs McGregor is a small woman and her husband is
more long than tall – it's like a Great Dane married a Cockapoo.

'I'm not sure about this,' Mrs McGregor says. They're
trying to be quiet. Failing miserably. I hear the sound of something metallic hitting the counter.

'She does look a bit young,' Mr McGregor replies. 'What is
she, twelve? She's got green dreadlocks and black lipstick, for
Christ's sake. What is that even – goth, punk, I don't know.'

'I was told we were getting an older woman with experience. I think we should—'

'Guys, I can hear you,' I call out. 'I'm right here, you know?'

gs go quiet in the kitchen. Very quiet. Only the noise boiling kettle filters through. I rub my hands on my ghs. Shouldn't have said anything, but I'm tired and hungry nd that makes me irritable. And I'm not messing about. I've come to do a job – I need the money.

The McGregors come back in with red faces and my tea. There's a slight tremor in Mrs McGregor's hands as she places the tray down in front of me. I grab a scone, bite it and feel better right away. Tasty, must be home-made, and just the right spread of butter on it too.

'I know you called for my grandma, but she don't do house calls no more. I'll take care of it for you,' I say, chow in my mouth. I wash it down with tea from a proper china cup. I'm even tempted to hold a pinkie out.

'We didn't mean to . . . It's just that we've had some people try to take care of this problem before and it hasn't exactly worked out as planned,' Mrs McGregor says.

'Who did you call in?'

'The bishop himself – Episcopalian.'

I get it right away. Those guys come in guns blazing, Jesus the shit out of everything, maybe even spray a bit of holy water here and there, chant some jazz from the *Book of Occasional Services* and shoot off. It's hit or miss with them: sometimes it works, sometimes it don't. But if there's something strange in your postcode, who you gonna call?

'These scones are exceptional,' I say. We may be here a while.

⊙ ⊙ ⊙

I've asked the McGregors to turn off the lights around the house, and the only illumination comes from a lamp in the corner of the room. The light creeps up the walls, painting a half-moon on the ceiling, and everything else is in the shadow of the lampshade. The telly's off, and in the silence we can hear each other breathe. The couple hold hands, sitting in the two-seater nearest the window, so I'm on my own on the big sofa.

Been here three hours already. It's not yet the witching hour, but I feel a slight chill in the air, the subtle drop of temperature that makes me reach for my coat, until I remember myself.

'How much longer?' Mr McGregor asks in a whisper.

I hold up my hand, stop him from speaking. He might as well be asking about the length of a piece of string. In any case, breaking the silence will only ruin things. Already asked them both to be good little church mice.

The chill in the still air hits them. Condensation vapour comes out of their mouths. They move closer to one another, the Mr throwing an arm around the Mrs. The little hairs on my arms rise, and goosepimples prick up all over my skin.

The picture of Thomas Carlyle clacks against the wall. The noise is awful in the silence. I sit up, lean forward and put my elbows on my knees, clasping my hands together. The lamplight flickers. The flowers on the mantelpiece rustle, shedding fresh petals onto the floor. A creaking noise comes from the wood beams in the ceiling. Something sickening wafts through the air, less a scent – it's a feeling of the forbidden, of sin, decadence, the smashing of a taboo that leaves an open wound on the soul of the world. The tongs strike the copper bucket, ringing out like a Chinese gong.

Mr McGregor makes a fist and bites down on his knuckles. Something turns the doorknob and a squeak escapes Mrs McGregor's throat. The door opens and shuts with a bang. It opens again and shuts. Opens. Shuts. The bucket. Picture. A statuette falls to the floor.

'God help us,' Mr McGregor wails, and crosses himself – left shoulder, then right.

Curtains fluttering, the locked windows rattling, commotion and chaos, small objects flung through the air. An ethereal grey figure rushing hither and thither in the dimness, knocking furniture over. This must be an old spectre for it to have the power to so touch the material world. I watch as it throws the door open again.

'Are you done?' I say, looking at the abhorrent apparition.

It looks back at me, all dark eyes, with an eerie tunnel running through its face in place of a mouth. It screams, a horrible squeal like a slow cut throat in a slaughterhouse. A wind rises in the room with its squeal, and it rushes towards me, mouth wide open from floor to chin as though it would eat me. The pages of a magazine on the coffee table flip open as the spectre bears down and stops right in front of my face with a terrible howl.

'I said, are you done, sir?' I reach for my backpack and stand up. 'This is quite the racket you're making here.'

It replies, screaming vile, broken sounds, an anguished cry of rage. Its approximation of a face is coated with grey smears of soil. And a scar runs across its throat, wide open like a second pair of lips. Old phantoms can be terrible to behold and this one's no exception. I study its form as I get the mbira from my backpack. It's an ancient musical instrument about the size of a small laptop. Mine's a simple one, without any adornments, just metal keys on a wooden block – thick like a heavy-duty chopping board. The McGregors are huddled together still, watching me. They can't see what I see, but the racket's stopped. The mbira's solid in my hands, the keys hard under my thumbs. I play a slow tune, 'Gavakava', something to bring the tempo right down, soothe tempers and ease the mood. I'm not here looking for a fight.

'Clap your hands to the beat,' I say to the couple. Then I turn back to the ghoul. 'We can do this the easy way or the hard way. It's up to you.'

It shrieks again, makes to threaten me, and I up my tempo, driving it back to the wall with a furious melody and pinning it there. I alter the harmonics of my music to capture the tether holding it to this world. The ghost howls in pain and I ease the beat back to my original slow melody. I have Authority here, and it gets the message. After years of haunting these grounds, it's felt the roots that keep it here cut out from underneath it. I'm basically removing a tree stump and that can be a bit tricksy, even with all the right tools. It shrinks before me into something small and sobs like a child.

'You're not supposed to be here. I don't know what unfinished business you have, but this is your last night on this plane. I'll give you two choices: you can either make a small request – one within reason – and leave of your own volition, never to come back. Or I cast you out to the Other Place. It's all the same to me. Speak now.'

There are many realms beyond our own, and the dead roam or rest there, depending on their kink. Ghosts with unfinished business stick in a realm glued to our world. But the Other Place is a one-way street – banish one *there* and they can never come back. The brochure for it promises the gnashing of teeth and other unsavoury stuff too, so the mere mention of it shows I'm dead serious.

It raises itself up from the corner where it's crouched, and I see at last the face of a young man, barely twenty. His fate was sealed by cutthroats years before this house was even built. And he was buried in a shallow grave in the field that eventually became the grounds of this place. Through its two mouths, one natural, the other made by a sharp blade, I hear his story and bear witness to an injustice that had refused to be buried by earth and time.

II

There's a body – can't even call it that now, a skeleton more like – under the crab apple tree at the bottom of the garden. It's lain there for centuries, rotting, turned by worm and wet as the roots of the tree tangled themselves round it. His name was Andrew Turnbull, and he lived, loved, lied, then died before his time.

I've seen enough to know we all die before our time, even if we live to a hundred and one. Keeps me in a job.

'Is it gone?' Mrs McGregor asks nervously.

'The bargain is you get Andrew's skeleton exhumed and reinterred on consecrated ground, and you do a service in his memory,' I reply, putting my coat on. 'A Presbyterian ceremony. He was a true Protestant, so none of that Episcopalian papish stuff.'

There's something like relief in their nodding. A bit of fear too. I guess anyone would be a little spooked if they had skeletons in their garden. Those are scarier than the ones in the closet. But, when all is said and done, my favourite part is the ker-ching of my fee. I finish buttoning up my coat, a surplus Germany army issue with the *Schwarz-Rot-Gold* on either arm.

'There's the small matter of payment,' I say.

'Yes, of course,' Mrs McGregor replies.

'Would you like a receipt?'

'If you please.'

I take the ducats she proffers in crisp notes. Twenty of them makes a princeling. Get that warm, fuzzy feeling lining my pockets with that. Don't normally make this much – then again, don't normally do this kind of thing. The day job's much more mundane. I get my receipt book and pen from my breast pocket. Scribble out 'special services'. Can't say what I've really done 'cause my licence to practise would be revoked if it got out. I hand it over to Mrs McGregor.

The couple follow me to the door, the three of us crowding the hall. I turn round and shake both their hands.

'Goodnight, folks,' I say. And I can't resist one last shot: 'Just so you know, I'm nearly fifteen.'

My birthday's not for another seven months, but I'm sure that sounds better than fourteen. Same thing really, it's not what you say but how you say it. Now, I just wanna get home, kick back and chill. Never linger after the job's done. The customers ain't my friends; I learnt that the hard way. I sling the satchel on my back and make for the streets.

Got a spring in my step back on Lanark Road. Can't feel no stress with dosh in my pocket. It's late and the streets are deserted save for two horses tied to the fence of the parish church nearby. Nice neighbourhood this. Low stone walls and hedges lining my route up towards the bypass. It's crazy dark 'cause the street lights are kaput, but the folks out here

THE LIBRARY OF THE DEAD

can afford a bit of solar power, so lamps glow through the windows.

I take out my phone, punch in the pod app and resume listening to my lecture. Only stick in one earphone, in my left ear. You don't wanna be so immersed that you forget what's around you. That's why I don't do headphones – sure way to get jacked like a sap. I like my podcasts and audiobooks: usually listen to history, science, true crime, lectures, all sorts of random stuff. I walk around all day and the way I see it, if I'm walking and learning then I'm doubling time. Easily turns a twenty-four-hour day into thirty-two 'cause I've spliced the other eight like two-ply toilet paper and got a bogof in the bargain. Just now, I'm listening to Arthur Herman's book on the Scottish Enlightenment.

I hear loud, confident footsteps behind me and remove my earphone.

Put my right hand on the dagger by my waist. I have to control my breathing. Once you start panicking, you stop thinking, and you've lost the fight already. Anyone tries anything tonight, I ain't screaming, I'm slicing.

'You there, stop,' a man calls from behind.

I pick up my pace.

'Police, dumbass. You either stop now, or we release the hound. Your choice.'

Bugger. Son of a . . . I stop. Turn back to face the harsh flashlight. I see two silhouettes and a mutt rearing on its hind legs. Pigs, man, pigs. Old fellas say they used to drive around back in the day. Didn't bother nobody. Once they got rid of the cars and these guys started walking the beat and riding horses, all hell broke loose. Best to let go of my dagger in case it gives them the wrong, well, the right idea.

'I'm sorry, officer. I didn't realize,' I call out.

They stroll over like they've got all the time in the world. One of them's whistling the theme track of *The Good, The Bad and The Ugly*. Puts the fear of all known and forgotten deities in me.

'What you think, Johnson?'

'Wilfully ignoring the lawful instructions of a police officer, evading arrest, breach of the king's peace.'

'Come on, it's not like that at all,' I say.

The dog lets out a menacing growl. I shudder. My hand instinctively moves back towards my dagger and I have to consciously stop it. Have to remind myself who these guys are and what they can do. The one called Johnson's six five, built like a brick shithouse, while the other one's a middle-aged guy with a walrus moustache. They walk with their legs spread apart, hi-vis jackets bright.

'Are these serious offences, Johnson?'

'I'm afraid so. Juvie's full up, so we won't have no choice but to throw her in with the big boys. Might be a few months before she gets in front of the sheriff with the system clogged up as it is.'

'That would be a mighty pity,' the cop holding the leash says.

'Nothing we can do. Law's the law,' PC Johnson replies.

'Guys, officers, sir, I didn't mean to . . .'

'Is she threatening a police officer, Johnson?'

'I believe she is.'

'I'm fearing for my life right now,' says the cop, his free hand resting on his holster.

They don't even bother to play good cop, bad cop these days, 'cause there's only one type of cop left.

The light's hurting my eyes. I raise my hands in front of me, then slowly reach into my pocket. I take out the money in there and hold it in the open palm of my hand. That's everything on me. Not hiding any. You don't wanna look like you're holding out on these guys, because if they find out, you're entering a world of pain.

PC Johnson comes over. There's static from his radio, and an inaudible voice talks for a bit before quietening down again. 'That's too much for a waif like you to be carrying around this time of night,' he says, scooping up my cash. 'Don't worry, I'll look after it for you.' I don't make eye contact, stare at his black boots, not his face.

He drops two mini-pennies back in my palm.

'The weak are meat . . . Get your arse home, kid. It's past your bedtime.'

'Thank you, sir,' I mumble and back away. The dog's pacing, straining against its leash. I turn and walk away. Just my luck this had to happen on the one day I actually make good money. Damn it to hell, I should have gone the other way.

III

They say fools and their money are soon parted, but goddamn. I really should have gone the other way. Round the B-road, through Wester Hailes and back out again. Dumb move. But I'm not psychic – I couldn't have known this would happen today of all days. It's like that song from the olden days about the old guy who won the lottery and died the next day. Flies in your bubbly and all that. I pinch my nose and frown.

At least I didn't get my arses kicked by the bobbies too, but I am so, so screwed.

I guess I'm a bit shook, been a while since Johnny Law's hit me with a shakedown. Nearly home now. Tar's cracked into a jigsaw puzzle on the bypass. Weeds have invaded it and grow proud in the fault lines. Been told by old fellas that this ring road used to have traffic jams miles long. Maybe that's true, but it's dead now.

Bits of metal poke up from where they had the middle barricade. Most of it was stripped for scrap ages ago. Yep, I used to be in that racket too a few years back. Now it's done, the hustle's moved on.

A light grey figure appears in front of me, so fragile, a hint of mist against the grim night.

Normally I wouldn't do business out on the street like this. But it's dark and deserted, my brain's scrambled, and I'm chasing the cash I've just lost, so I stop and take out my mbira from my backpack. This one's a new ghost. Probably far from its cemetery. It flickers like an old light bulb, trying to hold itself in this realm. Each micro-moment it gets sucked back to the land of the dead and comes back, it reappears in a slightly different position. Can't be long dead if it hasn't mastered how to anchor in this plane.

'Hang on, I've got you,' I say, warming up my instrument.

'Booga-wooga-wooga,' it replies.

Give me strength. I can't understand ghosts without the right music to unscramble their voices into words. All I get is gibberish until I fix on the right tune. But before we start, I have to give it the kauderwelsch: the terms and conditions. It's a legal requirement.

'Okay, I can deliver a message from you to anyone you want within the city limits, although at the moment I'm not doing the town centre, sorry. Terms and conditions – there's a three-tier charge for this service, banded in a low flat fee, a middle flat fee, and a high flat fee, plus twenty percent VAT. The band you fall into depends on the length, complexity and content of the message. If you cannot pay the bill, the fee will be reverse-charged to the recipient with a small surcharge. Please note: this service does not transmit vulgar, obscene, criminal or otherwise objectionable messages, but a fee may still be incurred if we decide to pass on a redacted version of the message. Do you understand?'

'Booga.'

'I'll take that as a yes.'

I thumb a few notes on the mbira, trying to figure out the right frequency for this particular spectre. She has a proto-face, something puffy for cheeks and two dim zones where the eyes should be. New deados go through phases. The hazy cloud thing first, then they work out to a humanoid figure. After quite a bit of practice they can even appear clothed or take on other forms. The guys who are dressed have usually been around for a while. Don't often get messages from them because they're less likely to have living relatives you can bill.

Me personally, I find the whole haunting business a bit pathetic. Like, if I died, when I die, I ain't never coming back to this shitshow. That'll be me done. Finito. I'd rather do other things with my afterlife. No way I'm coming back from the everyThere like some loser. It's your first stop when you die – a grim, grey place. Call it Hades Hotel, a sort of budget under-world linked to our own. But there's so much more beyond the everyThere . . . planes of light and music, mystical shit waiting to be discovered. However, once a ghost moves on from the everyThere, it loses its connection to our world forever – so I guess it must be tough.

I pick out the riff from Chiwoniso Maraire's song 'Mai'. She was one of my favourite mbira players ever and this particular tune is a vigorous jig infused with power enough to touch the spirit world. I can feel Chiwoniso in my thumbs as they dance from key to key, callus striking the hard iron under-neath. Ka-ra-ka-kata, ka-ra-ka-kata, ka-ra-kata. In ancient times, the mbira was used by the Shona to commune with their ancestors during ceremonies and stuff. Mine's made of a wooden board from the mubvamaropa tree with rusty iron keys laced against it. Pretty weighty.

She comes into clearer focus. I've managed to anchor her now.

'Tell me your name,' I say. It's important when managing visitors from the other side that you stamp your Authority immediately. That's why this is a command, not a question.

'Nicola Stuart.'

'Where you from?'

'Baberton, but I grew up in Murrayburn.'

Great, she's local. I'll take the commission, make a few shillings and that will be that.

'Can you pay, or do you want to reverse charge the fee to the recipient of the message?'

She swirls, her face turning from one side to the other. Then she flickers. I'm losing her, so I switch tempo to keep her earthed.

'My son, Ollie, Oliver, he's missing. He was missing before I . . .' Something catches in her throat. New ghosts tend to avoid talk of their passing if they can help it. Must be some PTSD type thing. 'He disappeared one day with his mate, Mark. Mark came back, but he couldn't tell us what happened. Can you—'

'Can Mark pay?'

'No, he's seven.'

'Your partner?' She shakes her head. 'You have anyone else at all who can pay?'

'My parents live in Sighthill, but they're hard up against it. We can't afford to.'

'Nicola, Nikki, Nik, stop right there. Let me level with you. I can send a message to anyone you choose, so long as they are willing and able to pay for it. That's how this thing works.'

'Please, you're the only one who can help me find my son.'

Zzz. What a waste of time. I'm past doing special services and certainly not for nothing. She must think I'm walking around with a big sign saying 'mug' or something.

'Sorry, I don't work for free. Everyone knows the score.' Nicola dims and two foggy arms come towards me in supplication, but she can't hold that form, dissolving back into mist. 'Let me make myself crystal clear, alright? I'm saying, I need to earn a living. That's what being alive's about, in case you've forgotten. My advice, call the police or find a clairvoyant. This ain't my hustle. RIP.'

I stop jamming. It's late and I'm knackered. I need to get a bit of shut-eye before I start work in the morning. Nicola's booga-woogaring, but I ain't listening no more. Night's giving way to day and the everyThere's gonna be tugging harder at her without me playing. I bail and let her fade to black.

IV

Smoke rising, the vague flicker of open fires. The scent of burnt charcoal and wood wafts through the air as I make my way up the road. Voices humming in alleyways, laughter echoing round corners. Sheep bleating and chickens clucking. This place has its own pulse, its own rhythm that sets it apart from the rest of the city. I jump over a drainage ditch and go past the statics on the periphery. They look like mini-bungalows elevated on stilts. Further on is the higgledy-piggledy mass of tents, prefabs, sheet metal dwellings, woodsheds and hasty constructions along the narrow lanes in what used to be a field.

The university up the way says we're an eyesore, that we shouldn't be here. Screw 'em. I step in a puddle and the water seeps into my socks. Just my luck. My steel toecaps stopped being watertight ages ago. At a glance, in this dim light, they look like a proper pair of Docs.

I make it to our caravan and a yelp greets me from the darkness underneath. I kneel and click my fingers and whistle. There's some panting in the burrow, but my girl River doesn't come to me. Her shining eyes watch from within. Total vixen. I should have put her in the pot ages ago, I think, getting up.

It's too cold to be fooling around anyway. Even the doorknob's freezing when I turn it.

Warm air greets me inside. I quickly check the windows are slightly open. The brazier on the countertop's burning lumps of coal. If you don't open the window, you go to sleep and never wake up. I suppose that's one way to go.

'Hey, Gran, how's your day been?' I say.

'Is that you, Ropa?' Like, who else?

'Yeah, I'm back.'

'Did you have a good day?'

'It's been ultra-great, thanks. Cast out a poltergeist.' I don't tell Gran about my encounter with Johnny Law. Her heart's not that great, she's on all sorts of medication, and she's not supposed to get stressed out lest it goes kaboom. I wouldn't know what to do without her, so I have to look after her.

'I hope you were kind. The lost especially deserve an ounce of kindness – sometimes it helps show them the way,' she says. Her voice is worn and crackles the way dry leaves crunch underfoot in autumn. Gran pats the seat beside her and I chuck my bag on the counter and plonk myself there. I rest my head against her shoulder. It's kinda squishy and comfy. She's knitting something and her elbow gently rubs against me. Looks like a little cardigan. Too small for us, must be for one of the neighbours' kids or something. I like the rainbow colours she's working into that. Gran don't see too good nowadays, but she can still knit. The patterns are all there in her head.

'Izwi?' I ask, after a few minutes.

'Under that duvet, fast asleep,' she replies.

'She make you tea tonight?'

'Yes.'

'Done her homework?'

'That too and all the chores you set for her. Why don't you rest, child? Have something to eat and tell me all about your day.'

I've already had tea and scones at the McGregors, so that'll save us some grub tonight. Means Gran can have lunch tomorrow, three meals instead of two. I relax and tell her about my visits, leaving all the bad stuff out. I don't wanna kill the vibe in our home. Gran umms and ahs to prod me along. When she listens to you like that, it's like the whole universe goes quiet just for her. Your voice is the only thing worth listening to, and only you matter.

V

I'm at the hob making oatmeal porridge. The electric tends to be erratic these days. We're not supposed to be on the grid, but for a king's ransom there's a guy on the estate who can sort it. Tethers you into the giant pylons running into town. It's fairly safe; only one trailer's blown up because of it so far.

Still a wee bit grim outside. The sun's hidden behind thick grey clouds blanketing the sky. Someone bangs on the door, brutal like. I look through the porthole window and see the troll, as we like to call him, outside.

'Alright, alright. Don't break the blooming door down,' I grumble.

I turn down the heat and go into the cupboard where I keep my jar and count the cash I keep in there. Not much, but it'll do for now.

'I'm coming already, shish,' I yell, 'cause the knocking resumes with even more vigour.

'Who is it?' Gran asks from her berth.

'It's no one, Gran. Go back to sleep.'

Some people. He already knows I'm coming out but he's still making a racket. If I ever raise enough dosh, we're outta here. Hasta la vista, morons, smell you later. No forwarding address.

I open the door. The morning air's a bit hazy and fresh. Birdsong and breeze. The troll's greasy green tractor's parked up front. I hand over my jar and stand with both hands on the doorframe, blocking the troll so he can't come in. He's our landlord in the purest sense of the word. He doesn't own our caravan, but he owns the land beneath it. I'm pretty sure this means we owe him ground rent. That means, technically and informally-illegally, we have a leasehold, which is more an English thing, really. Farmer McAlister figured out one day that he was sitting on prime real estate, after the first squatters moved in Hermiston way. Whereas a less savvy man might have called the law, he saw an opportunity – to leech money off us. It's easier than getting up mornings and tending the fields, which is what real farmers ought to do. The long and the short of it is that this is how His Majesty's Slum at Hermiston was born.

We call Farmer McAlister the troll not because he skims money off us, but because he actually looks like one. He has a big, bulbous red nose, pitted, with hairs spiking out of it. His ears are the bushiest this side of the equator, and his face is marked by deep lines. He's short and squat, spindly legs on a broad torso. I'm pretty certain he's the missing link.

'That's only half,' he says with a snort.

'The rest's coming,' I reply.

Would have had all that and then some, if it weren't for the fuzz last night.

He pretends to look around and scratches his temple.

'From where? I dinnae see it,' he says. 'I'm not a charity. Could be growing wheat and barley on these here fields. You want you and your nan to go on living here? Get it sorted.'

'You'll get your money,' I say.

'Aye, you're right about that, lassie. You'd be out on the streets if it weren't for me and dinnae forget it.'

The troll empties the cash into a little sack and tosses the jar back my way. He goes to his green John Deere, a yellow stripe running down the middle of its belly, and hops in. He's agile as a young man. He turns the engine on, cranks the gears and is off, the diesel engine roaring as he goes.

I've lost my appetite, but I still have to make brekkie for Izwi before she goes to school. Gran can't take her tablets, either, before she's had some of the hot stuff down her belly. I return to the hob and stir. I add peanut butter to the oats. Best way to make 'em.

'Have they found the boy yet?' Gran asks. 'Willie Matthews – they came around here yesterday looking for him. Been missing weeks now.'

'He's probably off sozzled somewhere,' Izwi replies.

'And what do you know of it?' I say. 'Hurry up and finish your porridge.'

I know Willie, nice kid, not a bad bone in him. The Matthews live in a trailer on the opposite side of the canal. Used to go to school with him back in the day. It's not like him to go off like that. But, hey, not my problem. *My* problem right now is getting my little sister to school on time. I tell her to take her satchel and kiss Gran goodbye before we set off.

Our cara's small outside and in. It's an '89 Rallyman from the days when they built things to last. It's a *really* small caravan, but still dope. Painted daisies and sunflowers on the sides that give it a cheery look. The tyres are flat and the grass around them's grown tall. The rims are rusted to hell. We're not going anywhere anytime soon. I place a bowl of porridge next to one of the wheels for River and hope I don't get my arm chewed off. I hear her sniffing the air from her burrow.

A few folks are wandering about. The day starts later when you've got no job and no school to go to. Most people are probably inside snoring or watching telly. Eddie, Izwi's friend, says morning. He's been waiting on us with an oversized rucksack which is his schoolbag. The thing goes all the way down to the back of his knees. Him and Izwi are both in Year 6; some days his maw takes them both, but today it's my turn.

Power lines reach down over our heads from the pylons above, like a giant way up in the sky's fishing down in our little houses. When it's windy the lines sway, and if they touch they spark and zap.

We make a steady pace to the roundabout and cross into the Calders.

Something moves in the trees ahead.

'Shush,' I say to the kids.

The birches are shorn of their leaves, but it's hard to make out what's in there. Then I see the squirrel clinging to the narrow trunk of one of the trees. Its grey coat blends in with the silver bark. I reach into my back pocket and take out my katty. Made it myself using dogwood. Used a nice Y-shaped branch, thick as a grown man's thumb. The wood's pale like bleached bone with lines running down it. I have two even lengths of rubber tubing attached, with a leather pouch at the back. The thing's top of the line. A real zinger.

I take a rock from my pocket and load it.

'You guys should look away,' I whisper to the kids. They don't 'cause that's how curiosity gets the cat every bloody time.

I still myself, breath slow and quiet. My arm's light as a feather. I draw the sling, adding tension as far back as the rubber will allow. My left hand's steady on the stem of the Y-wood. Doesn't even feel like I'm here. I'm not even thinking when I let fly the stone. It's like the katty picks the moment herself. The rubber goes *srrrrup*.

'Blimey, you got it,' Eddie shouts. He runs to the thicket where it's fallen. 'Cracking shot.'

My left arm's still outstretched, rubber dangling. My right hand's open like I'm Artemis let loose an arrow. Izwi's quiet. She doesn't like killing stuff. Kid's a vegan. Skinny as a needle for it, too. She turns away when Eddie comes back holding the dead squirrel.

'Will you teach me?'

'Nope,' I reply, taking it off him.

'Pleaaase.'

'Not gonna happen. You want your mum on my case when you take out your eye?'

Eddie pouts, but he'll live. I inspect my kill. Clean shot, got it right in the head. There's a bit of blood there. But the fur's alright. Gran will want to cure the pelt. Given enough of them, they're good for a lot of things – like small bags, linings for mittens, or adding detail to her knitwear. She's crafty like that. And this critter's a grey so I think I'm doing some conservation work. Protecting the red squirrels that are endangered and all that. I put the thing in my backpack.

'You know I have to,' I say to Izwi and put my hand on her shoulder.

She gently shrugs it off. This kid's softness gives her some hard principles at times. I'm just afraid the real world will chew her up if she carries on like this. No one can afford such strong morals. Life will break you in half.

Folks in the Calders don't like us lot from HMS. They look down on us. We only live across the bypass from them. Might as well be a mile away. They're, like, a council estate, the rough end of town, junkieville central, yet they still think they're better than us. Don't like their kids playing with us either. That's fine by me, but Sighthill Primary's still the nearest school and we've all got to share it. It's all proper flats around here, a whole estate of them. Three high-rises dominate the skyline. I'd give a kidney and half my liver for a place out here. But it's not like where I live. No one says morning or hello as we walk up to the school gates.

'Be good, alright, Sis,' I say as Izwi and Eddie enter the crowded schoolyard.

The fence around them, the barrier meant to ring the school from the outside world, was stripped and stolen during the great scrap metal boom. There was good money in it then and I made a duke or two off copper on the old railway lines. But I'd never have thought to hit a school like that. You gotta have boundaries. Ethical standards. Lines you simply don't cross, else you're just a douche.

The bairns make noise with their high-pitched voices. I

watch my two merge into the sea of preadolescents and then carry on. At least I can already tick one thing off my list today.

The bridge that runs between Sighthill and the Plaza's collapsed. Nothing's left of it but rubble. Now and again there's talk of fixing it, but it's just hot air, enough to lift a lead balloon. The pillars lie on the road like collapsed Greek columns. A ghostly wisp lingers in the shadow of a block of tar resting at an angle. It's watching me, shifting like steam from a kettle. Must be desperate for a deado to come out this time of the day. I ignore it and move on. Not on duty yet, and I don't have my mbira with me anyways.

I'm headed off to the pharmacy, see if I can get meds to fill Gran's prescription. She takes water tablets and simvastatin for her ticker. Then there's metformin for her diabetes. Went there last week and they said they'd run out of the cheap generic pills. Can't afford anything but that, so I'm hoping they'll have them today.

'Roparistic!' a voice calls from behind me.

'Jomo?' I turn around. He's walking with a small group of boys in black dress pants, white shirts and jackets, the uniform at the secondary section of the Wester Hailes Education Centre. 'Been a minute.'

'God save the king,' he says, suddenly remembering he's with people.

'Long may he reign,' I reply.

'I'll catch up with you guys later,' says Jomo, breaking off from the group.

'Jomo's got a girlfriend,' one of them jibes and they snigger like hyenas as they head towards the blocky building that's their school. I used to go there once too – well, I only did a year of secondary and that was enough for me. No, sir, as long as you can plus or minus your shillings, you don't need none of that nonsense in your noggin.

Jomo's had a spurt since I last saw him. He stands a wee bit taller, accentuated by his overlong afro, which no comb could ever run through. He's still a dork, though, with his glasses and acne all over his forehead. I got bumped up two grades in primary school and he was my bestie right up until I said sayonara to the system and split. Everyone in the class was older than me, and they were nice, but I got along with him best. Not seen him in a while, though.

He trips on his shoelaces coming towards me and I catch him.

'You might wanna tie those,' I say. 'Where've you been?'

We fist bump.

'I'm sorry, I should have called and told you. A lot's been happening and I haven't had the time to catch up. I got a gig at my dad's library in town. This is, like, the coolest place in the world. I'm surrounded by gazillions of books. It's only part-time, but still, I have to work weekends and after school sometimes.'

'You know that thing in your pocket that's masking your microscopic wang? It's called a mobile. You can use it to call or text from time to time.'

'I'm sorry, man.' His voice is uneven and screechy.

'Proud of you, Jomo. Maybe you can take me there one day, show me round.'

He winces and half smiles, sucking in air.

'I'm sorry, I would love to, but it's a members-only kind of place. They made me sign a confidentiality contract. Sorry.'

'You taking the piss? It's a bloody library.' He shakes his head and looks down at his feet. 'Whatever, eat my vag. Your class is about to start – text me and we can meet up or something.'

VI

It's a moonless night. Everything's shrouded in darkness. But flats are just visible in the distance, slivers of light escaping through gaps in their curtains. Anyone coming out here at this hour needs to have a big pair of cojones. I set up my weekly surgery in this play park by the old Hailes Quarry, near the pits. I've brought River with me just in case. Her warm body grazes my left leg.

I found River as a fox pup in the undergrowth out near Ratho. She was cute and I thought I'd fatten her up and chow her one day, but Izwi took a liking to her and we put it down to a vote. Gran swung it against me and that's how she survived. I sometimes think River knows what happened 'cause she's got a bit of an attitude. In the main, we're cool, though. I take her out with me some nights, 'cause you never know when you might need a second set of gnashers.

Used to be a real quarry here, way back before I was born. Supplied the stone that built tenements and stairs around Edinburgh. Then it became a giant dump until it got full and they covered it up and planted trees on it. A couple of years ago the miners started digging down here for scrap. Everyone calls it the pits 'cause they didn't bother to cover it again.

There's holes all over the place and a body or two's been stuffed in there. But when it rains, they fill up and look like pretty ponds – from a far enough distance.

I've been waiting ten minutes when my first client emerges from the lane along the canal.

It gives off a dull glow like a nautical light smothered in fog and it approaches in starts and spurts. One moment it looks near, and the next, further away. A sort of drunken ceilidh two-step. River pricks up her ears. She grows tense against my leg and whines.

'Easy, girl,' I whisper and stroke her red fur.

Three more lights appear in the distance. They flicker and slowly approach, but not before the first reaches me. It's an old man, butt naked with wisps of hair on the crown of his otherwise bald head. He blurs and slants away like a candle in the wind.

Repeat business, you gotta love it.

He comes right up to my face and says, 'Booga-wooga-wooga.'

'Hang on, Bob, I've got you,' I say, taking up my mbira.

'Wooga-wooga.'

'I said, I've got you, pal.'

My mbira's a small 22-key thumb piano. Used to belong to my biological granddad, but he left it to Gran, who passed it down to me. Been told he made it with his own hands. That was his thing, making instruments. Marimbas, mbiras, hoshos and ngoma. It was a niche trade, but he used to ship them all over the world. I twang a C minor, but can't quite get it to stretch, because it's cold and you get less zing than you would in the summer. You have to play around that, know what songs work in what season.

'You guys hold back there. For confidentiality,' I say to the lights in the distance. River barks to back me up. Then I give Bob the spiel: 'Okay, I can deliver a message from you to anyone you want within Edinburgh's city limits, although, at the moment I'm not doing the town . . . '

'Booga.'

'I'll take that as a yes.'

It's a mouthful, but rules and regulations, et cetera. Totally knapf, but what can you do? Now the kauderwelsch's out of the way, I can go about helping this deado. Dealing with them is soooo boring, though. It's always the same crap. *I wish I'd had a little more time. If only I'd known . . . Boohoo, why doesn't anyone remember me?* Me, me, me, me. And so on and so forth. Can't get no other job, though, so I'm stuck with this. I play a soft melody, soothing like fields of barley swaying in the breeze.

Bob shimmers, his harmonics blending with the music. It's like two waves meeting and superposing at the right frequency until they cancel out into unity. Bob's booga-wooga-ring morphs into a voice.

'Did they get my message?' he asks.

'Of course.'

'What did they say? Tell me, please.' He's anxious.

'It's a bit difficult, pal. They don't like the idea of you moving back in.' I'm trying to be diplomatic here.

'They are my family. I want to be with them. I can protect them forever.'

'I get it. I totally do, Bob. But face it, there aren't too many people out there who want to live with a ghost on a full-time basis. It's nothing personal. I'm sure they love you. In fact, they wanted you to know that.'

'What do you mean, people don't want to live with a ghost? That's discrimination, right? Am-I-right?' He's getting a bit worked up. I have to calm him down, de-escalate the situation. Ghostly tempers are the leading cause of intrafamilial hauntings, which is an undesirable outcome in my line of work.

'Think of it like when your kid goes off to uni. After that they get a job, their own apartment, maybe they even get married, you ken? You want them to grow, find their own feet, leave the nest, as it were. They move back in with you, that's failure to launch, pal.'

'They want me to go Beyond without them?'

'It's the same journey they'll have to make one day. I think it will reassure them knowing you've gone on before to suss things out. You'll see them again, Bob. Eternity is yours now, what's a couple more years?'

He thinks, aura pulsing like a lighthouse. I'm playing on, keeping the harmony going. Without the music, everything would collapse back into a pile of gibberish.

'Will you take another message through to them?' he says.

'That'll be billable,' I say. You must be upfront with the charges. That way no one gets messed about. I've met guys like Bob before. The ones who linger for a bit, not seeking closure, but because they can't handle change. They prefer stasis to progress. He left a nice family in a semi out in

Stenhouse. It'll take a few more sessions, messages back and forth, tears and so on, but it'll be okay in the end. More importantly, I'll get paid. This ain't no NGO.

I'm out till just after 4am when the activity subsides. It's important to do my business around the witching hour when supernatural activity's at its strongest. I take lots of messages: casual greetings, disputations, the usual family dramarama. There's a lady who wants her family to know the other side's alright. I quickly edit that in my head to tell them she said *she's* alright. Don't want them getting the wrong ideas. Hastening reunion's outside the remit of my services.

The last job I get's from a teenager called Kenny from Clermiston who threw himself off a bridge someplace. He takes the form of a gelatinous mass, kinda like strawberry jam talking to you. The kid's a poet. He's lovelorn and wants me to take a message to Claire who turned him down in high school. It's a tough case, but it ain't exactly the teen romance of the year. Poor Kenny wants Claire to notice him.

It's not my place to cast judgement on these things, but if she didn't want to know him when he was alive, what chance is there now he's an extradimensional gummy bear? Them kinds of relationships are hard, even with the best of intentions. But as far as I'm concerned, Kenny's problem is that classic teenage issue – he's run out of calling credit.

Claire's not willing to spend her pocket money on more sentimental doggerel about 'ectoplasm meeting flesh under the burning stars'. She doesn't want to hear any more about his naive hope of them settling on a farm somewhere and having half-human, half-spectral sprogs.

'Kenny.' I say his name firmly. 'This ain't no free service.'

'I know, but Ropa, I need to get through to her. Please take this one last poem, and if it doesn't work, I'll stop. This is killing me.'

'You're already dead, Kenny. That can't be helped. I'm turning the tap off 'cause you're way over your tab.'

'What do you want me to do?'

'As far as I'm concerned you have two options: move on or find shillings somewhere.'

'I thought you were my friend,' Kenny says.

I shake my head. Never give them an in like that. Emotional blackmail don't work on me. This is business, nothing more, nothing less.

'Don't come back here again without any money or I'll have no choice but to cast you out. RIP, man.'

I stop playing the mbira. I'm done with his broke ass. You have to be ice cold in this trade. Nothing for nothing, something for something. I get up off the swing and give River a nudge. She trots off just a little ahead of me. Kenny's red blob keeps up with us for a bit, shrinking smaller and smaller like the setting sun until it vanishes into the black night.

VII

I try to stay away from graveyards when I'm on the go. Easier said than done in this town. It's not that I have anything against them. It's just that, a) there's laws against solicitation (only registered mediums can do that), b) deados tend to go mental on their home turf. A ghostalker walking through a graveyard is like a stripper streaking through a football stadium. Doesn't make for good outcomes.

Still, them messages I take from deados don't deliver themselves so I have to go from address to address on my shift. This takes a lot more time than actually getting the damned messages. Wish I could do it by phone, but then I wouldn't get paid, and seeing the bearer in the flesh with a message from the other side is a hell of a lot more believable than receiving a cold call. In any case, I'm yet to meet a ghost that remembers a loved one's phone number; addresses are a different thing altogether, you can get that off them easily enough. Some stuff's best kept old school like this.

First up, I hit South Gyle.

Edinburgh's industrial zone's kinda meh. Run-down ware-houses, old offices turned into squats. Used to be bustling round here in the olden days. The big banks are still guarded, like they're expected to resurrect. No one works there anymore. A few charities have set up outreach missions here, soup kitchens and counselling places, salves and plasters for bums and drifters. Yeah, it's nice to know some middle-class lady cares, but that don't solve nothing for no one in the long run. I don't go to them places – I don't take no handouts so people can look down on me.

My first clients here are the Chowdhurys. Two sons living with their mum, wives and seven kids between them in a three-bedroomed crib on Torwood Crescent. It's one of the most lucrative gigs I've had so far. Been messaging back and forth since last summer.

The patriarch Mahdy Rahman Chowdhury died and left a shop on the Royal Mile. So far, so good. The eldest son Bilal took charge as the new head of the family. Mum's too old to work now. Problem is Devesh, goes by Dev. The younger lad's the one who worked in the shop with old Mahdy and feels hard done by by the whole thing. He's now Bilal's employee, yet Bilal, a software engineer, knows jack about the newsagenting trade. And that's all before I came in.

Turns out Mahdy left a will at his lawyer's which Mum kept schtum about, because Bilal's missus Asma is less inclined to send her to a nursing home. Mum gets on better with her and Bilal both as a result. So I come in with a message for Dev telling him where the will's at. Bilal and Mum take a disliking to this new complication and send me back with a message. They tell Mahdy his memorial service is off, as they don't much agree with the contents of said will.

The whole thing's a right mess and now there's lawyers involved on both sides.

I enter the house through the conservatory at the back, seeing as the open-plan living room/kitchen area has been turned into a massive dormitory for kids – ages ranging from two to fifteen. The Chowdhurys have laid out some treats at the table for me, like both sides are trying to curry favour. Who's gonna say no to chomchom and pantua?

But I'm impartial and scrupulous in all my reports. Though that won't stop me milking this thing as long as I can. Wills can be invalidated or amended, depending on the wishes of the deceased, if a licensed extranatural communicator is able to authenticate the intentions of the deceased within the first year of their departure. After that, the will is deemed binding. But, truth be told, the only people getting fat here are the lawyers. I just get the suds.

In Drumbrae I meet a postie hauling his sack down the hill. 'God save the king,' he mumbles on his way past. 'Long may he reign,' I say. It's pretty steep around here and when it's cold enough, you can ski on black ice all the way down. I'm going uphill, which takes quite a bit of effort. If my bike hadn't been stolen . . . Forget it. I'm mulling shit over when Nicola appears again under a weeping laburnum. Its spindly branches droop to the earth like a bride's veil obscuring her misty being.

Give me strength.

I go through to the nursing home on Ardshiel Avenue. A carer tells me to wait in the day room. I don't much like these places. The air's still and clammy in here. It's like I'm in a fog made up of intermingled absences that obscure the living. Traces of people who've been coming to this place to die for decades.

It's awfully cold too. The chill bores deep to the bone.

Shapes and shadows move in dark corners.

The important thing is to try and act normal. If you look at them, they see you. The presence of the dead is strongest where they died and where they are laid to rest.

I look at interesting photographs on the wall. Play with my nails. Anything to avoid them.

Half an hour later, the nurse comes in. It says Maureen on her name badge. I stand up and shake her hand. A blob's attached itself to her back. None of my business, I remind myself and focus on my business. It has two arms clenched around her breast. Them types of spectres are liable to attempt the occasional possession, given half a chance. I've never had to deal with that myself – Gran has – and you really have to know what you're doing if you're gonna play in that league. My thing's messages, hauntings, et cetera, so I'm keeping well clear of whatever's going down here.

'God save the king,' she says, a wee wheeze in her voice.

'Long may he reign,' I reply, and then I tell her why I'm here and who I need to see.

She listens with that caring face nurses are wont to have. Hard to read whether it's genuine or not.

'Mrs Gilruth is rather frail. She doesn't hear well, so you'll have to speak up . . . All the same, nice that you're here. She hasn't had a visitor in years,' Maureen says.

'That's fine, but just to check, Victor hasn't paid me, so does Mrs Gilruth have cash?'

'Oh no, no, no. You have to fill in an IB36. I'll countersign it and you can send it off to head office, along with a copy of your licence. You're a magician, correct?'

I shake my head. It would be highly illegal to try to pass myself off as one. 'I'm just a regular ghostalker – licensed, of course, but I don't do no fancy magicking.'

'Ah . . . it's still the same procedure for professions *ancillary* to magic, so you have to fill in the form anyway.'

Knapf, that sucks. I knew it, but I was hoping to pull a fast one. The IB36 for services rendered of a religious and/or supernatural nature has to be processed before whoever has power of attorney releases the dosh. It's a hefty form, but the worst thing is it takes up to six months before you see a mini-penny.

Mrs Gilruth's room is on the first floor, two doors from the stairs. Maureen announces who I am and why I'm there. Mrs Gilruth is a tiny old thing with a full head of curly white. Her feet barely touch the floor from the high-back chair she sits in near the window. It looks out to a nice garden below.

'The message is confidential,' I say to Maureen.

'You still have to include it in full on the form.'

I nod. That's the catch-22. Our messages are meant for the recipients' ears only and that's enshrined in the code of practice. However, for people in care and certain other vulnerable groups, we have to verify what we've delivered to the authorities in full. It's a fraud prevention mac-thingy. That's the thing about rules, though. They mean one thing, but are immediately superseded when the system feels like it. Maureen can't be in the room when I give Mrs Gilruth the message, but she has to read through and sign the form before it's sent out, so she'll see what I said anyway.

When Maureen closes the door, I sit on the edge of the bed near Mrs Gilruth.

'The message is from Victor, your husband,' I say.

Mrs Gilruth turns her head a fraction.

'Victor says, "It's almost time, my love. I've been waiting twenty years. I refused to board Charon's boat until you were on it by my side. We have all of eternity to look forward to, my darling."'

She turns her hand, palm facing up. I lean forward and place my hand in hers. It feels so fragile. Her skin is like paper.

'Do you want me to repeat the message, Mrs Gilruth?'

She smiles and shakes her head. Then she softly squeezes my hand, tired eyes gazing at the garden below.

Last stop, Silverknowes. I've just delivered an emphatic screw-you-both to a couple in a bungalow out there. Dead wife said she knew he was cheating with her best friend while she lay dying of cancer in hospital. She wanted them to know what vile people they are, and also to inform them that there's a special place in hell reserved for people just like them. I don't know if the hell part was metaphorical or not.

The couple weren't too happy about the message, especially

since they'd paid for the privilege. All I could say was, 'Don't shoot the messenger.'

I really should map out my routes better. Maybe start with the furthest delivery point and work my way back home. It's late, I'm tired and hungry. Through one earphone, I'm on chapter thirteen of the Scottish Enlightenment book, listening to stuff about Scots and the British Empire. Riveting read; the narrator's really good. He has this light Doric accent. This is a pirate copy as the official book never got an audio made, so the narrator's passion for the project sceps through. With some books, you can tell the person reading's an underpaid actor plodding through the pages 'cause they never got that big break in the soaps. And that makes for shitty listening.

The street lights are on tonight, the ones that work, that is.

I see Nicola's plume under the broken light near Holy Cross Church. Bitch is stalking me and my patience is wearing thin. I take out the mbira from my backpack and start twanging. Folks on bicycles go past at speed down the slope. A lorry rumbles by.

'You have the money now?'

'I'm sorry, but—'

'Look, Nicola, I'm gonna be straight with you. This isn't how we do things, alright? Now, you're new to this shit, so imma give your dead arse a pass. But you don't follow me around like this. Never, ever. Comprende?'

'Please, I really need your help.'

'If you have money and a message, then meet me at the pits. I'm there every Monday night at the witching hour.'

'My son's a really good boy. I wish you knew him like I do.

He's my world, my light, my everything. I can't find peace until I know he's okay. And he's not the only one this has happened to. If it was your child, your little brother missing, what would you do? I'm begging you, please find it in your heart to help me.'

'Meh. Tough world, get with the program. I catch you stalking me again, I will cast you out. That's a promise.'

I stop playing and walk away from her fading mist. You must be firm with deados. Never give them the time of day or they'll take advantage of your good nature. Inches stretch into miles. Nah. Rules is rules is rules, especially when they're my rules.

VIII

Sleet's falling. It sticks to the windows of our caravan in little dots and clumps. My face is reflected on the black glass, like I'm in a parallel dimension. Gran's on her berth, knitting. Bags of wool sit on the narrow strip of floor below. Izwi's lying on her back, playing games on my phone.

The berth is a U that runs along half the cara. It's upholstered in frayed fabric with flowers embroidered on it. Gran and I sleep on the parallel wings of the U and Izwi sleeps on the shorter side. Not sure what we'll do when she grows taller.

'Penny for your thoughts,' says Gran.

'It's nothing,' I reply.

'Your aura's off. Come sit next to me,' she says.

'I've beaten my top score, look Gran,' says Izwi, her voice too loud.

'Well done, baby girl. Now try beating that one also,' Gran says, a big smile on her face.

We have a small TV that sits on the far end of the berth. Gran's watching reruns of *Rumpole*. She's into legal dramas, the kind of shows you don't need to see with your eyes while knitting. All you do is listen to the dialogue and the picture paints itself in your head.

A text pings on my phone.

'Give it here, Izwi,' I say.

'I'm playing,' she moans.

I get up and snatch it out of her hands. Message from Jomo.

'Nooo, I was playing. Gran, I was playing,' Izwi squeals. It's irritating.

'Let your little sister play, Ropa,' Gran says. 'It's okay, Izwi, you'll get it back.'

'She does that to me all the time.'

'Get a job and buy your own damn phone then,' I snap.

The kid's throwing a tantrum, kicking around on her bit of the berth. I have a good mind not to give her the phone, but Gran gives me the look. The milky cataracts in her eyes bore right through me. I text Jomo quickly to say I'll meet him tomorrow after school, 'cause I'm finishing my run early. Then I toss the phone to Izwi.

'Say thank you to your sister, Izwi,' says Gran. I get a half-hearted thanks, and Gran turns to me. 'What's on your mind?'

I sit next to her. The skin on her arms is mottled with liver spots and moles. Makes her look a little like a leopard. The saggy flesh on her triceps jiggles as she knits.

'Thing is, Gran, someone's asking me to do some work for them. They've been proper stalking me.'

'Who's this person?'

'Dead lady with an axe to grind. She can't afford my fee, and I'm, like, sorry, but this ain't the Salvation Army. We've got bills to pay. But she keeps coming back.'

'She must be very desperate with nowhere else to turn,' Gran says, putting down her knitting needles.

'Nothing's free in this world. You do that for one, you have to do it for everyone else. I'm no mug.'

Gran exhales gently. Izwi shouts out something about dying in the game. Our reflections look distorted in the window opposite. Water runs down the pane, leaving streaks like tears trailing down.

'Don't make the same mistake I made a long time ago and lose yourself in the soulless pursuit of money, child. It's in the most trying times, when we ourselves have nothing, that we mustn't forget there are higher virtues like compassion, kindness and solidarity. Doing something when it is hard, because it is the right thing to do, matters more than doing it when it's easy. The world needs light now more than ever.' Gran puts her hand on my knee. 'You know your full name, Ropafadzo, means "blessings"? It's beautiful. I helped your parents choose it before you were born. It's a special name, and you are your name, child.'

Gran sets aside the cardigan she's knitting. She turns to me, clasps my cheeks in both hands, and I stare into her beautiful, cloudy eyes. She pulls me over and kisses me on the forehead.

'There you go, I've paid that woman's fee. Give her all the help you can.'

Gran lets me go and smiles wistfully as if she knows something I don't. I think I see a hint of sadness on her face, but before I can ask, she picks up her knitting and gets back into it, the needles clicking softly against one another. I lay my head against her shoulder, and she hums a tune, rocking ever so gently as she does. After a bit, I look up and kiss her cheek.

'There's your change.'

IX

A rustling movement comes from under the cara. Sounds like River's going on a wander. Fine, girl, you do you. Coolest thing about having a fox for a pet is that most of the time she does her own thing. Virtually looks after herself, she does.

I'm lying in my bunk, as I call it, with Izwi's feet in my freaking face. Should just put my head on the other side, but I don't. Can't sleep. I texted Jomo ages ago, but he didn't reply. Reckon he's in bed already. Now I'm just turning and tossing on this bunk like I've got something on my conscience.

Gran snores. Well, not *snores* snores, more like a light purr.

I've got a few deliveries to make tomorrow. Need cash more than ever. The troll'll be back soon. If it's not one thing, it's the other. Izwi's growing out of her uniform, but at least Clarice from the barn's got the hand-me-downs she's promised. Then there's Gran's meds, which cost an arm and a leg. Still no generic brand at the pharmacy, and I'm getting nervous.

So tired.

Still can't zzz.

'Gran,' I say. 'You awake?'

'No,' she replies.

'I'm going on a walkabout.'

'You know the everyThere's no place to play, Ropa,' she mumbles. 'It *will* try to keep you if you're not careful. The narrow lane connecting the living and the dead is supposed to be a one-way street.'

'I know what I'm doing, Gran.'

'That's what worries me. Be safe.'

I take slow, deep breaths. Relax my toes, my feet, my ankles, knees. I work all the way up my body, letting everything go limp. Loose. I close my eyes. Feels like I'm jelly. Every part of me's given up to inertia. There's no gravity, just oneness with the fields and flowers and fractals, everything inside and outside of the universe. I focus on my breathing to shut down my thoughts.

breathe in	breathe out	breathe in	breathe out	breathe in
breathe out	breathe in	breathe out	breathe in	
out	in	out		
in	out			
in				
out				

I flow with my breath, out and up and up and up to the ceiling. There's me and Gran and Izwi sleeping, our duvets rising and falling. I soar higher, through the rusty roof, a small brown dent where a pool of water collects. Chipped paint. Moss. Mild tingle as I go through the power line. Our neighbours' roofs, aerials and satellite dishes.

Higher still.

The city's bathed in an orange glow. Most neighbourhoods, there are dark spots here and there. But on a night when there's power you *almost* catch sight of the old city, the one you see in films from back in the day. Like, I remember watching *Trainspotting* and thinking it looked like paradise. I guess the world always looks more beautiful through a telescope. But if you use a microscope, you see things how they really are – up close and personal – and what you get is much scarier.

I soar over the bypass, over the trees, until everything below is concrete and glass and grass and water. The ocean far away reflects the silver light of the moon above. I descend back down to the ground gently, like a balloon.

It's so peaceful out.

The world around me transmogrifies, and the buildings melt away like ice cream in the hot sun. There's blots of green, white, brown, yellow and red, all the colours running into each other. The ground beneath my feet, the air around me, the sky above, look one and the same. An artist's palette, with splodges of oil paint bleeding together. I'm in the astral plane, with its many-coloured realms spread before me.

Focus.

The kaleidoscope enveloping me spins fast. I focus on where I'm going, where I want to be. I want to enter the grey dot – the realm that's hidden among the bolder, vibrant colours. I pour all my concentration right into it. It's hard, like threading a needle that's vibrating super-fast. I'm the thread, slim and nimble, and I wait for the right moment before making my move. I'm about to enter the plane of 'chaos', using the true, old meaning of the word. It meant 'void' in ancient Greek, the formless state that existed before our world was made – and that description fits this plane just fine. I'm going into the grey.

Into ash.

It's raining ash, as if from a volcanic eruption. Everything is buried in heaps and heaps of it. A desert of ash. But if there was a fire, it's long dead; not an ember burns. This place smells like stagnant marsh. It doesn't reek or stink – rather, it's stale. Something sits heavy in the air, gives it overwhelming mass, a pressure like being leagues under the sea.

Whoop-de-fucking-doo, I'm in the everyThere.

It's thick here, I'm in the middle of a dense fog. The air smothers you completely. North, south, east, west, up, down – those don't exist here. Shadows move. It takes a minute or two for my eyes to adjust, as when the light goes off and everything is black. After a short while, the room starts to take shape again. Bits of definition appear in the darkness. It's never a perfect picture, but just enough so you can move around.

Gran was right. I avoid coming to the everyThere if I can help it. This place makes me sick. I feel as if I'm decomposing and worms are eating my body.

Alien as the idea may seem, this plane of existence is grafted to our own like a stillborn Siamese twin. The two places are locked together in a deathly embrace. Gran says it's like the Earth and the moon, twinned for all time, one alive, the other dead. The everyThere is the shadow behind you at dusk, that ominous form in the corner of your eye, slightly out of focus, that you can never quite make out. It's the muffled sound that hails you, someone calling your name in an empty room when you're all alone; and when you turn, no one's there. The eyes you feel staring at your nape every second of every day. It is ever there.

The silver I see when I turn my head to where 'up' should be, a meandering line through the mist, is the Water of Leith. There are other lines of varying thickness running through the everyThere and branching off at right angles: water in pipes. There's the canal too. And the purer the source, the more it shines. Water cuts through both planes.

There are other things from our world, too, that you see in this spectral zone. The oldest trees, centuries old, appear as skeletons with deep roots. Old structures also appear: churches, castles, gravestones. These don't take on solid forms, but are formed of faint brushstrokes, indicating the decaying outline of something. Not the thing itself, but its echo. The really ancient ones stand out as black shadows in the grey.

I move through the soft ash, leaving no footprints behind. Footprints indicate progress through space and time. You can track where someone's been and gone. But here where there is no time, you cannot leave a mark. All that's here is complete desolation.

Ghosts trundle aimlessly. There's nothing to do here, there never has been, nor'll there ever be. I move among them, so many of them. They are allowed no rest in this place of no peace. To my eyes, they seem to walk above me, upside down. Or I see them below me, right side up relative to my orientation, or horizontal. They shuffle along at every conceivable angle – because there are no planes here. Instead all you have is a hall of mirrors, a mash of confusion. I search for Nicola in this infinite mass of the dead, which extends in all directions in this ghastly eternity, this place without horizons.

A grim skeletal figure approaches me. Its flesh is tattered, shreds hanging off it like a flayed sail flapping in the wind. I try not to be noticed, slow down, imagine what it is to be dead, to be insensate. The figure draws near, bares its teeth and snaps them. It's a voykor, the guardians of the everyThere who keep the living out. I see the head of a horse, white iris-less eyes where nostrils should be. Vulture's talons for hands. I drop my gaze and fight every instinct I have to run. Fear's screaming inside of me. The voykor's white eyes assault me as it tries to decide: dead or not. Its breath smells of rotting flesh. I let myself go limp and drift with the souls. Tell myself I'm dead, I'm dead, until I believe it.

Suddenly there's a strange movement in the distance. I don't look. I float along like a leaf in the sea. The voykor turns away, turns back to me, teeth gnashing. Unconvinced. The movement breaks the calm sea of shades, sending out ripples amidst the mournful dead. The voykor takes one last look at me, then, with impossible speed, it shoots off through the gloom. Three more voykor hurtle like comets from different directions. They fly straight and true towards a bright light, leaving dark shadows in their wake. The ash is thick. Running here would be as futile as running underwater. The voykor's gnashing teeth fill the air. They are hungry. This is what they wait for, foolish amateurs dabbling in astral projection, or unlucky lost souls in their sickbeds, slipping out of their bodies before their time. The astral plane is infinite, but if you end up in the wrong place, you only have yourself to blame.

This is no place for the living and the voykor make sure of that.

Then the most excruciating scream rings out. It's so horrid that even the ghosts stop to stare. Doesn't seem like it will ever stop. That's the cry of a soul being devoured. There's no coming back from that. It's like how Neo plugs his mind into the Matrix in the old film: you die here, you die out there. The voykor squeal with delight like pigs, snouts in the trough. Whoever's being devoured, their family will see them having a fit in bed. They'll fall into a coma, burn in a fever, a hideous grimace stencilled on their face. Then they'll die mysteriously and no autopsy will uncover why. Brutal like.

I'm about to exit the plane, no way I'm sticking around with all this kicking off, when someone touches my arm. I'm spooked, but a gentle voice calms me.

'Come with me.'

We end up resting in the shadow of an old church. Meanwhile, in my physical form, I'm pretty sure I've shat myself. Nicola looks around to make sure we're alone. She's formed half a face now. No hair yet, but a nice round elfin face that resembles how she remembers herself.

We're in a ruined place. It has stones and arches, but no roof. Steps lead up to roomless platforms. At least the voykor are not here. Faint echoes of a scream reach us, drifting out to the fringes of the everyThere.

'They'll be feeding on that poor soul for days,' Nicola says. 'It's horrible.'

'Where are we anyway?'

'St Edward's Abbey. That would be in Balmerino for you – the Scottish coast. My mother used to like taking weekends here, when I was little. We'd watch the waves rolling in together.'

'How did you know I was looking for you?'

'I knew you'd come. Goodness radiates from you. And ghosts gossip, you know? Living or dead, some aspects of our nature cannot be changed. We talk about which mediums to avoid, the talkers we like. We've got nothing better to do.'

'This place is terrible. Why don't you just move on, find somewhere else?'

'I don't want to be here, but my Oliver's still missing,' Nicola says. 'A mother can't rest knowing that, and at least this realm is closer to him than the others.'

'I hate to break it to you, but he could be dead. The city's a rough place.' I don't beat about the bush with her. She has to take it without the sugar-coating.

'I haven't seen him here.'

'He could be in another plane. Children go t—'

'A mother would *know*,' Nicola says, and there's a flash of rage. It's over in a blink and she mellows to sorrow. 'There are other mothers scattered around here – and they say something evil's happening in Edinburgh.'

'What do you mean?'

'I wish I knew, but it's just rumours I've heard. This won't stop with one or two children. Please find Oliver quickly. You should see what they've done to his friend Mark. The two boys were together when they disappeared. Only one came back.'

'Okay, I'll poke my nose around. Sniff the wind. Try to figure out what's going on,' I say. 'I'm not promising anything. This is outside my scope of practice.'

Nicola's half-face softens. She mouths a thank you. Then she tells me about Oliver and his friend Mark. I do my best to listen, even as the curdling echoes that fill the air chill me inside.

X

Chris Robson lives in one of the old barns amidst piles of coal, like Smaug guarding his treasure. Gran says when she was a kid she never saw coal, which is, like, weird. In the olden days people used to sit around indoors wearing T-shirts. They had central heating and everything. Rationed supplies still work in some small towns up north, but not down here. Most people get by with electric. The gas lines don't hiss no more. Most of our coal comes from Wales, but they opened up a new Scottish seam in Lady Victoria out by Newtongrange. It's simultaneously a working mine and a museum, 'cause it was turned into the National Mining Museum – back when they shut down production aeons ago.

'You'll be wanting your bucket filled, Ropa?' Chris Robson says. His clothes, face and hair are all coated in fine black dust. 'How's your nana?' he asks, scooping up the coal. There's charcoal and peat briquettes, too, but that's a wee bit out of my price range.

'She's good.'

'Tell her I put a few extra lumps in there just for her,' he says, lifting the bucket off the scale hook and handing it to me.

'Cheers, she'll like that.'

'Your nana told me I'd find the love of my life after the full moon. And I've started talking to someone,' he says, wiping his hands on the dirty cloth slung round his neck.

'Fancy telling me who, Chris Robson?' I ask, hoping to extract a morsel to brighten Gran's day.

'There's a queue here,' says a gruff voice behind me. It's Andrew Blackstone who lives out in the field near the uni.

'Hold your zebras, there's enough for everyone,' Chris Robson fires back. 'Tell your nana I said thanks. That charm's worked a dandy.'

He shows me the bracelet with wooden beads on his left wrist and I wink. Knowing Gran, it's probably just a fake artefact to give him a wee bit of courage. When it comes to love, people make their own magic, but it doesn't hurt to give them a nudge now and again.

I wanna get this pro bono thing out of the way, so I can get back to chasing green. Best thing to do is put it front and centre: slice, dice, and there's your ham and Marmite sandwich. Hence why I'm headed up to Baberton with Jomo and Izwi to go find Mark, the other kid with Ollie when he went missing. Reckon that'll be a good place to start. Hear what this Mark kid has to say and see where that takes us.

Jomo's quizzing Izwi on the planets. I turn my collar up, 'cause the cold's biting my neck like midges going mental. Still cold, but it's better than having the wind blow on it like that.

'Your roots are showing. You should dye your hair green again,' Izwi says.

'Shut it,' I say.

'I'm gonna tell Gran you cussing.'

'Fine, then you won't get to play games on my phone anymore.'

'Harsh,' says Jomo.

'Whose side are you on?'

I seldom get to hang out with friends 'cause I'm working all the time. Kinda nice to be out here with Jomo – I don't see him that often, especially since he got his new gig. Used to be just us two, top of the class when I was in school. Swapped retro-comics and stuff 'cause he's cool like that. Sometimes I miss it, then I think how great it is to be doing my own thing without no teachers telling what me to do. I prefer being the boss of me.

'How's the new job going?' I say, fishing.

'Half chicken, half duck – you know, so-so.'

'And?'

'There's nothing to say, honest. It's just a lot of stacking books, taking them back to the shelf – that kind of thing. It's rubbish.' Jomo's blinking a lot. Does that when he's lying.

'I'd like to come see it some time.'

'Me too,' Izwi says, tugging at his sleeve.

'It's really boring there. You wouldn't like it, it's just a big warehouse and the only people that visit are these stuck-up scientists. I'd get more excitement flipping burgers. We're nearly there now, aren't we?' he says, changing the subject. Not so subtle, kinda dumb too, especially since I know he's into science and stuff.

'Is that so?' I say. Jomo frowns somewhat. The strain is

killing him. He's never been that good at keeping secrets from me. I'll let him marinade a bit longer before I winch it out of him.

We come into Baberton through Westburn Avenue. I did a job up here not so long ago. It's a dope suburb. The houses have small gardens and whatnot. If I had *real* money, I wouldn't mind getting a crib for us someplace nice like this. I don't want a mansion or anything like that, but three bedrooms, pebbledash exterior and neighbours who don't want to borrow sugar all the time sounds like paradise.

A pigeon alights on a gutter. I could shoot it from here, but I don't want no beef going in to take it. Your lucky day, flying rat.

'Remember when you threw Isabel's bag into the canal?' Jomo asks. 'She still goes in the other direction every time you show up near college.'

'I admit, it was a bit excessive,' I say. 'But she deserved it. She was bullying you and someone had to set her straight.'

'Understatement of the year – you nearly got us both excluded. Is this the place?'

We're at the house on Baberton Mains Park. Well-trimmed hedges on either side separating it from its neighbours. It's got wide windows looking out onto the street, one of the few here without burglar bars. In the Southside, that's just asking for it.

'You guys know what you're supposed to do?'

They give me the thumbs up as we walk up the driveway and knock on the door. It's a white PVC door with a mail slot in the middle and a knocker higher up at chest height. 'Look cute,' I say, as footsteps come from inside. There's the sound of the latch being pulled. The chain clanking onto the door before it swings open.

'Can I help you?' a large woman asks.

'God save the king,' we say in unison.

'Oh, of course, long may he reign.' She's flustered for a sec. The sound of a baby gurgling comes from inside. 'What do you want?'

'My little sister here's a friend of Mark's from school, Mrs Jankowski. She wants to play with him,' I say. Izwi nods, looking up at the woman with her big eyes.

'Well, erm, he's not . . . How come we've not seen you before?' Mrs Jankowski says. There's something shifty about the way she fidgets about with her hands.

'They are very good friends at school. She really misses him.'

'Who's out there?' a man calls from inside the house. Must be the Mr.

'It's nobody,' Mrs Jankowski replies. 'Mark's very poorly and we don't want you to catch anything now. Goodbye.' She slams the door in our faces.

I make to knock, but Jomo grabs my wrist. He shakes his head and points to the ground-floor window. We move there and peek in. It's dim inside. One sofa's near the window, and another's at the far side, near the staircase. There's a TV on a stand in the middle, next to a faux fireplace. A kid's sitting on the far sofa. I can't make out his face; the lighting's too low. He sits very still. I wave, but he doesn't respond. There's something eerie about him, something a little off. I can't quite put my finger on it, just a general sense of weirdness. A door opens into the room and we abruptly turn to leave.

'That went very well, wouldn't you say?' Jomo teases, back on the main road.

I ignore him 'cause my spidey sense is tingling so much I need a backscratcher.

XI

There's always a plan B, C, then running all the way to Z and back up the alphabet in reverse. I've read *The Art of War* twice. It's my bible. Read the cheap Wordsworth edition, the one that comes attached to a version of *The Book of Lord Shang*. That one I didn't get at all, too much stuff about the law in it. Now if Uncle Tzu's right, there's always another way. Doesn't take Columbo to see the Jankowskis are hiding something. I have to find out what. Curiosity's killed cats, but they never mentioned kids. So I should be alright, I think, as I climb over the garage and land on the lawn. Chickens start squalling and clucking. The Jankowskis keep hens in the backyard. Makes me imagine warm eggs, freshly laid, as I dash across the yard to the back door and stick to the wall. I might nick a few for breakfast on my way out, I think.

Good thing they don't have security lights out back.

I wait for the chickens to stop kicking off. Make sure no lights come on in the house, or neighbours come out to see. I'm in a dark spot near the hedge. Max privacy for home owner and intruder alike. The kitchen door's way over to the right. Anyone comes out, I'm over into the neighbour's yard and gone.

I climb onto the kitchen windowsill. Steady now, hoist myself up onto the roof of the annex. The gutter barely holds my weight. I ease the strain by keeping one leg on the window-sill and the other on the wall of the annex, transferring my weight by degrees. Been a while since I've done this, but it's like riding a bike. Once you learn . . .

My gamble's been guessing the main bedroom's to the front and the spare to the rear. That's the standard layout of these places. I'm frozen against the wall when a door opens three houses left. The pebbledash catches my clothing. I'm gonna lose a stitch or two. Up here, I'm clearly visible. A man steps out in his dressing gown. I stick to the wall and make a poor impression of a chameleon.

The man lights up and inhales. I'm like, go back to sleep, go back to sleep, go back to sleep. He looks around, lost, his mind elsewhere. He takes a few deep drags and I can smell that ain't no fag from the smoke drifting my way. When he's done, he flicks the butt over his neighbour's fence. It traces a vivid orange arc, scattering sparks as it flies. The man goes back inside and shuts the door.

I exhale the breath I've held for what feels like a couple of days, then get back to work. The smaller window above me belongs to the bathroom. There's many ways to get into someone else's house. I'm talking ways to skin a cat. Lots of people, and the Jankowskis are no exception, keep the bath-room window open to let the steam out, or bad smells if they've taken a poo. I get my fingertips underneath it and swing it open as wide as it'll go.

This window's usually the smallest in the house. Here it's

a tiny rectangular thing, but there's one rule of thumb for getting into places: if your head can fit, the body will follow. Universal first lesson everyone learns when they're born. I lift myself up using my arms, pull myself in, head and shoulders. This is where it helps to be small and light. I'm half dangling with my legs sticking out. The ledge below has bath products and the toilet is directly underneath. I remove the aerosol canisters and shaving gadgets, all the crap they have on there, and stick them in the sink. Work as quiet as I can, problem being hard tiles and metal cans like to tap on meeting.

The tricky part's making sure I get a smooth landing. Could swear I was a gymnast in another life. The tiles are slippery, so I take care to have a good purchase as I work my way in. Bring my right leg in, keeping the left out for balance, and then I'm down, over the toilet and onto the floor. Pumpkin pie peasy.

I'm barely done doing my thing when footsteps approach.

Bailing out's impossible at this stage. I am screwed sixty-nine ways till Sunday. The floor creaks as the footsteps come closer and closer.

Bugger.

I hop into the tub and as quietly as I can, draw shut the shower curtain. The light comes on, just as I curl into a ball. The door opens, and someone walks in. The toilet seat clanks and they plonk on it.

The sounds. The horrors. The Luftwaffe dropping bombs on God-fearing villages. Chemical attacks by banned nerve agents. I endure it all, my dicky ticker pounding awhile. Now I'm thinking I should have locked the door – 'cause that'd have bought me enough time to abort the mission. Amateur move.

By and by, the war comes to an end. The toilet flushes. I hear a muttered tut, then the cans being righted and replaced on the ledge. Then the Mr or Mrs Jankowski washes their hands and leaves the room. Drowsy, they must not have thought much of the anomaly. Or thought the kid did it for some reason. People don't see things right in front of them if they don't expect them. Like this video I saw on the net where there's folks playing basketball and a gorilla walks past. But you just don't see it unless you're *told* it's gonna happen – because you just don't expect that sort of thing. Makes you wonder how much more we keep missing in real life. Best to keep your eyes peeled.

I stay in my position for a little while longer. Cometh the woman and all that.

After a bit, I tiptoe out of the bathroom. There's a closet on my right and the door to my left leads to the spare room. I keep to the walls – it's the quietest part of the floor, doesn't give as much as the centre. Downside of working nights is that sounds carry louder.

I get into the spare room and shut the door. A tiny figure's lying in bed.

Something happens, my way out's through the bedroom window. Never, ever go in without an exit strategy. Only Americans do that kind of cack, from what I've seen on the news. But that's plan B. Plan A's good, honest, salt of the earth, His Majesty's loyal subject, front door exit. C's too crazy to even contemplate.

There's plastic toys all over the floor. The duvet cover has a cute dinosaur on it. Someone's done good work drawing Pooh,

Tigger, Piglet, Eeyore and Roo on the wall. There's a picture of Mark among the cartoon characters. A plump little healthy chappie, radiating mischief and energy. Radium stars glow green on the ceiling. Didn't this stuff kill a whole bunch of girls working in a factory back in the dark ages? Still, looks pretty.

But something's not right. The room has the warm, churning odour of compost. There's a lingering miasma that sits in the air. Decay. Rot. Putrefaction. Like something has been excised, leaving a festering ulcer.

Mark's asleep. He makes little baby noises in his throat. I pull his covers down gently. Kids sleep soundly, takes a war to wake 'em, so I'm confident. That's until I see the freakiest shit ever. I'm talking a Cirque du Freak horror show. A wave of revulsion passes through me. No wonder Mrs Jankowski didn't want us seeing this kid. *Damn.*

The kid's body's normal, like a seven-year-old, but his head. It's old, like he's fifty, I don't know, sixty and some, perhaps? It looks huge on his little shoulders and neck. I stare, like, *what the hell?* His skin's got that normal, youthful glow, except it grows in lumps and folds. Not a spot or stubble on it. Baby flesh on a geriatric head? Cheeks sunk in like he ain't got no teeth. Jebus. There's no way this is the same kid Ollie was hanging out with.

I whip out my phone and take a couple of pics. Poor kid. I've got to talk to him, get some answers. Before I do, I cross the room, open the latch and make sure the window's ready, just in case. Last thing you need is the window jamming on you at the crucial moment. That shit they pull in movies of leaping through closed windows doesn't work in real life, unless you fancy being shredded.

'Mark, wake up,' I say in a low voice. I shake him gently by the shoulder. 'What happened to you?'

Mark wakes up slowly. He's drowsy. I tell him it's okay, hoping he won't freak out.

'Tell me where Ollie is, Mark.'

He opens his mouth. A burbling noise comes out. It's like, 'ek, ek, nyek', more primitive even than anything I've seen on National Geographic. He's trying to talk, but all that comes out is garble, with waves of foul breath that make me gag. I encourage him. He frowns. The frustration's getting to him. Christ, he's just a kid in them Pooh pyjamas. His old-man face contorts, a vein bulging in his forehead. Then he lets out a wail that sounds like a baby with a geriatric scratchy tone.

Time to bail – I make for the window.

XII

If there's one thing I don't like it's not knowing stuff. It gnaws at me and I have to scratch the itch one way or the other. Not that I'm nosey or anything like that, but . . . It bugs me, okay. A lot. Right now I'm frazzled and chilling at home. Izwi's gonna have to take herself to school. I make her sandwiches, while she helps herself to Frosties with hot water. Milk's off the budget at the mo.

Last night I sent Jomo some pics of Mark. This morning I get a reply saying, 'Super freakiest shizz eva.' Took the words right out of my thumbs.

I send him a 'Duh'.

He writes back: 'Progeria?'

I have to look that up 'cause he'll just brag if he finds out I don't know what it means. I'm doing a search on my phone when he texts again, 'U dt knw wt it is, do u??' and shares a link. Turns out it's a super-rare condition that makes kids grow old quick-quick. Some kind of genetic anomaly they're born with. Now, I'm no physician or anything like that, but the pictures of the kids on the net don't quite look like Mark. You can clearly see these kids are unwell: the baldness, oval shape of the head, weak chin, certain similar characteristics. That's not Mark. And Nicola would have mentioned if he was like this before.

'???' Jomo texts.

I send him a GIF of the finger going up and down.

'I'll c if we ve nytin in e lbrary.'

'Great, maybe I can come too. It'll speed up things. A kid's life is at stake.' I'm chipping away at him. He'll crack soon enough.

The local library in Wester Hailes was shut down long before I was born. It's now just a husk with smashed-up windows, graffiti and felled bookshelves. And if Jomo's place does science then that would be real useful. I wait for a ping back, but he doesn't respond. The ticks at the bottom show he's read my message. I send a '?' and put my phone to one side. Too zonked to get into it with him like that. I make sure Izwi's sorted and crawl back into bed after she leaves for school.

'You know why I knit?' says Gran. Her voice sounds distant.

''Cause you're old and have nothing better to do?' I reply.

She laughs, crackling and popping like pine burning on a campfire. Sparks of mirth fly from her and fill the room with a warm glow. When she laughs like that, it's as though her whole being pours forth, and her joy enfolds you and anyone near enough to hear it.

'You walked into that one, Gran,' I say, stretching out.

'I may be losing my eyes, but hands are important too.' She puts her needles down and holds her hands out in front of her bosom, her hands cupped as if cradling a crystal ball. 'We are mind, heart and hand. Through these our will is made manifest in the world. We shape it by touching it.'

Gran moves her hands, fingers clearly shaping something invisible. She tosses it to me and I catch it. It weighs as much as a bowling ball, and it warps the light like a clear lens. Looking through it, everything seems distorted.

'What is magic?' she asks, a question I've heard a million times before.

'What is magic if not the thing that connects us to the land and those who rest in it, the voices that whisper in the wind – our ancestors and their forebears?' I answer the question with a question, because Gran says in this there are no answers, only steps through and doors into myriad other questions.

'Is this why we weave our spells with our hands, just as we till the earth with our hands?' Gran probes further.

'Is this why?' I answer.

The ball in my hand gets lighter, softer, and melts, dripping into nothingness.

'Your turn,' Gran says. I hold my hands out, just as she did, and I concentrate really hard. 'Do you feel it yet?' she asks.

I'm trying to . . . I need to pick up Izwi's uniform . . . Concentrate, you numpty. I tense my fingers and try to feel the ball between them. What does crystal feel like, again? Cool, hard and smooth. I'm really trying to concentrate. Move my fingers the way Gran did. There's something, I can feel – no, that's just air. Nothing. I'm distracted by the sounds outside, my mind's restless pacing, the colours dancing in my eyelids.

'We are made of dirt and we return to the dirt when we die.

That's why, if you want to learn magic, you must start with the earth element before all else.'

I picture a freshly turned field in the morning. The harrow lines running straight through. Troughs, clumps and upturned roots.

'Now feel the earth, that's where you draw your power from. Feel it in your fingertips. Everything we are and will ever become is drawn from the land.'

In my mind, I'm trying to bend down and touch the earth. I want to feel the coarse soil, but there's nothing there. Gran's wasting her time. I can't master the chivanhu craft she's trying to teach me. I don't know how she does it so easily. Urgh, so frustrating.

'Remember, your hands must work in unison with your mind,' she says.

Sigh. Seeing ghosts is simple: you just have to know where to look. It's easy to pick out which shadows are real and which aren't from the blockage of light. I didn't even have to learn that. Just came to me. And it pays the bills. Don't know why Gran bothers. This magic thing's something else altogether. It's for gentlemen in top hats and penguin suits, not for the likes of us in a trailer park. Gran says her mum taught her . . . without books, no school or nothing like that. I'm thinking of earth. But I almost forgot – Gran needs her medication soon. I'll have to remind her to take it.

'You're not focused, Ropa,' she says.

'I'm sorry, Gran,' I reply, dropping my hands. 'It's too hard.'

'That's okay, my child.' Gran smiles. She has infinite patience like that. 'What matters is you are trying to learn the form. I was in my twenties before I mastered it. Just remember that when you go out to battle, you need a spear and a shield. The earth, which you must first master, is your shield, your refuge. Air and fire form your spear and arrows. Water is your sustenance. These are the four elements that make this plane, and don't you forget this.'

I nod along. She's taught me all this before. Truth is, I'm kind of embarrassed I can't do it. My knitting sucks too, but at least I can sew. I sometimes think I'm just not cut out for what she's trying to get me to do, you know. Like, I don't have a singing voice either, and couldn't hold a note if my life depended on it. It's all about having the right aptitude and magic clearly ain't my cuppa. Gran keeps trying and I don't want to disappoint her, so I go through the motions every week.

'What are you thinking?' That happens all the time. Gran knows how to read me.

'Nothing.'

'You're not really here. And you're wrinkling your nose, aren't you?'

'But you can't see that.'

'I don't need to.'

I tell her about the kid we visited, leaving out the part about breaking and entering. Make it sound like I saw some freak on the street, like the Elephant Man. She tells me she hasn't heard of anything like it. Maybe it's nothing, or it's some other genetic disorder, or something else. Gran says you always look to the natural before you check for the supernatural. That's the order of things and I'm with her on that. Dealing with a sick kid doesn't get me any closer to knowing where Nicola's Ollie is, though.

'Turn on the TV. It's time for *Siobhan's Game*,' Gran says when there's nothing left on the subject.

I press the red button and flip channels. *Siobhan's Game* is a local game show. Contestants get prizes of makeovers and cosmetic surgery on holidays abroad. Huge daytime ratings in Scotland. English viewers online are always complaining about the accents and it doesn't do so well south of the border. Gran's been watching it since she came to Scotland for uni. It's one of her favourite shows.

I ask Gran if she wants some chow, but she's cool, so I go to the kitchen end, near the door. It's only a couple of steps away. Berths at one end, some cupboards low and high to the right, the bathroom on the left, a hob at the far end, and that's us. Bit of a squeeze, but we get by like ninjas. I make myself a peanut butter and jelly sandwich, and return to sit with Gran. I can't sleep when the show's on. It's amazing how people can go on it and win the chance of a lifetime. Well, not everyone. The questions are pretty hard and the last person to win the big prize of a full body makeover was last summer. You only get one or two hitting the jackpot each year, others just get a nip and tuck, lipo or even a makeup therapy session. But I guess that isn't what we tune in for – it's really to see the losers, the ones who take a gamble and slip. Makes us all feel collectively better off, in my opinion.

'What's Siobhan wearing today?' Gran asks.

I tell her about the gold frock with incredible pleats and a flare at the bottom. Siobhan's a national treasure. She speaks with an old person's RP accent. She's from Gran's generation, but I swear she looks twenty years younger. And the longer the show goes on, the younger she seems – maybe getting some bodywork herself. That mane of hair, talk about incredible volume. Must take at least one full can of hairspray to set it up like that.

'She's stunning,' I say.

'That's what you get for lots of money and a bit of Botox,' Gran replies.

'Then you must be minted, Gran, 'cause you're more beautiful than Siobhan could ever hope to be,' I say and kiss her.

Gran chuckles and calls me a charmer. Then she gets up and says she has to use the bathroom. That's my cue to bail. The acoustics in this place ain't that great.

As I put on my boots, my phone pings. Message from guess who? Yep, he's cracked, the little shit. The text just says: 'OK: Bt U CNT Tell ny1 abt this . . . 4eva.' I can live with that. Nothing like a bit of emotional blackmail to get things going.

XIII

The auld reekie in the air tonight's louder than a Phil Collins song. It's a smothering blanket of nostril-blasting effluvia. I hop over trenches filled with raw sewerage, floaters bobbing round. Looks like the workmen started on fixing the pipes and took a permanent lunch break. Usually happens when they down tools after not being paid.

Tonight I'm breaking all my rules. I'm going into the city. Pain in the backside having to walk all this way on top of that – all 'cause some punk stole my bike.

The streets are strewn with litter as I pass boarded-up tourist shops, the kind of places where you used to buy a Jimmy hat and kilt towel back when, alongside overpriced shortbread and whisky. Don't get too many foreign visitors out in the city centre no more. Seen old pics on the net where it's looking prim and proper nice – them days are long past.

Pull up my hoodie and hide my face. I avoid coming to town these days because I have some ex-associates, whom I don't fraternize with no more. Just some bad old news, water under the bridge. Keep my eyes peeled just in case, though. Not easy 'cause we've got a proper haar tonight, laid on so thick I can only see my nose in front of me.

A figure in all white appears in front of me, just as I'm walking past an old bus stop with grey walls. Dude looks like Casper the Friendly Ghost.

'Hey Ropa,' Jomo says, with a little wave as I come nearer.

'What on earth are you wearing?'

'It's my uniform. No time to explain. Listen, what I'm doing with you is very, very illegal, okay? Promise me you'll never tell anyone, not a soul, not even your grandma.' I give him a thumbs up, like, whatever. 'I could get into so much trouble for this. You know that, right?'

Talk about being a melodrama queen. I get that it's a private library, but so what? And this ridiculous outfit Jomo's wearing makes it hard for me to keep a straight face. He proper looks like something out of the Old Testament, except he's got no beard. White cassock and black sheepskin slippers. He has a rope-like belt around his waist, sort of a cincture or something like that. It looks so ridiculous, I've actually forgotten to point and laugh at him.

'This is serious, man,' he says anxiously.

'Okay, I get it. I'm not about to mess up your hustle. I promise I'll behave. I'll try to be invisible, and I won't touch anything. Kosher?'

'It's quiet tonight, but there's still a few patrons in there. Don't talk to anyone. Try to look like you belong. If you see anyone dressed like me, go the other way.'

'You mean if I see a guy in a dress I should go the other way? What if they're wearing a kilt instead? This was Scotland the last time I checked.'

'Haha, very funny. Not. I'm gonna get you into a carrel so

no one can see you, and bring your books there.' He stops. 'This is *so* not a good idea.'

'Don't be silly. Let's just get on with it. Where's this library of yours anyway?'

I want to get off the streets quickly, before someone spots me. I'd thought the library would be the one up the Mound, along George IV Bridge. Didn't know there was a library this end of town. Jomo heads up the road, away from Princes Street. He looks around to check no one is watching before turning right into an archway, up the set of steps that leads into the Old Calton Burial Ground.

'Seriously?' I say, and I'm not amused. Jomo knows my hustle and he knows I don't dig cemeteries. Especially not old ones.

I see the ghosts all around us. Their pale shapes are distinct as they loiter over their graves. I keep my eyes on the ground, make sure not to look at them directly, make sure that they don't see that I see them. These are old ghouls, the ones I have no business with as they have no one left to bother in the world. Yet they still linger and refuse to move on, as if they're waiting for something. These guys are mental. They form themselves into the most atrocious shapes: skin dangling, clothes torn. Less ghost, more spectral zombie. They're angry and malevolent, filled with hate for the very life they so desperately long for. It's close, right there, but forever out of their reach. Their thirst is greater than Tantalus's ever was.

The sounds they make to one another are a guttural mess, and I try to ignore them. Me and Jomo follow the footpath deeper into the graveyard.

'Hey Abe,' says Jomo with a wave to the statue in front of us.

Abraham Lincoln stands tall on a plinth, his frock coat open, revealing a waistcoat. His right hand is by his side, holding a parchment, and the left is hidden behind his back. Thin face, that dodgy beard. He stands unbending and proud in the fog which seems now like cannon smoke heavy on the field of battle. Behind Lincoln are the spindly branches of a broad tree reaching for the sky.

'Come on,' says Jomo, beckoning. 'This is where it's at.'

'I don't know what your game is, but this ain't no biblio-theca, man.'

This is the stupidest thing ever. I can't believe he's brought me all the way out into town for this rubbish. The joke's wearing thin already. I could be home in bed chilling out. Already had a long day on the grind, doing my deliveries. Made it all the way to freaking Currie, right on Edinburgh's outskirts, only to discover my client wasn't there. So the last thing I need is this. Pal or no, Jomo's really got me wound up now.

I'm ready to give it to him, when he looks back at me over his shoulder, superior air and all, and takes out a massive antique key. He goes to the wrought-iron gate by a round mausoleum and I'm liking this even less. The soot-darkened walls are perfectly curved and it looks almost like a granary, a repository of sorts. Circles and lines decorate the top. Jomo fiddles with a padlock, which opens with a clank.

The ghouls have stopped to watch.

Jomo swings the gate open. It squeaks, hinges need oiling

badly. But this quietens the ghouls, as though they're in awe. I follow Jomo into the dark space within. Then he shuts the gate and locks it.

'Full marks for the creep factor, man,' I say.

'Welcome to David Hume's final resting place. Tread lightly . . . Erm, you do know who that is, right? Enlightenment philosopher?'

'Don't be daft – obviously.' I might not go to school, but doesn't mean he knows more than me.

He kneels and reaches for a stone somewhere amongst the pebbles on the ground. There's a rumble, as grinding machinery underground is roused to life. Cranks and gears. Slowly, a section of the floor opens up, revealing a shaft a little larger than a conventional manhole.

We descend down a steep staircase, and when we reach the floor six feet under, the tomb shuts above, plunging us into impenetrable darkness. I reach for my phone for light.

'No, wait for it,' says Jomo.

'What, where?'

'Look.'

In the distance, a light flickers to life on the right, then on the left. Bright torches continue to wink into being in their wall sconces, and it's like a dance, right up until they reach us. Then everything is illuminated by firelight and I can see that we're at the mouth of a long corridor.

'Come on then.'

'Hang on, did these torches just light themselves?' I ask.

'They did,' Jomo replies.

'How did you get them to do that?'

THE LIBRARY OF THE DEAD

'I don't know. They just do it themselves. Let's go, the really cool stuff's inside.'

The air down here is filled with the scent of incense and potpourri, as if to banish the foul smells of the city. I think it's coming from the Bowls placed along the colourful mosaic-tiled floor. Jomo walks briskly ahead, giving me no time to study the pattern properly. The walls are decorated with Celtic symbols and the triquetra runs along the middle of the wall. Other less common symbols trace their own trajectory. But nothing seems to fit together in this corridor. It's as though different artists had a go at different periods, creating something more like sophisticated graffiti than classically inspired art. It's an assault on the senses. The eyes don't know where to rest. There are no central points of reference, and maybe that is the point, to confound.

Each flame dies immediately as we pass it, plunging the route behind us into darkness. As they expire, the torches leave a trace of smoke, and the walls above them are charred with their shadows.

'We're somewhere under the streets now,' he says.

'No shit, Sherlock.'

The floor rises, so we are walking uphill. Life's happening right above us. People going about their business and we are underneath it all, in the bowels of the city. The corridor gives way to an antechamber. It's perfectly hexagonal with an arched entrance on every side. The narrow opening that leads back to the corridor occupies one wall. The one on the immediately opposite side is wider, with steps going up. Inscriptions in Gaelic mark the walls of the chamber. The calligraphy is stunning. It's as if the walls are pages from an ancient manuscript. The letters flow like a winding, cursive river seeking the sea.

I follow Jomo through the wide gap and up the stone steps. The walls here are bare, hewn out of bedrock. The only adornments are sconces bolted into the rock. The middle of the stairs are worn and concave, and with each one it begins to dawn on me where we really are. This is very much the kind of place the likes of me are not supposed to be.

'This is the Librarian's Walk. We ascend into the library. The readers have a separate entrance – they descend – but I couldn't take you that way because we'd get spotted,' he whispers. 'Ropa Moyo, welcome to the Library of the Dead.'

XIV

There's a nervous, Tiggerish energy about Jomo, a barely suppressed excitement. I get that. He was a wee bit jealous when I bailed out of school and got on the grind. Doesn't really get it, though; he thinks I can do whatever I want, whenever I want. I've tried telling him the grown-up world of work ain't like that at all. You still get all the rules of school even without the uniform.

Jomo's brought me here less for the mission, more to show off. It's his way of telling me he's got something going on too. I think it's dope, but I'm not gonna give it to him. I'm a bit of a dick like that.

'You thought you were the only one doing cool stuff, hey?' he says, as we approach a balcony. That seals it for me, so I keep a straight face. Jomo throws his hands up and rolls his eyes.

'Books and open flames – real clever,' I say caustically, pointing out the candles.

'Keep your voice down. You're gonna get me fired.'

I decide to use sign language and flip him V.

The room we're in is, like, super-massive. The walls curve around us; we're on the inside of a very large spherical chamber with alcoves, shelves, balconies and walkways running through the hollow space. And it's all made of carved rock. We've come out into the middle section, right on the circumference, where our balcony rings all the way round. A geodesic walkway runs across the middle. The rails are carved of the same black rock that makes up Calton Hill. Above our balcony is another balcony, and then a third, both tracing smaller rings on the inside of the sphere. Below us are two more.

This place was hewn into the rock, carved out. It's less a building and more a sculpture. There are chisel marks on the unpolished walls.

And carved into the rock face are plenty of bookshelves, for everything in this place just like the floors, walls and ceilings, and even the benches, tables, et cetera are sculpted from the rock itself. The shelves are packed with hardbacks. Row upon row of them.

The place is illuminated by hundreds of candles, some merely placed on the rock ledges, others held in candelabras dangling from the ceiling. The black rock seems to absorb light and spooky shadows cast by the different light sources cross one another. The only bright things in here are the numerous white marble statues lined up everywhere. Mythical creatures, naked men, nymphs and gods. The statues punctuate the dark stone like white ink on a black page.

The air in here's fresh too. No trace of the auld reekie. Must be ventilated from outside, so I imagine some kind of activated charcoal filtration system purifying the intake.

Trying not to geek out now.

Chill.

I'm so engrossed, checking stuff out, that Jomo has to tug my sleeve to get me moving again. Across the room, on the balcony below, sits a man at a desk reading some voluminous tome intently. He wears a top hat and tails dangle at the back of his seat. Yep, this place is definitely some posh wank. But it's also the biggest collection of books I've ever seen in my *life*. Fanny flutter alert. We keep to the shadows and I silently follow Jomo. He takes me into an archway, its ceiling carved with intricate symbols in Arabic-type script. The double door, five or so feet into the archway, looks thick and solid, decorated with solid brass studs forming patterns of squares. The floor's scratched where the door has scraped open and shut, and the base of the wood is frayed like a worn hem on an old skirt.

'This is where we'll hide you. Should be no one inside.'

Jomo takes a pair of white gloves from his pocket and slips them on before swinging the doors open. Bright light pours out of the room, making me squint.

'What is the meaning of this?' a man says coolly. He's just a silhouette against the light.

Jomo jumps back. He umms and blabbers incoherently, and as my eyes adjust I see it's his father, Dr Maige, standing in front of us. Orange after-images dance in my eyes.

'Hi, Jomo's dad,' I say, caught in the headlights.

He ignores me, staring straight at his son.

'Mr Maige, I asked you a straightforward question,' Dr Maige says. Jomo stands with his head bowed.

Yep, we've been busted, but so what? I'll just leave and that will be the end of that. No need to make a big drama out of it all. Just need to take some of the flak for poor Jomo, who's kinda scared shitless at the mo. Can't blame him, though – his dad is all straight lines and right angles. Even I'm kinda feart.

'I can explain. It's not his fault at all. I got him to—'

'Did I ask you to speak, Miss Moyo?' Dr Maige says in a flat, emotionless tone. He steps out and shuts the doors behind him, plunging us back into dim candlelight. 'I will deal with you soon enough. As for you, Mr Maige, you are an acolyte. Your job is to wash the floors, scrap candle wax, clean toilets, and do whatever else the librarians tell you to do within the remit of your responsibilities. It is not to bring outsiders to this institution – or tell them of its existence, for that matter. Those rules were explained to you day one, were they not?'

'Yes sir,' Jomo says, eyes cast down to his father's feet.

'Is there any part of that prohibition that didn't penetrate your thick skull?'

'Yes sir. No, I mean, I thought she could . . . Sorry.'

'You have no idea how much danger you've put your friend in,' Dr Maige says, his voice softening. 'You should have visited the house instead, Ropa Moyo. Mr Maige, tell Mr Sneddon to bring the Rulebook to the tomb, and after that, go and wait in my office. I'll deal with you later.'

XV

Me and Jomo have been mates since Sighthill Primary. Used to practically be neighbours back when I stayed up in Forrester, before we lost our house. I've been to their place loads. Mrs Maige is super-nice, but her husband the good doctor is stuck-up. Not that we ever got to see much of him anyway. He was always out. Or when he was home, he was closed off in his study, doing 'research'. Now and then he came out to tell us to keep the volume down or popped out at meal-times. Point is, whatever this is, it's going to be a slap on the wrist, that's all. Maybe a rollicking, but I can take that.

I follow Dr Maige down the floating stairs that creep along the walls, their glass banisters giving them a light, almost otherworldly air. His scarlet cassock reaches all the way down to his ankles and sweeps to and fro with each step he takes. There's a rigidity about him, his upper body so stiff as to appear motionless when he walks, hands fixed at his sides.

There's a scent of candle wax and old books in the air, which grows chillier the lower down we go into the heart of the hill. Here the rock is rougher hewn, as if the builders ran out of time and took less care with the finishing touches, compared to the smoother texture of the upper strata. These lower levels look much more primitive, cave-like and grim. The dark rock swallows the candlelight and defines itself with shadows in the cuts and cracks the chisels made as the hill was hollowed out, then filled again – this time with knowledge instead of stone.

We reach a landing, which leads to a wide open room, and looking up from here I see the walls of the Library curve all around us. A myriad of candles light up the upper levels like stars, constellations high above my head.

'Custom, then, is the great guide of human life,' Dr Maige says, stopping in front of a white sarcophagus in the middle of the room. 'This Library was built as the repository of all of Scotland's magical know-how. Many librarians and magicians have passed through these halls, and every one of them earned their place here. Look how the very rock we walk upon has been worn smooth by the feet of those great men on whose shoulders we now stand. This institution endures because of the rules that govern our incremental accumulation of knowledge from all four corners of the world. It is no longer about the individual; rather, it is about the whole. I stand in front of you as the keeper of such customs and traditions as are necessary to advance learning in our world. As such, I am bound by my office to treat you no differently to any other trespasser who violates the sanctity of this space.'

There's something chilling in his dispassionate delivery of these words. A quiet gear shift, ratcheting up whatever we're doing here. My gut rapid-fires signals to my brain.

'I hope Jomo doesn't get into too much trouble for this,' I say.

'You'd do well to focus on your own situation, Miss Moyo.' His brow knits, just a tiny fraction.

And what's this whole 'miss' thing anyways? He was even calling his son 'mister'. I can do formal, hell, even curtsey if I have to, but this takes the whole packet of biscuits as far as I'm concerned. A pair of thudding footsteps lumbers from a dim cavern to the far left of the room. If I didn't know any better I could swear it was a caveman, as a bulky, bow-legged figure steps out, lugging something heavy. The fat man huffs under the weight of the load clutched close to his chest. He wears a green cassock and has a large chain of keys round his neck.

'Here, if you will, Mr Sneddon,' Dr Maige says, gesturing at the sarcophagus, which is as tall as his waist.

Sneddon reverently deposits the hefty tome he's carrying onto the flat surface of the tomb. He's red-faced from the exertion, steals a quick glance at me and half-heartedly gives a little wave. The big, leather-bound book seems to have taken a battering over the years. Tattoo-like spirals and symbols run across its cover, which features neither title nor author. It's at least a foot thick and that's a lot of pages. The whole thing is held together by a bone-like exo-binding running from the spine, supporting the covers like a ribcage.

Dr Maige moves round to the other side of the tomb and opens the book, while Sneddon supports the pages on the other side. It's a bit surreal, standing here in front of a solid, white marble sarcophagus. The top is flat as a rule, and the base is embellished with intricate designs and artwork. I figure this is where these librarians or occultists or whoever moved Hume, after occupying his grave. The whole thing's pretty macabre for my tastes, and that's saying something.

'You are here under charge of trespass, Miss Moyo,' Dr Maige says.

'Technically it's not trespassing if one of your staff brought me here,' I reply, and Sneddon gives a subtle nod.

'How you got here is irrelevant, according to the Rulebook. Once here, you must answer for your presence. The fact of the matter is that you are neither a practitioner nor registered theoretician in a recognized field of scientific magic, therefore you have no right to be in this Library.'

'I'm a licensed ghostalker, that's got to count for something,' I say.

Dr Maige flips to the back of the book with difficulty. It's cumbersome and the pages filled with small print rustle as he does so. You can almost hear the book itself groan as though it has been disturbed from deep slumber.

'A peculiar area of practice. Let's see what the Rulebook has to say about that. There is nothing in the list of recognized professions, but I will check in the compendium of allied professions on page 3259.'

I wonder what manner of rules are in that huge tome and who wrote them all down?

'Here we are. "Ghostalkers, otherwise known as Visionairs, Talkers, Hauntmail, et cetera. The Registration Act of 2003 has seen this esoteric profession given recognized status outwith the Society as part of the Allied Professions. It is noted here that while it is accepted that these artisans receive messages from the Other World, within their scope of practice, they

THE LIBRARY OF THE DEAD

merely act as a passive communication conduit. And thus they cannot be said to be practising magical science any more than a telephone wire can be said to be communicating. For this reason, the Library does not permit into its ranks members of said profession, since this potentially opens the membership to anyone who might notice an extranatural occurrence, however minor." That settles that.'

'The young lady has no advocate. Perhaps we should adjourn until one is found for her,' Sneddon says, in a quiet, timid voice.

'What's all this talk of lawyers?' I say.

Now I'm feeling *really* nervous: a) I couldn't afford one, even if I needed one, and b) I'm really beginning to think I misapprehended the gravity of this situation.

'Mr Sneddon, may I remind you of rule 89.2-1, which clearly states anyone of sound mind over the age of seven can answer to the head librarian for their infractions. Miss Moyo, I assume you are over seven years of age.' Dr Maige checks several pages and places a finger on the relevant rule. 'You're not a member of this Library, am I correct?'

'Hey, I'm just—'

'Yes or no?'

'No, but—'

'Record as wilful trespass, Mr Sneddon.' Dr Maige looks at me but I cannot see his eyes as candlelight reflects against the lenses of his glasses. 'The penalty for trespass is hanging by the neck until you expire. Do you have anything to say in mitigation, Miss Moyo?'

Screw this kangaroo shit; I reach for the katty in my

back pocket. The options are pretty clear to me: take out Jomo's psycho dad with a shot and outrun Sneddon, with the secondary option of using my dagger in a melee. No way am I gonna stand for this sort of rubbish. I have a clear shot as I pull a stone out of my right pocket, and prepare to lock and load. Dr Maige cocks his head a fraction, like he's read my move and is waiting for me to make it. Almost as though he's already calculated the projectile motion, including air resistance.

I load and fire true, straight at Dr Maige . . . but my stone slo-mos, then halts, hanging in the air between us. I gasp. Like, what the actual fuck? Sneddon bows his head and touches the bridge of his nose, as though somewhat embarrassed for me.

Dr Maige reaches out, plucks the stone from the air and sets it aside on the surface of the tomb.

'Where were we?' he says.

Someone brushes past my shoulder. I'm so startled I jump. He's a man in a tailored herringbone tweed suit. Its beige-brown colour makes me think of clay-pigeon shooting, for some reason. He walks up to Dr Maige and stands in front of him, blocking my shot. I'm pretty certain I was gonna have a second go. Maybe. Well, if I could stop my hands from shaking.

'I see you're letting the riff-raff in, continuing with the same progressive policies as your predecessor.' The man's 'R's are really strong, and the words come out like *rrr*. 'The membership will take a dim view of this.'

'You're mistaken, Sir Callander,' Dr Maige says, but the man turns away from him and faces me.

He has jet-black hair, obviously dyed 'cause his face is wrinkled, and his eyebrows are bushy. His teeth are yellow-brown, stained black near the gums, but they are still all his own, and when he comes near me, I can smell the tobacco smoke that's sunk into the fibres of his suit.

'I detect the aura of the chivanhu craft about you, girl. Such an old and discredited form; one of no use to the modern practitioner. If you're to progress within the Society, you'd do well to begin your studies with a firm foundation in Thomson's *Thermodynamics*.'

He holds his left hand in the air and a black book appears. He offers it to me and I'm forced to pocket my ineffectual katty to take it. I'm also like – how did he do that? Sleight of hand? He can't have hidden it up his sleeve, the book's too big. Pretty neat, if I wasn't about to be hung by the neck until I expire.

'It's basic. Shouldn't be beyond your level of comprehension – if you haven't already irrevocably damaged your potential with that chivanhu folklore twaddle.' He gives me a long and meaningful look through bushy eyebrows, like he's assessing me or something.

'Sir, may I remind you of the sanction against practising magic outside the underHume,' Dr Maige says severely.

'I am well aware of those kindergarten rules of yours, Dr Maige. This was a trick, not a spell,' Sir Callander replies caustically and walks away, heading for the stairs to the main Library. As he leaves, he shouts out, 'Make wise use of your time in the Elgin, girl.'

Okay, that's it, I'm even more baffled now. There's a pause, for Sir Callander is like a great big ship that's just passed

through, leaving ripples in its wake. And that look he gave me
. . . like he had somehow been expecting me, or something.

Even the impassive Dr Maige seems annoyed as he closes
his book. Something resembling a smile starts to form on
Sneddon's face, but one look from Dr Maige is enough to
snuff that out.

'It turns out she is a scholar after all, and must be
admitted,' Dr Maige says flatly. 'But because of the dubious
circumstances of her arrival, and her attempt at violence
against an employee of the Library, I rule that section
307bxi applies. Under this, she is disqualified from full
membership for a year, and can only be granted associate
membership with limited privileges. Furthermore, she is
to be fined fifty ducats retrospectively for the infringement
prior to admittance.'

'A pound of flesh is fair enough,' says Sneddon with a sigh.
He gestures to the Rulebook and says, 'I'll return this to where
it belongs. Then I'll get her to fill out the forms and give her a
membership card.'

Dr Maige leaves then, to my huge relief, heading into one
of the many yawning caverns gouged into the walls. Sneddon
takes me back up the stairs to a reception area. He goes behind
the desk to a metal filing cabinet, retrieves some paperwork
and stacks it in two piles on the desk. One's a membership
form and the other's a nondisclosure agreement. The papers
are way too thick to read, so I go straight to the end.

'Give me a pen,' I say. I'm just going to sign this shit and go
home. I'm late already.

Sneddon takes a grey pen from the drawer in the desk and

comes over to my side. He takes the blue lid off and says, 'Give me your hand.'

'Why?'

But I give it to him anyway and he grasps my thumb firmly. He presses the pen against it, something goes click. I feel a sharp prick.

'Ouch, what the hell, man?'

A drop of blood bubbles up and I make to suck my thumb, but Sneddon stops me. The damn pen was a blooming lancet. He squeezes more blood from my thumb until the drop expands, threatening to run off.

'Put your thumbprint here and another one on this form,' he says, guiding my hand to the paper.

I stick my thumb on the pages and leave my red prints there.

'Welcome to Calton Hill Library, also incorporating the Library of the Dead,' Sneddon says, the corners of his lips rising slightly. 'Right, here's a plaster for your thumb. Now, let's get you a Library card and check out that book Sir Callander gave you.'

He goes back to the drawer and then hands me something resembling a desiccated ear. It's fleshy and slightly warm to the touch. Yep, that's most *definitely* someone's ear. Jomo's got a lot of explaining to do when I next see him. Then again, I did pester him into getting me here, still . . . Screw it, I pocket the ear and ask for the exit.

'Will you be settling your membership fee and your fine now, or shall we expect it upon your return?' Sneddon asks, pointing to a third document on the table.

It's the invoice for my membership fee, which is equivalent to, like, six months' wages – and only if I hit target every month. The fine alone's my rent, and there's no way my indigent arse can afford the rest. It's a no go for me.

'How about I don't join your Library and we can just call it evens?' I say.

'You've already signed the paperwork,' he replies.

It sounds like a posh threat to me and after the rodeo with Dr Maige, I'd rather avoid any more trouble. For now.

'I'll pay you later,' I say.

'Very good. Oh, and before you go, you should know we're very strict about late returns here. We don't do amnesty,' says Sneddon.

He stamps the book Sir Callander gave me and hands it back with a pointed look. Even in his high-pitched voice, I can tell this is damn serious. If the penalty for trespass is death, I wonder what it is for a late book – the breast ripper, Spanish boot, Scold's Bridle? I'd rather not find out.

XVI

Back home now. Never been happier to be here. Despite Jomo's psycho dad trying to have me hung by the neck until I expire, I'm still no closer to finding Ollie. On the upside, I have someone's ear in my pocket and a plug at the Library. Squares things up nicely, though I'm still a little miffed with Jomo for putting me in that situation. That's why I'm ignoring his texts. I'll let him stew a bit. Still, the sun don't wait for no one. It's morning, birds singing and all that malarkey, and I reckon it's about time to change the cassette in our toilet. Such are the joys of permanent caravanning. But, hey, our lives are one big journey, right?

Gran's watching reruns of *Murder, She Wrote* on telly and Izwi's at school. I sometimes join Gran, 'cause I dig old school stuff like that, and retro video games too, when I have the time. It's nice to see what it was once like, before the catastrophe. Pure glam.

'Just nipping out to sort the potty, Gran,' I say, heaving myself off my bunk.

'Have fun,' she replies.

It's freezing outside. The sky's a brilliant blue, without a single cloud in sight. I dig days like this – warmer with clouds swapped for freezing with light. I don't mind the temperature much, so long as the day's bright. I open the hatch on the side of the caravan that contains the cassette for the toilet. Done this a million times, but with frozen fingers it's a bit of a pain getting it unclipped and sliding it out. Smoke wafts through the crisp air; seems someone's got a fire going.

River pokes her nose out from behind the wheel of the caravan. Must have heard me fannying about and has come to see what's what.

'Come on, girl,' I say to River, after I pull up the handle so I can roll the cassette along. It's like a little cabin suitcase, complete with wheels. I feel the liquid sloshing about in there. At least it ain't frozen 'cause that would be a pain in whatever orifice that stuff comes from.

River trots in front of me, stopping occasionally to sniff at something and poke her head into the bracken.

There are more homes, trailers and freight containers in the field on the other side of the canal, running along the M8. I take the path as far as the bridge, where there's a massive septic tank. It used to be a slurry pit for animals. Suppose that don't make no difference. Poop is poop. I open the grate and the cold nips my fingers. This sucks ass. I have vague memories of indoor plumbing, flush toilets and running water. Never mind your Library of the Dead, that's real magic right there: press the lever and away your poop goes. You don't even need to worry about it. That's the height of civilisation, if anyone asks me. Forget your phones, TVs or computers – nothing beats the good old-fashioned flush toilet.

I spread my feet apart for balance. Press the button at the

back of the cassette as I pour. It lets the air in so there's not so much splashback. Takes less than a minute to empty. I use the tap next to the pit to rinse the thing out and give the valves a clean too. I know I should lube up the hole that connects to the toilet valve, but . . . Maybe next time. I'll use wood ash to mask the smell, which works better than coal. There's technically chemicals for that, but the troll goes radge on account they kill the bacteria in the tank and he has to pay for the honeysuckers out of his own pocket.

I stifle a yawn.

When I'm done, I take the cassette back to the caravan, slip it in the hatch and shove till it clicks in place. Check the water levels while I'm here. Tank's low. To make it last longer, we wipe instead of flushing, but I still need to top it up. That can wait for now.

I say bye to Gran through the window and head off to Sighthill. Need to visit the Stuarts, Nicola's parents, and see what intel they can give me. River comes with. She doesn't have a collar or anything and she's free to do her thing. I am a bit surprised because mostly she prefers going out at night. She's independent like that – goes out foraging for her own meals too. That takes a certain amount of wiliness and I respect her for that. Can't afford to carry no deadweight out here – though I feed her scraps whenever I can.

I follow the Calder Road over the big roundabout and onto the estate proper. One earphone plugged in, listening to an old *The Life Scientific* podcast – with the astronomer royal speculating on the multiverse. I like that kind of stuff. Science. I'll listen to anything if it's good. Gotta fill my noggin with learning since I don't do no schooling. Gran didn't much like it when I bailed from the establishment. But I told her that just because I was out of some government building didn't mean I'd let myself go, you know. They say the brain is like a muscle: use it or lose it. At least now I get to decide for myself what I wanna put in there. Honest Abe was an autodidact and he went on to become 16th president of the whole United States once upon a time. If it worked for him it'll work for me too. Funny thing is, the more I learn, the more I feel that I know even less than all there is to know. It's like, you reach the horizon, only to see the damn thing keeps on stretching further out. A bit messed up if you're just trying to find the pot of gold at the end of the rainbow.

A lone seagull flies over me, heading from Sighthill to Calder. It beats its wings a few times and coasts across, to the wrong side as far as I'm concerned.

The bird swings in a wide arc and soars over the flats, looping back towards Sighthill. I pull out my katty and load a stone. I track its flight path, rubber drawn to the max. If the Mongols could fire arrows on horseback, I sure as hell can do it walking.

Just a bit more. Come on. I need you closer, right there in the Y targeting system. A bit more . . .

River trots ahead, ears pointed, and gets ready. We've been hunting together before, mostly rabbits and squirrels, and she's a good retriever.

Then an updraft lifts the seagull higher, just out of range. Damn it.

I let off the shot in frustration anyway. The rock flies

harmlessly beneath the bird and all I can do is put my katty back. I'm relieved, though, that the shot went off as expected. Wouldn't want to keep doubting the laws of physics, after my visit to the Library. That way the loony bin lies.

The gull would have made for a nice supper. I once read somewhere that there's no such thing as seagulls. It's a made-up term, because what you really have are different types of gull, all with their own names. Maybe I jinxed myself by calling it the wrong thing. Nah, stuff that. Everyone knows what you mean by the term. Call it yellow-legged gull or herring gull, everyone's like, what you on about?

To be fair, they don't taste that great anyway. In the city they hang out at rubbish dumps, or tip bins over and eat all that filthy jazz instead of fish or grain and organic stuff. After you've plucked and gutted one, you have to soak it in saltwater with a bit of vinegar overnight to try and suck all that gunk out of the meat. That helps with the flavour issue a bit. Some folks like to roast 'em in the oven; I prefer to debone and fry them with copious quantities of onion, garlic and spices to mask the flavour.

I make it down to Sighthill Drive and find the red two-up two-down house Nicola told me about. It's got a cute little box hedge and the gate makes a horrible squeak. The hedge catches it so the gate only opens halfway, but that's all River and me need to get in. There are smiling garden gnomes standing about on the tiny patch of lawn. Empty milk bottles sit at the side of the door for collection, which opens before I can knock.

'God save the king,' Mr Stuart says, wearing a severe look. He's Ollie's granddad, one of them elderly geezers you can tell was a badass back in their prime.

'Long may he reign,' I reply. I fish out my licence and give it to him. 'I'm here on behalf of your daughter, Nicola. Is Mrs Stuart also in?'

'Come on then,' he says, making way for me. He frowns a little when River steps in, but there's no way I'm leaving her outside. 'First left to the sitting room.'

I have to call River back, because she's headed into the kitchen. I pop into the living room and find Mrs Stuart sat on the sofa, reading a copy of *Country Life*. There's pictures of a younger Mr Stuart in full military gear on the wall over the fireplace mantle. Above him's a massive portrait of the king, also attired in uniform, sash, medals and all. Then there's pictures of Mrs Stuart, Nicola and Ollie. And on the mantelpiece, I spot a mini-Union Jack proudly flying next to china dolls and a commemorative plate featuring the last queen of England. I guess Mr Stuart's one of them soldiers that came up from down south during the catastrophe, got billeted here and never left.

'You have a visitor, Susan,' Mr Stuart announces, pointing to a seat. I settle down and River takes her place at my feet.

'Hello duck,' she says, beaming at me. 'We don't get too many visitors these days, Niall.'

'This girl's one of them clairvoyants. I think she has a message from our Nicola.'

'Well, I'm really here about—'

Susan stops me. 'Would you like a cup of tea?'

'I wouldn't say no,' I reply, hoping there'll be a biscuit or two thrown in the bargain. These guys aren't rich, though, so I don't press 'em for nothing. I'll just take what they offer.

Susan gets up from her seat slowly, and makes a little 'oomph' once fully risen. She's wearing a floral dress and orange cardigan, bright and summery for this time of the year. She uses a walker with three wheels to help her move. Maybe her hips are bad; it reminds me of Gran. Must be arthritis, 'cause Susan's fingers are twisted and bent, like the gnarled roots of a tree. There's a slight tremor in her walk, but with each step she takes, the joints loosen up, and she's much steadier by the time she reaches me.

'My, what a curious dog you have. What breed is that?' she says, looking down at River.

'It's a fox, dear,' Niall replies.

'Oh, will the fox be having tea as well?' Susan asks.

'She'll eat anything,' I reply.

Foxes are like people, like that. They'll take whatever is at hand. That's why they're the great survivors. Bigger and stronger animals like bears and wolves were all wiped out, but foxes live on. They found nooks and cracks in our cities and towns when people chopped down the forests and destroyed their habitats. The key to surviving is taking what you can get, living off the land the best way you can. Can't afford to be picky these days.

Niall moves his jaw up and down. Has to be because his dentures don't fit right. I look at the picture of Ollie, trying to study his face. Kinda cherubic, with flushed cheeks and blonde hair. Small lips rounded to an O as if he's about to blow. I don't need to see the cake out of frame to know it's a birthday picture.

'We were at the brink, and he held this country together after we lost Belfast,' Niall says, talking about the king – he must think I've been checking out his portrait. 'You young people don't remember what it was like back then.'

He abruptly stops speaking. I don't prod him, because grown-ups don't like talking about the catastrophe. Niall was in the army. He'd have been in the thick of it when things went down. But I'm not here for a trip down memory lane.

Through the window looking onto the back garden, I spot a trampoline. Ollie must have played there. They haven't bothered to pack it up. It sits there as a reminder, rain or shine, near the wooden fence.

'Nicola's asked me to find Ollie for her,' I say.

'You?' he scoffs. 'The police don't care. So what can you do about it, lass? I bled for this country, but they won't lift a finger to find my grandson. I'd have done it myself if I could, if only I were a few years younger, but I can't get far these days.'

'I can try . . . Nicola can't move on before she knows he's okay. Could his father have taken him?'

'No chance. That deadbeat's in Saughton Prison for protesting against *our* king. That's treason in my book. They should have him shot, a bullet to the back of the head – that'd have been the end of it. He's no man, didn't even have the decency to be there when his son, his own flesh and blood, was born. What do you say to a cockroach like that?'

I take a different tack.

'What do you remember about the day Ollie went missing? Was there anything at all unusual?'

Susan comes back in with tea and a plate of digestives balanced on the lid of the basket on her walker. She hands me the mug and places the plate beside me. They don't have a coffee table. I presume this makes it easier to move around the room.

'I'm sorry we don't have milk. The milkman stopped coming a few months ago and it's hard to keep going out for it. Too much bother. We only do a monthly shop, isn't that right, Niall?'

'The girl doesn't want to hear about that. She's asking about Oliver. Nicola won't move on until he's found.' He tenses up and balls his right hand into a fist. There's a restrained current of anger coursing through him. I get the feeling that if he were only ten years younger, he'd turn this whole city upside down until his grandson was found.

I give River a digestive and she gobbles it up greedily. Yank my fingers away just in time.

'A few weeks ago, Ollie was playing out back with his friend – what was his name again?'

'Mark,' I say.

'That's the one,' Susan replies, voice breaking a little. 'They were on that trampoline out there all the time. See, Nicola was at university, doing her nursing, so we looked after Ollie whenever she was at her placements or such. He was a good little boy, wasn't hard work caring for him. Then they disappeared. We thought he might have gone to Mark's, but his parents came calling and they didn't know where he was either. It's all too distressing.' She wipes her eyes with the back of her hand.

'Did Mark's parents tell you anything when he came back?'

'They say he just turned up at their doorstep one evening and he was in rough shape, like he'd had the life drained out of him. Never seen anything like it.'

'These things simply didn't happen in our day,' Niall says.

'Did you hear anything – did they cry out at all when they were taken?'

'Not a peep.' Her lower lip quivers.

I figure they would have been taken by someone known to one or both of them. Taking one kid would be tricky enough, but two at once, with adults in the house? That would have to be a face they knew for sure.

I was listening to an old American podcast a few months ago. They were talking about a kid who went missing somewhere in Minnesota in the nineties. He was never found and the wrong guy was arrested, and even though he was ultimately not charged and set free, the townspeople persecuted him for it for years. Anyway, it turns out, if you don't catch them within twenty-four hours, your odds go down to infinitesimally close to zero. And that's with the police involved, 'cause things was different out there back then. Here, where no one cares, you get better odds playing the lotto than putting a picture of a missing kid on a milk carton.

But I made a promise to Gran to help, and so I have to at least try. If Mark came back, then there's hope for Ollie yet, however slim it may be. I just have to get Sherlocking about the whole thing.

The tea tastes like cow piss, but Susan made the effort, so I'll drink every drop. I give River another digestive and ask to see Ollie's room.

It's a tiny rectangular upstairs room, with a window looking out back and a pine single bed. There's pics of Ollie and his mum on the wall above the bed. I unstick one and pocket it. Football posters too – including a massive one of Tynccastle Park, the Jambos' home ground; I ain't impressed with that. Hibees forever. I also see crayon drawings. A box of toys packed away. Canvas wardrobe taking up a lot of space in one corner. Dirty sneakers under the bed. I sit on the mattress, take a good look around the room, and try to put the pieces of this puzzle together. It's all pretty normal here, which means stuff don't add up right now. Can't quite put my finger on it. What the hell happened to the wee man?

XVII

Outside snow falls.

Fine flakes slanting in the wind.

Been a couple of years since we last had any snow. Folks say that's because the planet's warmed up a few degrees and it's getting warmer still. But you forget all about that when you see the way snow fills the air. River steps out from her burrow and takes tentative steps. She pauses, front paw raised. Then she springs, nipping at the flakes. She prances around, battling this strange new foe left and right. Tail swishing this way and that. It's her first time too – must seem wondrous to her.

After showing her adversary who's boss, River returns to her burrow underneath my feet.

Gran's playing Ali Farka Touré. I'm not sure which song exactly. I know him by the sound of the kora. The tune's something timeless. Its swirling patterns gather up together and then break apart again. Gran says he's from the desert, but his music is snowflakes forever falling out of step with time. It takes you away, makes you forget everything. Who you are. Your worries. Until it's just you in a dreamy haze, the endless pure white of the snow desert. You linger in the music until

THE LIBRARY OF THE DEAD

the world calls you back and you remember yourself again as the song ends.

I wanna learn a stringed instrument. I know Chris Robson has an old violin going spare in his caravan; he used to be a classical musician, played in some orchestra, till he fell on hard times. You get a lot more hauling coal than playing cello. Maybe I could try it – see if the harmonics work for the deados as well as the mbira does? I've already got calluses on my thumbs, so . . .

'Izwi, have you done your homework?' I say, turning from the sink. She's got her face buried in my phone, playing *Plimo Close*. 'I know you can hear me.'

'I'll do it later,' Izwi mumbles.

'No, you'll do it right now.'

'Fuck's sake,' she says.

'Excuse you?' I put down the pot I'm washing. 'Am I hearing French in this house? I'm sorry, *je ne parle pas Français*.'

I leave the sink and stride across to stand over Izwi. Gran looks up.

'It's okay, Ropa. She misspoke,' Gran says. 'Let me talk to her.'

I point at Izwi, soapy water dripping from my finger onto the floor.

'You do not use that language in this house or anywhere else for that matter. Do you understand?' I say, my voice hoarse.

Kid blanks me like this is some sort of joke. Kinda cute in her defiance, but I'm not standing for any of that. Don't like having to do this, but you don't mess with big sis like that. Next the little shit will be cutting school and running with the slum urchins. If I don't make sure she's okay, who will? This whole thing falls on my shoulders; I've seen girls younger than her end up on the flesh market – and I'm not going to let that happen to my little sis. It's just her and Gran, they're all I've got.

'Do you understand me?'

Izwi sniffles, and then the waterworks come on, large tears streaming down her cheeks. I'm not buying that crap, not today. I rip the phone out of her hands.

And where's she getting this lingo from anyway? Scrap that. My problem isn't really with the swearing; everyone does it. It's knowing when to do it and when not to, and in front of one's own nan is definitely not one of them places you ever do that shit. She's a smart kid, but she's gonna have to figure that one out herself. With a little help from big sis.

I open my mouth again, but Izwi beats me to it.

'I'm sorry,' she cries out.

'No, you're not.'

'Ropa, let it go,' Gran says.

'I'm sorry, I'm sorry, I'm sowieee.'

Izwi slides over to Gran and buries her tearful face in her bosom. I'm ready to give her a rollicking of sergeant major proportions, but Gran holds her hand out and stops me. She puts her arm around Izwi.

'I'm sorry, Gran. It's just—' Cat puts two-inch nails in my tongue.

'It's okay. I understand. Get back to what you were doing,'

Gran says, very gently. 'Me and Izwi are going to have a little chat about how the anteater lost his tongue.'

Allah, no, that's worse than anything I could have done. I remember that story from the time I said my first 'fuck'. Something about a hip anteater who ends up pissing off the ancestors because of running his mouth off, on account of his long tongue. Of course, that had disproportionately disastrous repercussions for said anteater.

A new song starts up and the drums sound like someone thwacking someone else.

Gran starts on the story, Izwi's arms hanging round her neck. I toss the phone on the counter and get back to my dishes.

I know that's Ballaké Sissoko playing because the sound of the music is now falling cherry blossoms blowing in the wind through a courtyard, curved multi-layered pagodas, and courtiers scurrying about in silken garments.

After I've finished cleaning our kitchen and packed everything away, I open my backpack and take out the book Sir Callander gave me: *Thaumaturgical Enquiries Concerning the Thermodynamic Aspects of the Second Science* by W. Thomson. There's a title that could tranquillize an elephant.

Gotta set an example, since I've just ragged Izwi about her schoolwork. It's not easy 'cause I'm out long hours and stuff. Some days I get home late and she never gets to see me on the books. Doesn't help that I much prefer audiobooks to proper paper. I wasn't always like that, but needs must and all. There's a world of a difference between reading and hearing. I mean, you extract the same juice out of the fruit of knowledge – whether it's coming off pod or page. But with audio, I like hearing the sound of someone else's voice. I like having a guide with me through the maze. And I can also do other things while I listen, whereas when I read, that's it. There's no multitasking there and I ain't got no time for that.

After a while, I look up from my reading. Thomson blowing my mind. Gonna have to tell Callander that. It's already like my third eye's been opened and I can see the world afresh. Thomson says magic isn't inert or organic, something that just happens – it's the result of centuries of 'progressive scientific refinement'. It's only mystical to the uninitiated; for the modern scientific practitioner, it's plain as algebra. Fair enough, the book is dry and preachy, with that early nine-teenth-century authoritative tone, but it's so good I'm whizzing through.

The magician is like the engineer who, through a thoroughly scientific understanding of natural and supranatural law, shapes the world according to his will. The great questions of this age will be decided by wands and incantations.

This stuff's *brill*.

I know where I've been getting it wrong. First principles and all that. Gran's been trying to get me to do this earth stuff, but as Thomson points out, fire is the first true magic. Why else was Prometheus so viciously punished by Zeus? Chained to the rock where his liver was devoured daily by an eagle, only to regenerate and go through those tortures over and over, day after day after day.

The modern thaumaturge is the modern Prometheus.

See!

So, like Thomson's saying, back in the day when man was living in caves and trees, he was at the mercy of the elements. Wasn't no difference between humans and animals back then. And fire was this fearsome thing that happened when Zeus's thunderbolt struck the earth, and they would flee from it wailing and weeping. This pretty much remained the case until man was, like, screw this – wrested the reins from the gods and tamed fire for himself. Only then could man fire up Hephaestus's forge and master the elements, including matter itself, which changed the world with devastating force. Fire made civilisation possible. The gods weren't too happy about all that, especially top dog Zeus, but at least they got cool temples and burnt offerings in return.

Man, this shit's deep, like. Old Thomson does like to drone on in highfalutin language, like they did back in the day, but he hits the nail square on and it opens your eyes.

So, if I'm getting this stuff right, the first spell a magician must master is the making of fire. Everything else flows from that knowledge. And this is where the science mojo comes in. Making fire ain't no hocus-pocus, poof and it's there kind of thing. The laws of thermodynamics kick in. Magic can neither be created nor destroyed. The magician doesn't make fire happen; instead their task is to alter the state of entropy within a given system.

I get that, so far so good. It's like the magicians don't create the spark, but rather they shift things to a state of higher entropy. Kinda like pushing stuff to a tipping point, stuff that was gonna happen anyway. If you burn a piece of wood it releases energy, carbon dioxide and water vapour, leaving a pile of ash, thereby increasing the overall entropy of the universe. 'Cause entropy is, like, a funky way of saying chaos, 'cause all stuff kinda gets disordered over time anyway. If you clean your house, it gets dirty again, and so you have to expend energy cleaning it up all over again. Stuff also breaks down and rots away to simpler forms. That's what Thomson's on about . . . I think. The magician tips things over to the next state through the quadrat of will, focus, energy and knowledge.

The book's saying spells are merely scientifically proven methods of achieving a 'nexus of the quadrat' though language, thereby increasing the likelihood of the desired entropic shift. Basically, you need speech – the right words, said and ordered in the right way – to cross the thermodynamic threshold between the ordinary and the extraordinary. I have to understand what it is I want, and the full scientific implications of the spell, before I can do this. See, that makes a whole lot more sense than what Gran was trying to teach me without words.

This stuff's pure fire. Every neuron in me noggin's blazing up like it's the fifth of November! I need to learn more. This is the real thing –stuff Gran can't even dream of teaching me 'cause she's not a real magician who went to school. Damn, I'm bloody loving it.

XVIII

Gran's pretty cool, though. When I grow old I wanna be just like her. During the day, there's always someone knocking on the door of the trailer. They bring her wool, her favourite thing in the world, and she returns socks, hats, gloves, jumpers and whatnot. Doctor said she should exercise more, and I don't think he meant sitting on her berth all day knitting. It's like when they used to chain medieval monks to their desks and force them to copy texts – except she loves it. That's what Gran is, a knitting monk. And that rainbow-coloured cardigan she's been working on's coming along nicely now.

Nice out today. The sky's clear and bright. I can almost taste spring, though that's a while away yet. Izwi's still mad at me, though. Boy, can that kid hold a grudge. Wouldn't even let me walk her to school or give me a kiss before she left. Shot off with Eddie and his mum Marie instead. Through the window, I gaze at the snow-capped hills on the horizon. I can see lines and ruts in the earth, dark patches running against pristine white.

I remember when I was little and Gran got a call out to a farm near Dolphinton. The farmer came in a diesel pickup truck to get us. They were among the precious few allowed to get fuel on account of they needed it for their business. Imports were squeezed, and the king's men were rationing what was left of the North Sea reserves.

His name escapes me, but the farmer was desperate. He'd got Gran's number from a friend of a friend who knew a guy. Gramps was out shooting craps or some such. I only remember seeing him nights. Lovely man. He had a special scent. It's only when I grew older that I realized it was the smell of bathtub gin. Can't fault Gramps, though, 'cause he was a happy drunk. Anyway, Gran had to take us along since there was no one to look after us at home.

The A702 winds like a snake through villages and small towns. There's houses along the road whose front doors virtually open onto the tarmac. I sat in the middle, sandwiched between Gran and the farmer. Gran carried Izwi on her lap. The farmer had a long flowing beard and wore a tweed flat cap. His face was taut and tense, and he took the bends at such speed we were thrown from side to side.

'Fancy some baccy?' he said to Gran, offering a baggie.

'Don't mind if I do,' she replied.

I'd never known Gran to smoke, but it was chewing tobacco and she put a thumb's worth in her cheek. Never seen her take the stuff since, either.

We flew past fields full of sheep and heather. Drywall and fences. Hills rose and fell. Burns ran alongside the road and passed under it. Stumps stood sore where pine had been harvested and birds flew in the distance. The car hacked up phlegm when the farmer missed a gear and spluttered as we turned onto a dirt road sloping down into a steep gradient. I remember 'Ryecroft Farm' stencilled on a wall, and I can still see the weather-beaten sign in my head.

We bounced up and down the lane, going over a small stone bridge and through puddles from recent rains. 'The Black Mount runs through here,' said the farmer, pointing left to a range of nearby hills, their tops disappearing in the clouds. There'd be quite a view from the hills. We passed scrub and eventually reached a grove surrounding the farmhouse where he lived.

A woman in wellies came out to meet us. She wore stone-wash jeans and a sleeveless jacket. Her hair was raven-black, cropped short. The farmer said she was his wife and that he thought she'd be relieved to see us. As soon as he stopped, Gran got out and spat like a cowboy. She kept the lump of tobacco in her cheek.

They had a modern brick bungalow on their property. It was long and straight, but nothing extravagant. Four, maybe five bedrooms. It had that fresh look buildings have before they settle properly on the land. The bricks hadn't yet taken on a bit of moss or grime. The gutters were shiny. The house was attached by a new corridor to an older stone cottage with slat roofing.

The farmer's wife – whose name was Kathleen, if my memory serves me right – came up and shook Gran's hand. When she got to me, she smiled awkwardly and patted my head.

'It's been a nightmare,' Kathleen said, turning back to Gran.

'I heard, but these things often have natural causes. Show me the damage.'

'If it's natural, I'll eat his hat,' Kathleen said curtly.

She took us to the back of the cottage, where a Douglas fir had fallen and smashed part of the roof. The building itself was intact, a testament to the craftsmanship of them builders of yesteryear, who made things to last. Gran traced the tree trunk down to its roots. She crouched low down, keeping Izwi on her knee. There was still a good bit of earth stuck to the roots. The ditch left by the uprooted tree was half filled with muddy water. I looked in and saw my face and the sky reflected.

'Could be the wind that made it fall. These trees are very old,' Gran said.

'The trunk would have collapsed if the rot had got to it. And look at the size of that hole. The earth's firm here,' the farmer replied, stomping the ground for show. 'The wind don't explain the broken windows either. The way sheep go crazy when put in that barn overnight. The dreadful sounds we hear in the dark. It's unbearable.'

'How long have you lived here?' Gran asked.

'About six months,' the farmer replied.

'Eight,' his wife corrected him. 'That's when the mortgage came through. Only took seven years to get one.'

'Did the previous owners say anything about these issues?'

'Not a bloody word, the cowards,' Kathleen said.

'We're not the kind of people who believe in things that go bump in the night anyway,' said the farmer. 'Goddamn it, I'm an atheist.'

Gran stood up and nodded. 'That might be why it took months for the attacks to start. Their activity grows stronger over time. And if you're not a believer, you often miss the early warning signs that something unnatural's going on.'

A strong wind blew in from the hills and the trees swayed. Gran walked over to the barn, which was the largest structure in the courtyard, a little removed from the houses. There was a broken harrow, its round discs rusting. Bales of hay. The husk of an old steam tractor.

Dusk was setting in.

Gran handed me the baby. There was something about her expression. It was hard to tell what she was focusing on, though something had obviously captured her attention. We all followed her gaze, but clearly none of us could see what she was seeing. She stood at the barn doors, not staring at them, more looking *through* them, maybe at something inside. The timbers groaned and the farmer's wife flinched.

Gran turned back – her attention suddenly with us again – and said casually, 'I believe you promised dinner.'

The dining room window looked out through the trees onto the imposing hill beyond. It was a dark mass against the sky now that night had descended. Gran went to the bathroom to change Izwi, while I sat at the table waiting for food. A fire was raging in the wood burner in the living room.

We had stovies and mushy peas that night. The rich aroma of potatoes, onions and home-made lamb mince filled the room. I parroted Gran's compliments to the farmer and his wife.

After dinner, Gran cleared her throat. She drank some wine and began to speak.

'A vile and horrible deed was done upon this land many

generations ago. The woman who lived in that old cottage went to the barn one morn. It was another barn, not the one you have now, which stands in its stead. The woman, carrying her baby, went to look at the animals. There she stumbled and the wee bairn fell out of her hands and hit its head upon a rock.'

Even though the fire was roaring, the room seemed to drop in temperature and we all shivered. Sometimes it felt like Gran was a wee bit too good at telling stories.

'My, she wept like the wind tearing through those poplars now. And hearing her distress, the villagers came and found her with blood on her hands. They were torn. Some said it must have been an accident, while others suggested darkly that she did the deed. But seeing the truth of her grief, they let her be. Not long after, another misfortune befell her: her eldest son drowned in a shallow creek not far from here. A double tragedy was taken for a sign of something more sinister in those days.'

The wind rattled the shutters, and the rafters above creaked ominously. I leaned closer to Gran.

'They named her witch and demanded just punishment. But before they sent her to be dunked, she put the rope to her own neck and swung off the rafters in that old barn. Those are the horrors this soil has seen, and the soil remains soaked in those horrors, for she was not given the comfort of a Christian burial. No such kindness was shown to suicides then. Or witches – which is what she'd been named. She was damned either way.'

There was a chilled silence in the room. Kathleen put one hand to her collarbone.

'The older boy I did not see, but the woman and her unbaptized bairn have joined the people who are not in the light. It is them we must help,' said Gran. She stood, ready for business. Although first she opened the baby bag and took out a bottle of milk. 'One of you must stay here with the baby. The other will come with me.'

Kathleen chose to go with Gran, much to the relief of her husband. I was happy to stay, shaken from the tale as I was. But then Gran called me out and said she needed my help.

Gran and Kathleen each carried a solar lamp. Kathleen unlocked the barn door and swung it open. I was shitting myself, knees shaking and all. The talk of witches and dead babies had left me spooked out. Didn't much like all the noises coming out of the darkness beyond the lamplight neither.

'I need you to be brave, Ropa,' said Gran. She stroked my cheek. '*Whatever happens*, hold that door open.'

I nodded, and she and Kathleen went inside. Their lamps illuminated the hay on the floor and the wood beams that criss-crossed above. It was damp and smelled of animals, though none were inside. Gran held her light high up above her head. For a short woman, she cast a long shadow across the barn. Then she walked to each of the four corners of the building, before finding a place in the dead centre.

Them days, I couldn't yet see the people who are not in the light, never mind talk to them. All I saw were Gran and Kathleen standing in the middle of the barn. In the lamplight, their shadows crept to the walls.

'Mairghread, it is time now,' Gran said in a strong voice. The wooden timbers above buckled and groaned, and the farmer's wife crossed herself. 'A great wrong was done to you, that is true. Yet you hold not just yourself in the dark, but your child's soul, too. These people are not the ones who wronged you—'

The hay beneath their feet stirred. It circled across the floor, resembling dust devils, though there was no breeze in the barn. A milk pail fell on its side and rattled.

'Those who wronged you are long gone and the grief you hold onto is not ours to assuage.'

The barn began to quiver. Wood clattered against wood. Someone was pushing hard against the door I was holding, trying to close it. I bent my back and with the palms of my hands firmly against the wood, I pushed back. I started sliding backwards, then found my footing and held firm against the unseen force.

'Enough now!' Gran said testily. If we were in a tempest, then she was the thunderclap. 'I said enough, Mairghread. I will cast you out by my Authority if I have to.'

The force pushing against me relaxed and I swung the door fully open once more. The hay settled and the barn became still. My heart was pounding. The farmer's wife was pale. She held her lamp close to her chest, mouth agape.

The silence that followed was even more unnerving than the rattling.

'Go now, Mairghread. You have no business in this realm anymore. I set you free from your pain and your just rage. I bestow on you warmth and love, to take with you to the halls of your ancestors. When you reach their vast lands, where the grass is tall and the cattle are fat, where the sun rises twice a day, once from the east and once from the west, they will weigh your heart against a feather and find it lighter. Be on your way now. All is well.' Gran's face softened as she pointed towards the open door.

I felt something cold brush against me and make its way into the yard. A moment or two later, something small crawled past my ankles. Gran stood with her feet apart for a minute or two longer, staring into the darkness, before she was satisfied. Then she put her hand on Kathleen's shoulder and told her it was done.

When we left the barn, Gran thanked me and told me I'd been brave. My hands were bleeding from the splinters that had dug in.

XIX

I meet up with Nicola at the pits to give her an update and vague reassurances that I'm on the case. The only thing I can think of at the moment is to use my plug at the Library. Someone there might know what's going on. I'd be on it 24/7, an old briar pipe in hand, deerstalker hat on my head, if I had the dosh. But I have to earn my bread. The troll's riding my arse and I have to come up with the rent soon, else we're gonna have to find a way to move our flat-tyred caravan somewhere else. But I'm doing the best I can, and I let Nicola know that Niall and Susan were asking after her before she's sucked back into the everyThere.

River's playing guard fox, but she doesn't react when Mrs 'It's not Ms, it's Mrs' Drummond comes over. She's a matronly ghost, huge bosom, wide hips, bun at the top of her head and half-moon glasses on the tip of her nose. I'm not sure if ghosts have ophthalmological conditions, but I've seen all sorts in my day: heads dangling, severed limbs, that kind of shit. They manifest in whatever form they feel most comfortable, so who am I to judge? She's a regular. Back in the day she was a proper amazing baker. Ran a wee cakery up Bruntsfield way. It closed down 'cause no one knew her recipes and it just wasn't the same with the new owners after she passed.

'I'm sorry to bother you,' Mrs Drummond says. 'I know you're awfully busy.'

'That I am,' I reply. I have a soft spot for her. She's been a great customer for months, and her grandson, to whom she sends messages, always pays without complaint. That's my kind of people.

'It's just, rather, I'm not sure, you see.'

'Before we start, I need to make sure you are aware of the terms and conditions of the service, et cetera.'

'Why, yes, of course.' She pulses, which I take for some level of indignation. 'I'm happy to give you other recipes, you know, but the Battenberg sponge . . . Oh, I don't know.'

'We've tried all that and you're still here, Mrs Drummond.'

'Well, I know that!' she says. River's ears prick up. 'I'm sorry. I must control myself. It's just. Aww. I've already given up the mirlitons, the Victoria sponge, pithiviers, ginger cake, my Madeira, even the brandy snaps à la crème. Does it have to be the Battenberg? They won't know how to do it properly if I give you the recipe anyway. They'll mess it up, make changes. Oh, this is too much.'

I tap my foot on the ground. Will it work? Won't it? Why not? Other impatient ghosts wait their turn, flickering in the night while I deal with her. It's taken me a while to build up my practice to the stage where I now have a dozen waiting to be seen. Gotta build up a solid reputation, even with the dead. They may not have TripAdvisor reviews going on, but they don't take kindly to being messed about, so I try to keep my whole thing professional.

'Mrs Drummond, I have a plan,' I say.

◉ ◉ ◉

The next evening, after a hard day's tramping around delivering messages, I hit the Braids, near the golf course. It's mondo-posh, the kind of place where the council still bothers to send the sweepers out and there's neighbourhood watch stickers on every other gate. Then again, I suppose everywhere's posh compared to where I'm from. But these guys have long since untethered from the rest of us. They're ascended into a different stratosphere, where the air's so thin you need a respirator to breathe. It's a slog walking past the grand houses this end. And most of them hide behind tall hedges or walls with razor-wire on top, so you can't even do any good snooping.

My feet are killing me already – my kingdom for a bike, anyone?

I come to a monster detached two-storey, mock-Edwardian house and press the buzzer. Have to do it for a bit before Colin picks up and I smile at the camera. The electric gate whirrs open and I find myself on the drive with a Tesla four-wheeler plugged into the port near the house.

The front garden alone could fit a fair few caras, I reckon.

Colin's holding open the front door, wearing a slightly puzzled expression. He's in chinos and a purple-white jumper, nice as anything Gran could knit. The Scotch slippers on his feet don't quite match.

'Look who the cat dragged in,' he says in a silky voice.

'You have no idea what the cat's got, man.'

'I thought you told Barry we had the last recipe.' He steps aside to let me in and I ask him to hold the door.

'There's someone with me,' I say.

'Who? Where?' He looks around.

'Say hi to Mrs Drummond,' I tell him, pointing at her standing on the threshold. Colin squints and looks through her, then back at me. 'I know, I know, but she's right in front of you. Be polite and say hello.'

'Hello?' he says, a bit hesitant in case I'm pulling his leg.

'She says, "Hello Colin, I've missed your toddy",' I say, and add, 'Now walk past him so he feels the chill. That might convince him.'

'Brrr,' says Colin, shaking his shoulders as Mrs Drummond moves right through him. 'Oh my.'

I'm gonna have to use my mbira to keep her earthed. Don't think she can hold on much longer using her own resources. I shiver a bit myself, as the house is lukewarm, just on the cusp of bearable. I imagine it costs a princeling and some to keep it heated, even with solar panels on the roof. I go into the lounge and plonk myself onto the long-ass four-seater. The giant cushions on it are super-comfy. These guys have it made. They work in television – not as actors, but behind the scenes where the big money is. They have a giganormous flat screen, longer than our caravan, mounted on the wall. Bookshelves you need a ladder to reach the top of. Pictures of them getting married, honeymooning in Cuba. There's them climbing Everest. Mrs Drummond hovers next to me and if I look to my left through her, I can see out the French doors into a back garden lit up by security lights.

Barry comes in wearing a Scotch dressing gown that matches Colin's slippers. Cute. Barry's hair's wet and I imagine him leaving a candlelit bath in a bit of a hurry.

127

Mrs Drummond smiles seeing him, and for a flash she almost looks alive.

'It's about the chapel-window cake. I told you, Lin,' he says, voice just a few octaves from eardrum perforating.

'Your grandmother says "Sorry I was holding out on you",' I pass on.

'She's here,' Colin adds.

'*Here* here? In this house?' Barry asks, looking in completely the wrong direction.

I point, so he knows she's right beside me. Barry sure as hell can't see shit, but he smiles all the same. I suppose one doesn't get to be a top TV exec without some imagination.

'Bloody hell,' Barry says, then immediately checks himself. 'Sorry, I meant, hello, Grandmother dearest.'

I swear I hear Mrs Drummond laugh for the first time ever. She's fading, though, so I pick up my mbira. I explain briefly about harmonics and all that jazz, and jam a soft riff off Sekuru Gora. It immediately stabilizes Mrs Drummond's wave. So far, so good, but I have to get to the business side of things. The customers ain't my friends. Just something I need to keep reminding myself, like a mantra.

'I'm sorry to cut in, guys, but we have to deal with payment,' I say.

'We can do that later, can't we?' says Barry.

'Sorry, it's company policy. I'm not allowed to . . . ' Naturally, I don't say I'm the company, but pinning it on some distant faceless corp always does the trick. 'Because this is a specialized service, outwith the normal "message to end user" protocols, I will need to ask for a dozen dukes now and an additional ten shillings for every extra hour after the first.'

Colin and Barry hold their hands up in unison, like the Corsican Brothers. Once I've been paid, it's straight to the kitchen.

If I thought folks in the Braids were living in a different town, in this kitchen I see they're clearly in a different era altogether. They've gone for a woodsy, dated feel. Oak everywhere – from the table to the cabinets and dresser that run the length of the opposite wall. Copper pots and pans, an antique black cast-iron kettle on display. The only thing out of step with the period feel is the steel-finish panel light dangling from the ceiling above the breakfast bar.

Mrs Drummond asks me to emphasize that the making of the Battenberg cannot be rushed. Ever. She even offers to come back another day if Barry and Colin have other plans – an offer that is politely and firmly refused.

'Oh, I don't know about this,' she says to me. But before I can relay the message, she gives me a stern look, fingertip on lip. 'They're going to mess it up. I just know it.'

'Be cool,' I reply.

'We are cool,' the guys say together. They're at the cupboard picking out bakeware.

'I wasn't talking to you,' I reply, thumbing my mbira.

Another thing they have in abundance out here is food. I'm talking a fruit bowl with imported stuff. Dates and red grapes! That's crazy. Colin opens the double-door fridge to get the eggs and it's jam-stuffed. The glowing light makes it look like pirate treasure. I've never seen so much cheese in my life.

These guys are living the dream. I'm clearly in the wrong blooming profession.

On one kitchen shelf they keep a stack of recipe books and, just below that, an impressive spice rack that the Maharajas would have envied.

There's aprons hanging at the door and the guys insist I wear one as well. I want to say no, but then again, he who pays the piper and all that . . . even if it's a lame tune. It says California on my apron, and shows a buff dude with oiled up muscles, riding a wave on a surfboard.

Mrs Drummond's pulsating and I'm afraid she might bail on me, so I quickly say, 'Let's get this party started,' and give her the thumbs up.

'You are not to share this recipe with anyone,' Mrs Drummond says, and I relay it to the guys. 'You have ground almonds?'

'I was thinking maybe we could try ground rice to get that coarser texture,' Colin says.

Mrs Drummond expands like a balloon, and I'm afraid she'll pop and cover us all in ectoplasmic goo. I shake my head vigorously and tell them we have to do it her way or it's the highway. Barry preheats the oven to 180 degrees. I take a seat at the head of the table and start relaying instructions.

Reckon I'll squeeze an extra two or three hours off this racket. The flatscreen TV on the wall's showing an interview. Some upper-class geezer's talking to Siobhan about her new memoir, *Becoming Siobhan Kavanagh*. Everyone just knows her as 'Siobhan', right from the old days when she was a Page 3 girl, before she morphed into a national treasure. She hovered over that fine line between sex bomb and girl next door when she was younger. Now she's like the cool aunt everyone wishes they had, with bags of money to boot. Her empire includes fashion, beauty products, TV shows, philanthropy and even ghostwritten novels – not written by actual ghosts, of course. But in this interview, she says she wrote the memoir by herself, every single word. I'll wait till the rush is over and it's in pirate audio, then maybe me and Gran will listen to it together.

'You guys work in telly and all. Ever met her?' I ask.

'Lots of times. My company has co-produced some shows with her. She's a queen in every way,' Barry says.

'I'd give a kidney and half a tit to meet her,' I say, catching myself because Mrs Drummond gives me quite the stare.

Barry laughs. 'Trust me, I've met people who offered more than that.'

While I'd never be tempted to give away someone's family recipe, confidentiality and all that, I think the key's in the butter substitute and the choice of jam Mrs Drummond insisted on. In her opinion, it's an ingenious deviation from the traditional Battenberg. Colin looks a little concerned, with his furrowed brow. I reckon he has other ideas about how this whole thing shoulda woulda coulda been done.

The mixer whizzes. Colin crushes dried raspberries to a powder. He makes quite the show of it. I have a go at rearranging the flowers on the table while I take a break. My thumbs are killing me. The metal keys of the mbira are hard as heck.

They add eggs to the mix, bit by bit. Mrs Drummond's hovering near the ceiling now. She seems to be in some form of acute psychic distress and I change my tune. Ghost sweat appears on her face.

'Gently, make sure you keep the air in there,' she says, and I pass on the message.

'We know what we're doing,' Colin says.

'Tut,' Mrs Drummond goes. I don't bother relaying that one. 'It looks a bit thick. Add a drop of milk, please.'

After they're done, the guys divide the mix into two separate bowls. One's for the almond, and the raspberry goes into the other; it will give one of the cakes that pink colour.

If Mrs Drummond is to be believed, the Battenberg is the greatest thing ever created in these here isles. 'Queen of cakes,' she calls it. I'm more partial to good old carrot cake myself. I also don't mind walnut cake. Then there's Victoria sponge. Hell, throw in fruit cake. I'll have any cake, even cakes that aren't cakes, like cheesecake or Nutella crunch cake. Not that we get much of any kind of cake, full stop. The ingredients ain't cheap.

'Would you like to dip your finger?' Colin asks, and I don't need to be asked twice.

I stick my index finger into the red mix and taste the stuff. Divine.

'Really, guys, really?' says Barry.

'I know you want to,' Colin says.

'So mature, both of you,' Barry replies, moving the bowls out of reach.

They bake the cakes for half an hour, and Colin makes tea.

Gran used to bake too, before her diabetes went crazy, and prices rose. A thick, rich, heady scent rises from the oven. It takes me back to the days when Gramps was still alive, and we had a place out in Forrester Park. Used to be nice . . .

'Tell my grandmother we miss her,' Barry says soberly. 'It hasn't been the same. I'm so sorry she never got to see her grandkids.'

Colin puts an arm around him and they touch heads for a second. Mrs Drummond's welling up again. I rest up on the mbira for a bit. Sometimes the sound of silence is the best song. Only the low hum of the oven fan breaks through. I look out the window, past our reflections, into the garden.

When the cakes come out steaming, I swear my mouth waters. Colin and Barry leave them to cool and make marzipan together. I get to help by spreading the jam around the lengths of cake after they cut it into four equal strips. Barry neatly sandwiches them together again, making a geometrically perfect plus sign of melted apricot glaze in the centre, which sticks the pieces together. There's pink then yellow on top, and yellow then pink on the bottom layer. Yum.

Barry rolls the whole thing up in marzipan and, voila, Battenberg cake.

'I'll hand it to them, they've done well,' says Mrs Drummond.

'Look at it,' I reply. 'It's brilliant.'

'Okay, better than well, but the proof is in the pudding.'

Mrs Drummond has a point there.

'Guys, she says we have to taste it. For scientific purposes, of course,' I say, in a completely dispassionate tone.

Colin cuts three slices and I tell him to get a fourth, which we place symbolically to one side. Ghosts can't eat, obviously. As far as I know, the only real offering deados can take is spilt alcohol, on account of water being able to traverse the two planes. But it's the thought that counts.

I take a man-sized bite and beauty explodes on my tongue. I totally get why Mrs Drummond wanted to take this thing to her grave with her. It's manna, it's ambrosia, it belongs in the seventh heaven. So light and jammy and almondy and tasty. A symphony of sweetness and delight. Mrs Drummond hovers appreciatively as we dig in.

'I can feel her spirit in this thing. My God,' says Barry, through a mouthful of cake. 'Takes me back to my childhood summers when the days were long.'

I stand up and turn to Mrs Drummond.

'How do you feel?' I ask.

'Light as a feather.'

She lifts up and glows brighter still. It's like dawn rising on a clear day. The lights in the room flicker. Mrs Drummond floats up and up. Then she scatters into fine powder like self-raising flour, sailing through the ceiling. I jump off my chair and run to the window where I see her ascend higher, her essence merging with the stars. There's nothing holding her down now. Let her fly. She is free.

And for me, that means on to the next one.

XX

I'm heading away from Edinburgh's West End when an electric whirrs past me. Been bogged down chasing green all day, and I've neglected Nicola's task. Mrs Drummond's grandkid has paid me quite a bit, though, so I can get back on it. It's time to revisit the Library. It means going through the city centre again, but needs must and all that.

The cold slips in through the soles of my boots and my feet are ice blocks as they plod through the latest snowfall. There's a mass of people trudging down Princes Street, coats wrapped tight round their bodies. Our feet crunch on the snow, now a fist deep. It sticks to your face and catches on your eyelids, blinding you. My ears sting, and still it falls, burying the litter and dirt that decorates these streets. It's ironic how as the city decays, the old stone quarters and those ancient buildings hold out better than the newer steel and glass structures. These are the parts that will remain long after everything else is gone. They are its soul.

I put my hands in my pockets and even the stones I keep ready there, as ammo for my katty, are freezing. I pass by a group of women, all bearing daggers openly sheathed by their sides. Since the bad days when folks were looting and raping, it's been law here that a woman may carry a blade – no longer than six inches – on her person for self-defence. A man can swing his schlong, whatever the length. The king decreed it and so it remains up and down the land.

There are mule-drawn carts and donkey wagons trundling along the street, headed back out to the crofters beyond the bypass. Tramline's still there but I ain't seen one go by for yonkers. Folks on bicycles struggle through the ungritted street and police on horseback trot through, leaving steaming droppings on the fresh fallen snow. It's late and the shutters are up on the shops to my left. I'd give anything for a mug of hot chocolate about now.

The cold air drives away the auld reekie, which blossoms on warmer days. It is at its most intense when there's enough heat to raise foul odours – and these mix in with smoke pouring out the city's chimneys, creating the foulest fog this side of the equator.

I run my hand along the wrought-iron fencing that runs beside the new loch. Old fellas say all this used to be a garden filled with flowers of all sorts that bloomed in a riot of colour. The only thing that remains now are petrified trees, whose forlorn branches still stand out above the waterline. On a bright day, you can catch sight of the steps and statues submerged below. On more peaceful nights, lights reflect on the still surface of water. The new loch formed after the council offices in the East End collapsed. Their rubble forms one wall of the dam. The west side was sealed when the train tunnel was blown up by separatists, and the water now runs on until it submerges St Cuthbert's Church in the West End.

In the depths, you can still see bits of the famed glass roof of Waverly Station. Triangular peaks and troughs like waves beneath the water. Underneath are locomotives frozen in time, arriving or departing from the platforms below. This mirror world all belongs to the loch now. The trains that do run can only come in as far as Haymarket and no further. Calton Road runs under the bridge and now plunges into the water like a tributary. Occasionally a piece of luggage floats up, drifts to shore and makes the news.

I make my way onto Calton Hill, clamber up the slippery steps until I get to the unfinished Parthenon, and climb up the base. This was meant to be a perfect replica of the temple in Athens, but the cash ran out, so all they did was pillars and lintels and not a lot else. It's deserted up here. Not a soul in sight; not unexpected, given the weather. Sneddon told me which pillar to find after warning me that I was not permitted to use the librarians' entrance Jomo took me through. Something to do with protocol, yadda yadda. I find the right pillar and walk around it, but I can't see anything but smooth stone. I'm looking for something, a button to press – I don't know. Sneddon didn't give many specifics.

I'm *sure* he said the third pillar . . .

I place my palm against the pillar, thinking maybe I should call Jomo to figure this malarkey out when a hairline fracture appears. As I discover next time, this forms the outline of a narrow door. Then a whole section of the pillar I'm holding onto vanishes into thin air, and I stumble down the rabbit hole. The world spins sickeningly around me and I squeeze my eyes shut.

After a moment, I open my eyes and brave a quick peek. Calton Hill has vanished and I find myself inside a small room with a fire roaring in the fireplace. A little old man in a maroon bellhop outfit, complete with round cap, is sitting on a stool beside the only door in the room. It's closed. He startles from his sleep, grunts and curses, then regards me with drooping eyelids.

'You're new,' he says with a drawl. 'Library card?'

I give him the ear Sneddon gave me and he punches a pinprick hole in the lobe before passing it back. He gestures to the passageway and mumbles, 'Through the Abyssinian entrance and down the stairs.' I'm about to thank him when he shuts his eyes, drops his chin to his chest and promptly starts snoring.

I pick up my phone and step under an archway with the inscription:

'SCIENCE IS THE GREAT ANTIDOTE TO THE
POISON OF ENTHUSIASM AND SUPERSTITION'.

Beyond is an expanse of stone stairs, with more wise quotations visible on the walls on either side of me as I head downwards. I recall what Jomo said about the readers descending into the Library, whereas the librarians ascend into it. These stairs are steep and large, like they were designed for really tall people. Either that or I'm much shorter than I thought I was. The steps make me feel like a child as I carefully make my way down to the reception. There are faded murals on the walls too. Crucifixes and haloed heads.

In reception, Sneddon smiles like we're old pals when I walk up to the desk.

'Miss,' he says.

'Hey, Mr Sneddon,' I say. I'm sussing him out to see if there's going to be any of that 'hanging by the neck until I expire' malarkey. If they dare this time, I'm getting the first punch in.

'Wonderful to see you again.' That'll do for me.

'I need to see Sir Callander,' I say.

'I have no idea if the secretary is coming in today. When he does come in, it's usually later than this. You can leave a note in his pigeon hole if you like.'

'Cheers, but I think I'll wait.' I start walking away.

Sneddon clears his throat and I stop.

'I don't mean to be indelicate, Miss Moyo, but there is the small matter of the money you owe the Library.' I shrug. I don't have that kind of money at the moment. 'If this isn't a suitable time you may go through, but I must warn you there are additional fees imposed if it goes unpaid for much longer. We wouldn't want you to part with any more than you have to.'

'I'll sort it some other time,' I say, bailing. They might as well draw blood from a stone.

Don't really know where I'm supposed to be heading, but Jomo mentioned something about a section for medical texts. Reckon I'll find a few books and set myself up someplace where I can keep an eye out for Callander. Seems like these guys don't do orientations or nothing like that. I'm sort of slouching as I walk around, so I straighten up like I know what's going on. Gotta fake it till I make it.

'Hey there,' a husky voice hails me.

I look around and see no one, nothing but endless rows of

dusty books.

'Over here.'

'Marco,' I say.

'Polo,' she replies.

I glance up and see a girl in a wheelchair directly above me, looking down with a Cheshire cat grin. She's fully upside down. Like, attached to the ceiling upside down. Our eyes lock and she waves. I snatch a quick peek at the floor beneath my boots just to check the gravitational situation, and then look up again, bending my neck as far back as I can. The girl waves again and I wave back like a muppet. She points to the wall by the far row of shelves and wheels herself towards it. I'm kinda weirded out by the whole scenario, but I roll with it.

The girl's strapped in with some sort of harness around her thighs that stops her from dropping out. How exactly the wheelchair Peter Parkers on the ceiling is beyond me. She reaches the wall and descends until she hits the floor, and wheels towards me. Upright. Normal. I point to the ceiling.

'It helps me concentrate,' she says, coming right up to me. She taps her forehead. 'Gets blood flowing to the nut.'

I raise my eyebrows.

'Seriously, it's cool. I have a special dispensation for spells of an ambulatory nature. It's sort of like a blue badge.'

'Uh.'

She's got short hair dyed silver with a purple fringe. Her clothes are a hippy riot of colour. Orange pants, green Converse shoes and a psychedelic tie-dye top that hurts the eyes. She wears tons of bracelets and a beaded necklace.

'You're Melsie Mhondoro's grandkid, aren't you? I've heard all about your gate-crashing antics. Plenty of loose lips in this Library. You have quite the orenda about you too, wow.'

I have no idea what she even means by that, but I keep it cool. Don't wanna look ignorant in front of a nineteen-year-old hippy. She unclips the straps on her harness and packs them in the folds of the wheelchair. Then she offers her hand.

'Priyanka Kapoor, healing and herbology at the Kelvin Institute.' I shake her hand. She has an iron grip. 'You can call me Priya.'

'Ropafadzo Moyo, ghostalking, erm, home-schooled, I guess.'

'People do that?' Priya says and clasps her hands with delight. 'How original. Word of advice, hot lips: next time call your craft *practical necromancy*. This place is a *snob-fest*.' She finishes off with a flourish, 'Though most of the scholars are alright, really.'

'You can call me Ropa.'

'I was gonna call you that anyway. Come with me, I have to see what you've got.'

I don't have time to think, so I follow Priya as she wheels through the section. I'm happy to latch onto someone for the time being. She seems okay. Maybe she might even teach me the ropes about how all this works. There's something about her round, open face that you can trust straight away. But I also sense an edge to Priya. Following her feels like white-water rafting, and she's the free-flowing river whose waters run deep. I think of hidden rocks and churning white spray.

Priya takes me to the stairs, which are more human-sized

down here.

'Want me to help you down?' I reach for her chair. 'Is there a lift somewhere?'

'Pfft.'

Before I can grab the handles, Priya's off. I panic and go after her. The wheelchair clanks down the stairs, gaining speed. Her head bobs from side to side. The chair's bouncing and clattering, making quite the racket. And even though I'm taking two steps at a time, I can't keep up with it. She's definitely gonna fall and hurt herself, while I stand by like a bloody lemon.

'Oh my God,' I cry. The noise of the wheels as they hit the stairs is insane, then it ends with a bang when Priya reaches the floor below. I'm a few seconds behind, experiencing a heart attack.

Priya swivels her chair, which is still moving away from me, and turns just as I land on the floor.

'Look at your face,' she says, laughing, and slaps her thighs, tears rolling down her cheeks.

I stop to catch my breath. My heart's pounding in my ribcage. I bend over and touch my knees. Total fuckery this.

'You could break your neck doing that,' I say, collecting myself.

'Can't be any worse – I've already done my spine in two places,' she deadpans.

A 'shh' comes from somewhere behind the bookshelves.

'Follow me,' Priya whispers, still giggling.

We wind up in the underHume. It's so called, as far as I can tell, because it's literally under the sarcophagus of David Hume. There are catacombs and locked doors. The doors are metal, and some of them have bars. Has the feel of an old dungeon and the ceilings are so low a tall man would have to stoop. I follow Priya into a cave-like room with bare black stone walls. It's the type of place ancient man might have used for a slumber after a hard day's hunt. Instead of a club, I have a backpack, and I place it on the floor, which is swept and polished pristine.

'So, how come you know my nan?' I ask Priya as she closes the door.

'Don't be silly.' She frowns like I've said something really stupid. 'Stand there, right in the middle. I've been looking forward to this, ever since I heard about you.'

I go to the spot she's pointing at.

'Well?' she says.

'What?'

'Do something.' Priya balls her fists and flicks her fingers.

I give her the stare. 'You think I'm a performing monkey?'

'Don't be a bore. Do some magic, come on.'

I stand, dumbfounded.

'That's not how it works,' I say. 'I just talk to dead people and deliver messages, that's all. And there's no dead people in here, as far as I can see.'

Priya wheels herself along the wall. The titanium frame of her wheelchair glistens in the light. The wheelchair's very spick and spanny and, for some reason, it makes me think of pictures of Sputnik which I saw in a book on the space race. The tyres are chunky with deep treads and her seat is custom upholstered with funkadelic comic-strip imagery.

'They wouldn't have let you in if you couldn't do manipulatory magic. That's active, not passive.'

'I'm learning to make fire.'

'A bit kindergarten, but go on, show me the colour of your flame.'

I need to find the right formula, words from the incantation that agitate the inflection point, so I go to my bag and reach for my copy of Thomson. I have the page bookmarked. Apparently, back in the day, spells and magical instruction were authored in Greek, but after the Scientific Synod of 1893 there was a move to English. Which is great for me because I can't read a lick of Greek. I find the right page and place the book on the floor.

Okay, here goes. I hold my arms to each side, palms facing the centre of the room, and incant:

'Spark of Prometheus from the eternal flame of Mount Olympus, I call upon thee to light this forge of mine.'

Nothing happens. Okay, that's cool – it's not like I've actually done this before. Here we go, for real this time. I concentrate and raise my voice, repeating the incantation word for word. Thomson says this vocalisation is crucial for the novice.

'*Spark of Prometheus . . .*' I'm picturing fire from the '*eternal flame of Mount Olympus*', which is the anchor of the spell. Most basic spells have three parts: the approach, the anchor and the accelerant – AAA. Get one of them wrong and poof, no magic.

I'm trying to get the right rhythm and flow of words, so I can get into the zone, but it doesn't help that Priya's gawking with no small amount of condescension written on her face.

'*Spark of Prometheus* . . .' I'm trying to put in the vital energy needed to cross the thermodynamic potential into action. My neck and shoulders feel tense. I'm trying to get the words right. I try. And try.

But nothing happens.

After a few goes, I decide I've had enough of making myself look like an arse and give up.

There's clearly a gap between knowing the spells and performing them. I know what I'm supposed to say, but that's not good enough. I'm not used to flunking, but maybe magic is the one subject I'm not good at. Doesn't matter if it's Gran trying to teach me or some toff in a book. Maybe I'm just not cut out for this.

'That's it?' says Priya. She has a smirk on. 'Neat party trick. *Spark of Prometheus*, woo.' She giggles.

'Cut it out,' I say.

'Your face cracks me up . . . Okay, I'm sorry, I'll stop now. I'm taking the mick. Don't mind me, I'm stupid like that. No, but seriously, that's why I don't dig Thomson.'

'What do you mean?'

'He's all about the homogenization of magical practice, which was all the rage in his time, trying to reduce the art to simple mechanics. It's very old school.' She wheels herself to where I'm standing and shoos me back towards the wall. 'The problem is, there's no way around his long shadow when you're starting out.'

'I enjoyed reading it, actually,' I say, a bit unsure what she'll think of me now. I feel like my pants are on the floor.

'If you like that sort of thing, then maybe you should try Montague and Chandrasekar's *Foundational Aspects of Scientific Magic*. It's a bit more contemporary, and after that you can follow up with their *Further Aspects*. You should get them both together if you're a fast learner.'

'Thanks.'

'Here, let me show you,' Priya says, parking her chair and putting the brakes on.

She goes all zen. 'Find your nexus point first,' she says. 'The words are supposed to be a channel to your will, not its surrogate.' She exhales and inhales. It's kind of meditative. Her gaze is fixed to a point in the room somewhere between us, a tiny dot in the air. Only now do I notice how green her eyes are, turquoise as a tropical sea. She takes her time. Four, maybe five seconds pass.

'Flame on,' she says with a snap of her fingers.

A tiny spark appears in the air between us. I gasp and Priya gives me a triumphant smile. The spark flickers, then suddenly it shoots towards my book. It strikes the top corner of the open page, which catches alight instantly. The flame's the translucent green of burning boron, and it looks properly witchy.

'Oh, no – quick, get it!' Priya cries.

For a moment I hoped it might be an illusion, but acrid smoke rises from the page. I hastily stomp on the book with my boot, killing the flame. It doesn't smell like normal fire. It's intensely chemical, pungent enough to make me scrunch my nose. Carefully I inspect the damage. Thomson's a bit singed, but the pages are intact – though I've left a dirty boot print on one page. That's one small step for man.

'Sorry, I didn't think things through properly,' Priya says, cringing. 'That's why these rooms are bare. It's to prevent accidents. The spark tries to find something combustible, so it can manifest fully into flame. Here, let me perfume that before you return it, otherwise Sneddon will have a fit.'

I hand the book over and let Priya do her thing. Once she's satisfied I can pass it off, she gives it back.

'Shall we go up for a munch? I'm famished,' she says.

XXI

The Library cafe's an elegant alcove on the third level, on the far side of reception. It looks out into the sea of books, as well as marvellous sculptures of warriors with javelins and maidens bearing hydriai, or ancient Greek pottery jugs. There are a dozen round tables with chairs set for two or four, and black and white pictures of historic Edinburgh line the walls. It's cosy and intimate with tons of bibliographical charm, given the setting.

To my surprise, Jomo's at the counter, wearing a dotted red and blue pinny. I thought his job was sexier than this, like doing magical research, or I don't know. He looks pretty glum, but he perks up as Priya and I take the middle table.

'Miss Moyo and Miss Kapoor, lovely to see you today.' He sounds so pretentious that I raise my eyebrows.

'Mr Maige junior,' Priya says.

'Hey Jomo,' I reply.

He shifts from foot to foot. 'You're supposed to call me by my surname. It's the rules.'

'The same rules that your psycho dad was going to use to have me hung by the neck until I expired?'

'Yet here you are looking as fresh as ever,' he says, with a smile that drops off when he sees I ain't playing ball. 'Look, I got done too, man. The old man went ballistic after you left. He read me the riot act and everything. Do you know that for bringing you here, my sentence is two years' labour without pay? My hair's gonna be grey before I make a single shilling – the Rulebook covers what I did as well.'

'Cry me a river, Jomo.'

Priya has a mocking half-smile on her face. She turns from me to Jomo, obviously amused.

'I'm sorry and I love you, man,' says Jomo gruffly.

'Aww, how cute,' Priya says, clapping her hands, which makes her bangles ring. 'Kiss and make up.'

'I love you too, Jomo.'

He holds out his fist and I bump it. I could only maintain the front for so long. This place is awesome; I should be thanking him for hooking me up in the first place. But I never do sentiment on an empty stomach. We go over to the counter, which is laden with so much grub it's ridiculous.

'How much is all of this?' I ask, 'cause there's no prices and I'm squeezed.

'It's on me. I took one look at you today and thought, we've got to fatten her up a bit,' says Priya.

'Cheers.'

'It's cheap and you can eat all you like,' she says, handing her desiccated ear to Jomo.

'All you can eat?'

She nods.

I'm like Moses and manna, poor children of Israel. I've never said no to free food in my entire life and I'm not about to start now. Crustless sandwiches, canapes, whatsymathingers, salady stuff and spring rolls, and fruit too – even tropical things like mangos, which we don't get anymore. I'm in shock and experiencing giga-levels of awe at the heaving table. Waste not, oh knight of the round table . . . I unzip my bag and pinch a bit for Gran and Izwi too.

'That's for later, when I'm doing my studying,' I say. 'I don't want to have to keep coming back here.'

'Healthy appetite, I like that,' says Priya, who only takes a few sticks of celery and some apple juice.

I follow with my plate loaded like it's the Last Supper. We leave Jomo at his post. Apparently he has to stand there like a dick for the next hour and clean up after. Yahweh, this hot chocolate hits the spot too. I sip and scoff myself, while Priya picks at her greens.

Two middle-aged men sit near the entrance. One of them wears a gold and black cravat under his loose-fit white shirt. He has an old school Hulihee beard, moustache running down the sides with a shaved chin. It makes him look like a relic from the American Civil War. I get this vibe of film sets, mirrors, smoke and red carpets coming from him; limousines and expensive perfumes.

'That spark you made?' I say over the chow. 'Did you use the wrong incantation?'

'A classic beginner's mistake is to assume the magic lies in the words. If it did, any literate idiot could recite a spell and it would work. The words are merely an aid, not the thing itself. You could say "Abracadabra", or whatever your flavour. Eventually you find what works for you.'

'Hmm . . . I still think it would have been better to strike a flint if you really wanted a workable fire.'

'Ouch.' Priya bursts out laughing and covers her mouth. 'Fire's not my strong point, I admit. You have to look at it this way: all magicians are athletes. You have your sprinters, long-distance runners, high jumpers, shot-putters, swimmers, gymnasts, curlers, steeplechasers, catch my drift? Now, a sprinter can also throw the javelin, but they might not be that great at it. A dressage rider is practically useless as a rhythmic gymnast. There's very, very few decathletes who do many things well, and of those, fewer still can actually match or surpass specialists in their given area of practice. I think in my year at school, we had only one general practitioner. If arson's your thing, a pyrotechnician can cause a conflagration with a blink.'

'Yeah, and I just talk to ghosts. It's lame,' I say.

'Embrace it,' she replies.

Jomo walks past us to serve a table of toffs who've just come in. They're young guys in their twenties, talking loudly as if they own the place. I find myself shrinking a little and have to remind myself to sit up straight. Jomo's fake posh accent as he addresses the toffs grates on me. This kind of place does that to you. I ain't gonna lose myself and start acting like someone I'm not just because they let me in here. No bloody way. Come in, get my books, get my knowledge, and I'm out, back to my own. Priya's alright, though, I like her. The rest of them can go suck dick.

'You're a doctor, right?' I say.

'Healer. Potato, potahtoe.'

'What can you tell me about this?' I ask, taking out my phone. I flick through my photos until I find the one of Mark, and show Priya. Her eyes widen.

'Oof, he's had a hard paper round.'

'What happened to him?'

'Clever photo manipulation,' she says, quickly sliding the phone back to me.

'It's not. I took that picture. There's a kid called Ollie who's friends with this boy. He's only seven and what happened to Mark might be happening to him right now.' If it hasn't already happened. 'Can you help me?'

Priya wipes her mouth with a paper napkin and releases the brake on her chair. She looks at the watch on her wrist. For some reason, she looks super-nervous, but then it's gone in a flash.

'My, is that the time? Been nice seeing you, Ropa, but I have a date with a guy who dances the tango. Call me some-time, mwah.'

I don't get a chance to say anything before she's off, weaving between the tables at incredible speed. It's like watching Pac-Man in the maze, and in a sec, she's gone. And I realize she didn't give me her deets.

I'm about to get up and go after her, when I notice blue ink scribbled on my left palm. It's a phone number. I punch that into my phone, save it and send a wee text with my details back. I suppose healers are like doctors. They don't do work for free. Only saps like me do. Anyway, I have someone much better in mind for this. Someone I think can actually help.

I'm feeling a bit sluggish as I stroll through to reception.

Could use a nice hammock to lie in for a few weeks while I digest all the food I had, like a python. I had to stop myself going back to get more grub when Jomo started giving me weird looks. He asked if I was a human or a rubbish bin. Fair enough. I dump Thomson on the counter to return it and hand over the books Priya recommended I check out.

Dr Maige's there, in his red costume, going through some paperwork, a stern look on his face. Only now do I notice bits of khanga sewn into the cuffs and hem of his dress. It's subtle and tastefully done, and I have a feeling Mama Maige was behind that. The doctor doesn't strike me as someone overly concerned with matters of style. He looks up when he's done with his papers.

'Miss Moyo,' he says coolly. 'Are you enjoying our facilities?'

'Yeah, now that you're not trying to hang me by the neck until I expire,' I reply.

'A trifling incident. Protocol makes this place what it is.' There isn't a hint of remorse in his tone.

Screw you. 'I need to see Sir Callander.'

'Associate members like yourself may not fraternize with the secretary.'

'He's just a secretary?' I say.

'He is "just" the secretary of the Society of Sceptical Enquirers, Miss Moyo. But more importantly, Mr Sneddon has noted with concern that you have not settled your subs.' He leans in and adds quietly, 'Of course, we both know you can't afford them, don't we?'

What a douche. I open my mouth, ready to blag, but Dr Maige holds up a silencing finger.

'Come with me,' he says.

At this point, I'm getting tired of following people around like I'm some sort of tail. But I don't really have a choice, so I follow the doctor through a maze of long corridors lined with bookshelves. He moves deliberately and not without grace, the hem of his dress flowing at his ankles.

'So, you're a magician too?' I say, when the silence gets unbearable.

'I would never stoop so low. I am a mathematician,' he says *with* no small amount of contempt. 'Galileo once said that mathematics was the language in which God had written the universe. I'd go further and say that even if the universe itself did not exist, mathematics still would. Magicians are nothing but glorified tinkerers, children playing with chemistry sets. And had you the aptitude and the means, I would sooner set you on a different path.'

Dr Maige tells me he came to Edinburgh to do a PhD in some esoteric branch of mathematics as a fresh-faced twenty-something-year-old. It's hard to picture him as anything approaching youthful. At the time, he thought he'd return to Tanzania to take up a coveted post at Dodoma. During his studies, his supervisor Professor Rifkind got him a part-time gig in the Library, which the prof also headed. It was all going according to plan until the old guy choked on his beef stroganoff and died one evening. The Society asked Dr Maige to act as head librarian while a suitable replacement was sought to relieve him. Dr Maige agreed, to honour the supervisor he'd been especially fond of, and because he needed the money to supplement his stipend.

'I am still waiting for relief,' he says drily.

He takes me to a little door decorated with gilded vine leaves, which creep across its surface. They're lifelike, as if real leaves had been dipped in gold. Loud, angry voices come from within, and a strangely familiar woman's voice remonstrates, speaking over everyone else. The whole thing's pretty heated, but Dr Maige knocks on the door firmly regardless.

'What is it now?' Sir Callander calls out. 'Can't a man have a moment of peace? This place was a *library* the last time I checked, and it's no place for Society business.'

The good doctor asks me to stay outside and stoops to enter, for the lintel is barely shoulder high to him. Through the gap in the door, I see their long shadows square up.

'Miss Moyo would like to see you urgently,' Dr Maige says.

'Am I supposed to know who that is?' Callander replies irritably.

'She's your charge and that grants her certain rights.'

'What on earth are you talking about?' asks Callander.

'You were her advocate, thus, ipso facto she is apprenticed to you.'

'I did no such thing.' He lowers his voice a notch.

'You interceded for her at the hearing, vouched that she was a practitioner of sorts, even though she has neither been to a recognized school, nor does she hold an accredited qualification. And so, in the eyes of this *august* institution, you are in effect her master, since her membership is bound to your word alone, sir.'

'This is preposterous.'

'Would you like us to consult the Rulebook?' There's a

touch of smugness in Dr Maige's tone, a certain one-upman-ship.

'I didn't realize . . .' Callander's shadow recedes and retreats behind a desk. 'The business of apprentices is – is an outdated and ridiculous affair. But I'll humour you all the same, Pythagoras.'

There's a loud huff from the woman who'd been sighing and pacing all through Dr Maige's interjection. She casts a long, graceful shadow on the wall, elegant hat on her head, hands resting on her hips. It's a perfect stencil, a beautiful outline, but I can't help thinking it looks a bit predatory too.

'Since you have no intention of doing the right thing in a matter that greatly affects small busigicians up and down the country, I have no choice but to take this to the committee. Once I'm finished, proposition eight will not see the light of day,' she says.

'That's what I've been trying to say all along. I can't unilat-erally stop it being passed,' Callander replies, exasperated.

'Come on, Patrick,' the woman says, and I realize there's another man in the room. 'There's no point in us wasting any more time here while he prepares to stiff some other poor soul.' I wonder with a start if she means me. 'The Society mustn't interfere in practitioners' private business. That's how it's always been and it should stay that way. Good day, Sir Callander.'

'Ms Kavanagh,' he replies wearily.

The door opens fully and I step back to allow the woman stooping to pass. She wears the latest haute couture: a stun-ning royal purple dress. The gems stitched in place dazzle the eye. Once out of the door, she adjusts her hat, and I see, to my huge surprise, that it's Siobhan Kavanagh – from Gran's TV game show, no less. Wow, she looks even better in the flesh. Doesn't seem a day over forty, neither pimple nor pore on her face. That luscious hair. Swoon. I whip out my phone and ask for a selfie. Sir Callander glares at me from inside the room, but I ignore him. The man behind her emerges in a zoot suit so baggy he might have stepped out of a time machine.

Siobhan leans into me and smiles. I press the shutter and get my picture. Gran's gonna be proper surprised.

'Thank you. My nan and me watch your show all the time,' I say.

'You are a beautiful little creature and you have manners too. I can always tell a good egg when I see one. Pity you're a bit too old now, but us girls must stick together,' Siobhan replies, showing her teeth in a smile. In a bit of a daze, I wonder what she means – I'm not *that* old. She lowers her voice to a whisper. 'That man in there is a dinosaur, a misogynist to the core. The remnant of a bygone age. I've dealt with that kind all my life and beaten them at their own game. Don't let him or any of these fools grind you down.'

She strides off with the guy in the zoot trailing her. Me heart's pounding. I'm in awe. Goosebumps all over me. I've been touched by small screen royalty.

XXII

I'm still in a bit of a tizzy when I walk into what I suppose must be Sir Callander's office. Dr Maige stands with his hands behind his back looking rather satisfied, like a poker player who's bluffed an opponent with a stronger hand into folding. The room's chilly and has floor-to-ceiling shelves on two sides, stacked with ancient manuscripts. A banner featuring a black unicorn rearing up against a blue and white background hangs proudly on the wall behind the oaken desk.

Sir Callander moves to a liquor cabinet in the corner and picks up a tumbler. He throws in ice from a handy ice bucket and pours two fingers of whisky from a glass decanter. He offers it to Dr Maige.

The doctor shakes his head disapprovingly and says, 'Never with ice.'

'Suit yourself,' says Callander, taking a gulp. He turns to me. 'Right, let's have a look at you. Such a skinny wee waif. You must be freezing in that. Here, an old friend gave it to me many moons ago – probably before you were even born. I shan't be needing it anymore.'

He reaches over to the coat stand near the door and takes down a black woollen scarf with multi-coloured square blocks and circles running through it. It's an old thing, with a misaligned pattern and the wool's motheaten. I'm insulted – the thing belongs in a bin – but I take it, 'cause one has to be nice to rich old people. They throw you scraps off the table, so you bow and scrape and say milord and all that crap.

'Cheers,' I say, stuffing the old thing in my jacket pocket.

Callander waves his hand dismissively.

'Before I leave, I feel it's only proper that I inform you that due to the nature of your association with Miss Moyo, Sir Callander, the Library holds you responsible for her subscription fees, joining fees, and any other costs she might incur during the course of her membership. You will also be involved in matters of discipline and monitoring her general conduct here,' Dr Maige says matter-of-factly. 'We will be expecting prompt payment of the first.'

Sir Callander grimaces, and I'm not quite sure if it's the whisky or this. He narrows his eyes and nods. I feel a huge sense of relief – not like I was ever gonna be able to come up with the money for my subscription, anyway.

'As for you, Miss Moyo, I'm sure one day your dominie will explain the mechanics of the scattering field in this space, which renders useless any photography. Nothing that happens here leaves the hill either. You will tell no one anything about what, or *who*, you see here. I assure you, we have remedies for any infractions.'

Dr Maige stoops low and slides out of the door, making sure to shut it behind him. I take my phone out, flick to my photos and am gutted to see my selfie is nothing but a blur of pixels, some kind of Pollockian expanse. That's so messed up.

159

I'm now stuck in this awkward silence with Sir Callander. The only sound is his breathing. Maybe he's still annoyed about having to pay my fees. He sits on the edge of his desk, regarding me as one might a piece of dirt on the floor.

'I may humour Dr Maige, but if you want to learn magic, girl, my advice is for you to enrol in one of the four schools and learn it properly. Understand?'

'That's not why I'm here to see you,' I say. There's only so much of this dismissive shit I can take.

'What do you want, then?'

'I thought I'd ask you about some weird stuff that's been going on about town. Thought you could help, since, you know, you're the man and everything.'

'Don't be nonsensical. My time is precious, girl.'

He finishes his whisky and holds onto the glass, swirling the ice so it clinks against the sides. In his presence I feel an awesome turbulence, the sign of an incredible force that can displace anything in its path. If there's anyone who can help me, it's gotta be him.

'There's kids who've been turning up old in the city. Like someone's taking them and sucking all the juice out.'

Something passes over his face, but he quickly regains his composure. I'm not sure whether I saw surprise or annoyance – or something else entirely. He knits his brow and glares at me.

'Hogwash,' he says.

'I've seen it with my own eyes. There's a kid who looks older than you are, yet he's barely seven. I can show you, Sir Callander.'

'Listen to me very, very carefully. All magicians in this country operate within a strict regulatory framework. Such idle talk as this threatens to bring Scottish magic into disrepute and I will not have it. Do you understand?' I wilt beneath his intense gaze. Then he softens, just a fraction. 'How did you find the Thomson?'

'But I really think you should—'

'Did you read that book I gave you?' He stops me mid-faff and I know we're done with my questions. I nod. 'What did you think of it?'

'Good, I guess,' I reply, deflated.

'And who are you reading now?'

'Montague and Chandrasekar.'

'An excellent choice. They are brilliant communicators and you will find that, alongside Thomson, they offer an elementary instruction. See the ice in this glass I'm holding?' He stretches out his hand so it's right in front of me. 'The ice is going to melt eventually. The room is warmer, therefore a thermodynamic equilibrium must be reached. After that, the laws governing the enthalpy of vaporization will ensure that, given enough time, it will all turn to gas. The most straightforward spells are the ones that follow those laws. In this case, the practitioner could merely accelerate the process by which the water warms up. This would make its molecules vibrate faster while the room imperceptibly cools, losing energy in response. It's a seesaw: if one goes up, the other comes down, until their temperatures match.'

He runs a finger down the glass to remove some of the condensation formed on it, and in front of my eyes the waterline begins to rise, just as the ice melts. It's like a time-lapse video happening right before me. The water from the ice cubes fills a little more than a third of the glass and Callander sloshes it around. Then, incredibly, it begins to boil, steam curling into the air. I'm still taking it in when he stands up, comes forward and ushers me to the door, opening it to show me out.

Once I'm in the hall, he bends to look at me. I feel the air around me grow warmer, as if the sun itself was shining in the middle of July.

'It's easier to create chaos than to install order. Any halfwit – and the great majority of magicians you will encounter here are that or worse – can do third-rate magic. The real science begins when you can turn the arrow round to face the other way. Here, thanks to Maxwell's demon, the scientist can turn the water back into ice. But you are a long way from that just now. Focus on the basics first and the rest will follow.'

I don't understand any of what he's just said, but the heat in the air dissipates, as the water in the whisky glass refreezes into a single, solid chunk of ice. Without warning, Callander throws the glass my way. It hits the floor, shattering ice and all into a hundred pieces.

'Clean that up, will you, girl,' he says, slamming the door shut.

What a certifiable bawbag. I'm proper radge at the moment, standing here with all these broken shards at my feet. I'll have to think of some other way of finding Ollie on my own. No one else in this town gives a toss.

XXIII

It's hard juggling everything I've got going on at the mo. I've got the Ollie thing and I really want to help his mum. But I've still got to chase guap to make rent, like I ain't Bruce Wayne here – I'm simply doing the best I can. So I'm minding my own business, playing loyal conduit to the dead, when I get a message from Priya the next afternoon. She's asking to meet on Regent Road later. Kills my night, 'cause I was gonna watch a movie with Gran and Izwi, but I make my way there anyway.

We meet up by the monstrous St Andrew's House. It's blocky and grim, as one might expect from something built on the site of an old prison. Somehow, it seems to have imbibed the soul of that ghastly institution into its fabric.

'Sorry about the other day – for rushing off,' says Priya, scanning the empty streets. 'There's stuff you can't talk about in public, motormouth. That picture you showed me – I've heard rumours in the barras about something real bad.'

'Go on.'

'I don't know, but that kid you showed me might be linked to something I've seen before,' she says.

'So why haven't you told anyone? I tried to tell Callander, but he wouldn't help.'

'Callander's a bureaucrat and he'd never do anything that might attract attention from London, Ropa,' she says. 'Scottish magic is in a precarious position. We chose the wrong side during the troubles, and now, if word of anything like this gets out, we're toast. That's why none of the honchos in the Society will go anywhere near something like this. If it's not official, that means it never happened.'

'We both know it's happening.'

Priya glances around to check no one's watching us.

'Follow me. There's something I need you to see,' she says.

I follow her down the stairs and through Edinburgh's narrow lanes until we cross through Canongate to Holyrood. If I had issues with coming to town before, well, this is the part of town I'm definitely not supposed to be going through.

We emerge at the foot of the Royal Mile, the heart of Edinburgh's Old Town. It's a shabby place. The concrete walls of the now-old 'new Parliament' are marked with graffiti, and there's a gaping hole through the main entrance, called 'the king's knock'. It was made by a shell from a Challenger tank when separatist MSPs holed up in the building, rejecting the crown's authority after the restoration. Parliament looks like a wounded animal sunk on its haunches after the hunt, just before it expires. It's forever caught in that moment. As the wind blows, you can hear its rattly gasps through the yawning cavern.

The forty separatists were smoked out at dusk with teargas, like rats, and lined up against the walls facing the Palace of Holyrood. There, they were offered the king's peace if they recanted their erroneous creed. But they rejected it, and were summarily shot.

There are pockmarks where the bullets went through. It's said their blood was the first graffiti to paint the walls. Blood is the strongest ink. You can't erase what's written in blood, ever.

Priya keeps on straight ahead passing into Holyrood Park. I think she's heading for the hill at its centre and its most isolated point – Arthur's Seat. Despite being surrounded by snowy open land, we are still just a stone's throw from the Palace and Parliament. We pass the pond – or St Margaret's Loch, to give it its grander name – and there's no more ducks or swans in there. All eaten. Me and my mates bagged a few ourselves back in the day, sharing in the king's bounty. Spit-roasted them to perfection. Been ages since I've seen a swan about.

'Can you push my chair?' says Priya as we come onto the steeper part of Queen's Drive, below the hill.

'I've seen you wheel yourself upside down on the ceiling, and you want me to push your chair?' I reply.

'Don't be a dick,' she says.

'Touchy, are we?' I step behind to help her up the steep road. 'How was your date, anyway? The one you blew me off for.'

'It was great. We danced all night long, but he's not really my type.'

'What's your type then?'

'I'll know it when I see it.'

Camelot comes into view, the camp sprawling around Dunsapie Loch. I'm bracing myself 'cause there's quite a few folks angry with me out here. Nothing else for it but to keep my spine straight – in for a penny and all that. There's wood fires going, and smoke rising through the winter air. Camelot is the somewhat ironic name given to the largest tent city in Edinburgh. It has no fixed demarcations, borders or form. The residents come and go as they please. At the moment, there's a few hundred of them with ridge tents, dome tents, inflatables and the like. They are ultra-colourful, a riot against the white snowfall.

She's been razed to the ground thrice by the city fathers and thrice she's risen again like the phoenix of yore.

Me and Gran and Izwi lived here for a while until the riots, when we moved to HMS Hermiston, which is a lot quieter. That means a lot safer. There ain't too many families left here now; it's mostly rough sleepers and itinerant men. You can hear them coughing inside their tents. It's like that entropy stuff Callander was on about. Things keep changing 'cause they have to. The only thing that's unchanging's death, and no one wants a piece of that real estate.

An accordion's playing in a group camped in front of a bonfire. Someone wolf-whistles. I stop.

''Ere, beautiful, be a good little girl and come sit on my lap,' says a man drinking from an olive canteen.

I take my katty out, load it, and shoot the ass end of his canteen just as he's mid-swig. The canteen twangs as the rock hits metal and a spark flies. The man cries out, drops the flask and gingerly examines his mouth for bleeding. He growls and makes to stand.

'The next one's going through your eye if you so much as take a step, knobhead.' I've reloaded and drawn my katty to the max, rubber straining against my hand.

'If you knew who she be, you'd believe her, pal. Sit yersel
doun if you wanna keep them binoculars, and mind that gob
of yours,' a voice says from the camp. 'Good to see you again,
Ropa. Dinnae mind him, he's new and disnae ken what's
what.'

'Great shot,' Priya says. 'Where do you know this lot from
then?'

'Long story. Alright, Cameron.'

I give Cam the nod, ease my katty and head on towards the
large circus marquee with flags fluttering up ahead. You don't
let no one diss you here or they chew you up. Never give 'em
an inch or they take the whole nine yards, and then some.
Been a year or two since I was last here, but while people may
come and go, Camelot remains the same. And the code they
live by don't change either.

The tent's red and yellow stripes radiate from the apex
down. The entrance has the picture of a grinning showman,
arms open, welcoming you in. Here goes . . . I roll back the
tarp and follow Priya.

A festering odour hits us just past the box office. It's the
kind of thing you get in a hospital, scrapes the back of the
nose. At one end of the tent is a wrecked-looking sitting area.
Metal and plastic from the damaged seats jut out in a messy
matrix. There's crates and stuffed animals, wooden manne-
quins and drapes hanging from the roof.

A couple of heavies watch us as we walk in. Guy with a
mullet lies passed out on a bench. F knows who the juggling
guy is wearing the McDonald's clown outfit while riding a
unicycle round the tent. We're not interested in them. A child

in a dirty white nightdress is crouched on the ground, playing with a doll. But at the centre sits a man on a throne, in front of a brazier burning ash wood. He's staring into the flames, lost in thought, and though Priya says hi, we wait for a very long time for him to speak.

'Green hair now, is it? You look like a decaf Hulk,' the man says at last. The fire reflects in his eyes. 'Why did you bring her here, Priya?'

'Is there some history here that I don't know about?' she asks, looking at me. 'Bit of a heads-up would have been nice, pal.'

The man's called Rooster Rob, but he also goes by Red Rob. He runs a racket around town. They call themselves the Clan – and they do a bit of stouthrief and hamesucken, pickpocketing, moving merchandize and beggaring. Red Rob trades in anything except human flesh. Uses young lads, mostly, but I used to work for him too. It was the best job I ever had, 'cause we were all like family then. He's pushing forty and has a red mohawk with a beard to match. He wears rainbow-coloured fingerless gloves, and a navy overcoat on top of an old jumper. His boots are red Docs that match his hair.

The tent's too big to warm with a single fire, and the holes in the canvas don't help either. Rob's right leg's crossed over his left and he slouches in the faux throne – pilfered from a film set. Its yellow paint is chipped. Above it sits a carved bald eagle.

'Heard you was too good for us, Ropa Moyo. Left for the suburbs,' he says. 'Now here you are, back in the company of a magician no less.'

'Hermiston Slum, actually,' I reply.

'We know that already.'

'It's good to see you again,' I say, moving closer to the fire to warm my hands.

Rob looks down at me. 'Is it now?'

'I'm sorry I left like that.'

'Water under the bridge. We stole your bike. So there, we're even.'

'You guys did *what*?'

'It's over there, in that pile of junk. You can have it back. We didn't sell it, because we always knew you'd come back to reclaim your duthchas,' he says, sitting up. 'You might forget who you are or where you from, but the Clan disnae forget. Not one of our own.'

This ain't the reception I was expecting . Used to see broken noses, jaws and eye sockets back in the day if you crossed the Rooster. Must be mellowing in his old age.

Rob reaches for the half-empty bottle of red wine at the foot of his throne and drinks. Then he offers it to me. I take a sip. It's harsh and fruity, home-made. I hand the bottle to Priya and she swigs before handing it back.

'I come here once a fortnight to do some voluntary work, looking after people who can't afford healthcare. It means I get to give something back, unlike the rich bastards I treat at my usual job,' says Priya, before turning to Rob. 'Ropa's seen another child like the one you showed me. That's why I brought her here. She can help us figure out what's going on.'

Rob walks over to the child playing in the corner. She's barefooted and her face is covered by unruly hair. Kinda looks like the *Ju-On*. But maybe I watch too many old films. Rob takes her by the hand and brings her to us.

The stench gets worse as she draws nearer.

'You might wanna change her nappy,' I say, wincing.

'If only,' Rob replies.

He sits back on his throne and the girl clambers onto his lap, putting her arms around his neck. As she rests her head on his chest I see her face and recoil involuntarily. Rob's watching me closely. He pushes her hair back so we can see her clearly. The head of an old woman on a child's body.

'This be Lizzy's child. You remember Lizzy, don't you?' I get the dig and nod. 'She died of the cough last summer. You didnae come to the funeral.'

'Oh God, it's Katie . . . no,' I say.

My chest tightens and my heart sinks. Lizzy was my friend, she was one of us. One of them. I'm no longer part of this, but it doesn't mean I don't care. And Katie – I used to babysit this kid. Washed her, fed her, changed her, sang her lullabies. She used to play with Izwi too. We left, they stayed.

I move closer. The stench of decay and corruption is unbearable – and familiar. She smells like Mark, but this is so much worse.

I stroke Katie's hair and she makes a rumbling sound that breaks my heart.

'What happened?'

'It's not your concern anymore,' Rob says.

'Don't. Please.' I choke on my words.

He exhales and reaches for the bottle. When I lived here, he wasn't much of a drinker, but now I see he's drinking to forget. Trying to flush something out of his mind, but the bottle's a poor tonic for that.

'We got sloppy. Katie was your replacement, Ropa. Everyone here has to earn their keep. So what choice did I have? She was tiny, nimble, climbed even better than you, believe it or not. Slipped through windows like a rodent, she did.' He drinks and offers the bottle to me, but I shake my head so he hands it to Priya. 'I scoped out this house and thought it was a go. This place had so much loot right on display through the window. It's like they were inviting us to come and get it. A job like that could feed the entire hill for months, so I sent her in. She never made it out.'

'Why didn't *you* go after her?' I'm pissed off.

'Aye, I wanted to, but the lads were too afeared. Said they saw a dark shadow there, Old Nick himself. You know us, we don't scare easy, but that place did it in for us.'

'So, you left her, to cover your own hides?' I snap. 'What happened to one for all?'

'You dare talk to me about one for all, Ropa Moyo?'

Something awful simmers in the space between us. Broken promises, resentment. I might not be of the Clan anymore, but Lizzy's child didn't deserve this. Lizzy used to tell me all she wanted was a better life for Katie. Kept hoping she'd find a rich fella to take them away from it all. She was older than me, but so sweet and simple. That's why I liked her. Even now, I see something of her in Katie's eyes, and I do all I can not to weep.

'I thought we'd lost her forever,' Rob starts up again. Something heavy drags down his words. 'Anyway, one of the lads finds her wandering about dazed in the flesh market a few weeks later, and brings her home.'

I have to sit down on a bench, feeling even more sick to my core, now it's someone I know.

'You should have told the police,' I insist, knowing full well how stupid that sounds. You're more likely to get your skull smashed in by them lot before they lift a finger to help you.

Rob doesn't even bother responding. He plays with Katie's hair, running his fingers through the tangled mass. A bird flies up in the rafters, hitting the canvas, trying to find a way out. It flits from one side to the other, and then settles on a steel beam. It casts a strange shadow in the firelight, as all the smoke gathers high up.

'Give me the address, Rob,' I say. 'I'll square it.'

'You could always come back, ken? Hell, no one else has your kind of skill, the knack you have for telling whether a place is empty or no, or how lightly they're sleeping.'

'I can't. I promised.'

'I'll double your take to a fifth. How about that?'

'Just give me the address,' I say.

The Rooster takes a good long stare at me and I eyeball him back. There's flames burning bright between us, fire in his eyes. Everyone in the tent falls silent, watching, waiting. I hold firm until Rob blinks first.

XXIV

I remember Gramps by the scent of gin on his breath whenever he carried me. The way his stubble was rough against my face. There was mischief in his blue eyes, a constant twinkle, like he was in on a joke no one else knew about. His hair was thinning, and you could see his scalp as well as you can see the skin under the hairs on your arm. On cold days, I remember him sitting down with a hot toddy in front of the radio talking about Hibs. That's why I love the green shirts even though I'm on the wrong side of the city.

Used to take me to Easter Road on match days, too. I remember being swept up in the crowds, sitting on his shoulders as we made our way to the stadium, surrounded by hats, banners and scarves. Never mind the fact we lost more often than we won, we sat in the stands cheering, jeering and cursing our lungs out. When we couldn't go to the games, he refused to watch on telly, preferring to tune in on the wireless.

'Your heid's always gonna give you a better picture than any screen,' he'd say.

When the commentator was speaking, the images always got jumbled up in my mind, especially for away games. The stadium always looked like Easter Road to me regardless, bare earth where the grass had worn away in the six-yard box at either end. But I'd sit there at Gramps's feet, him leaning over to hear better even though the volume was maxed. I could see the strips in my mind, but seldom the faces of the players. Sometimes I celebrated the wrong goals and he'd laugh and call me a traitor.

Gramps wasn't my real granddad, though. Not biologically anyway. My real ones died before I was even born.

The thing about the dead is you can never bring them back. Doesn't matter how much you love them. Never mind how much money they had or what good they did in this world. Doesn't matter how much you pray or which god you turn to. It's set in stone. One shot is all any of us ever get, and I've seen enough regrets from beyond to know how true that is. My real granddads went to where the grass is long, but at least we had Gramps.

Gran says she met Gramps in a pub on Rose Street. Claims there wasn't anything romantic about it, especially since all he talked about on the day was urban mining, which was his thing. 'Do you know there's gold in sewerage?' he said, by way of an opening line. That was epic, in my opinion. I picture them sat on a bench in the quiet corner of a pub, some place with a low ceiling and massive wood beams. A few punters on stools near the bar, with the place virtually dead.

That's how love happens.

Sometimes I think Gran is a lonely swan. She sits in the caravan all day long. If you don't talk to her, you see her eyes twitching, like maybe she's searching for something, watching the past roll by on the microfilm in her head. She laughed a lot more when she was with Gramps. He was a happy alkie, never got loud or angry. But when he was sober, he seemed to lose his mojo. Got all spaced out and disconnected. But put the bottle to his lips and the batteries were recharged.

We were happy until Gramps lost the house on a gambling debt.

Gran calls it his demon. An impulse he couldn't do anything about, no matter how many times he promised to quit. It was the only thing I ever heard them argue about. He hid betting slips from Gran in different corners of the house. She took away his mobile to stop him from gaming on it.

But he always found a way. The demon came calling to him every second of his existence. Gramps played the lotto too, but he always missed by a few digits. If he bet on a horse, it always finished a close second. If he played the accumulator on football, he'd match all his games bar one – where an underdog invariably upset a sure thing. He was always just an inch from hitting the big time, so we'd be rich and never have to worry about money again.

There were days Gramps would say he was off to meet a friend or colleague. But if you walked past the bookies, you'd see him there, anxiously watching the screens. On days he won, you knew because we'd get sweeties and Gran would get a bottle of wine. But these small winnings were so much less than the sum total of all he spent chasing the pot of gold.

When the sheriff officers came to kick us out, Gran wasn't even angry. She bowed her head, resigned, like she knew it would happen all along. Gramps had hidden the court notices until it was too late. Gran packed our things into the caravan and hitched it to the car we had, before it broke down and we sold it for scrap. It was like a little adventure at first, moving around the city, camping in supermarket car parks, disused industrial lots or by the beach, before being moved on. Gran tried to be cheerful in front of us, but I could tell she was suffering.

We didn't take Gramps with us. Gran told him he had to make his own way from then on.

No goodbyes. No divorce. No tears, or anger, or recriminations. They were beyond all that.

Last time I saw Gramps was at the Royal Infirmary, hooked up to drips, an oxygen mask on his face. His skin was sallow and sticky. Eyes jaundiced and weary. His hands were cold to touch and he hardly had the strength to squeeze my fingers. Gran sat at the foot of the bed and said nothing back when he mouthed, 'Sorry.'

The last thing Gramps bequeathed us was a hefty medical bill.

His name was John O'Toole. He was cremated, and we scattered him in the Water of Leith like he wanted, so he could make his way to the sea. Gran said she'd rather have flushed him down the toilet. Maybe he could find his precious gold in the sewers. She laughed at that, but I couldn't tell whether she was serious or not.

After Gramps died, I started seeing things. People who weren't supposed to be there. Spooked me out when I saw my first deado hovering over her unmarked grave in broad daylight. Most people don't know what that feels like. This gift, this curse, to see what shouldn't be seen. Some days I find myself asking if it ain't all just an illusion and I'm really a straight-up loony.

Gran told me that my real granddad on her side, the one I never met, was a Memorykeeper. It's some ancient Shona order that used to do sorcery or some such. Apparently he remembered everything, right from the time he was in the womb. Every single second of his existence. It sounds cool, but now I'm older, I think that was a curse too. Sometimes there's stuff you have to forget so you can live.

It's only when I smell gin or see Gran lonely that I think of Gramps. The first days it was hard. Thought I'd see him in the Other World, but I never did. Reckon he knew Gran was mad at him, so there was no point in lingering.

I hope he found his way to the land of the tall grass.

XXV

I wanna go in swashbuckling and see what's happening at this place Rooster Rob told us about, but Priya's been stalling. First it was, 'Oh my, I have a J.O.B. and I work long hours,' and now it's, 'I'm at a conference in Aberdeen. Wait for me till the weekend.' But time's a wastin' and the whole thing's boiling my piss now. It's not like I don't have a job too. Fair enough, I'm not some fancy healer, but the sooner I find Ollie, the sooner I can get back to making real, actual cash and get the troll out of my pubes. Priya's super-cautious about the whole thing. But she's my best hope, being an actual magician and all that. I figure when shit goes down, I'm gonna need the Guns of Navarone with me. I guess I just have to hold on.

Time sure has a way of grinding to a crawl, though, when you have something hanging over you like this.

Message pings from Jomo asking when I'm coming back to the Library. My phone's plugged into the charger, which helps. The battery's nearly full. Even though it self-charges with kinetic energy when I walk, sometimes the battery still runs out from overuse and I'm on it a fair bit. It's not a problem when

I'm on the go, but when I'm home, I have to use the electric.

I text him a 'Soon', with a smiley emoji, and get back to surfing the net. It's what I do in my downtime. Business is a bit slow at the mo, and I should be out hustling, but I need a break. That, and a new pair of feet.

I'm sat on the step outside our cara, cleaning my bike. I have half a mind to ask Rob for a new pair of boots since I've pretty much worn mine out tramping about half the city. They didn't even oil my bike or anything. Rust's setting in and I'm gonna have to fork out for some remover. Messed up my brakes too while they were at it. It's been a bit of a mission fixing it, but once I have it sorted, that's half my problems binned. BMX don't make 'em like this anymore. I feel chuffed, like an amputee who's had a limb sewn back on.

A bit nippy out. Stupid scarf Callander gave me's still bulging in my pocket. I should throw it away or something, but I keep holding onto it. Maybe because no one ever gives me anything. I've had to grift and thrift for everything I've got. Reckon I might fob it off onto someone else in exchange for a shilling or two, if I can get Gran to fix it. Waste not and all that.

I get up and go back inside, leaving my bike parked against the side of the cara. Still a bit more work to do, but we're getting there. I shut the door and fish the scarf out of my pocket.

'Hey, Gran, can you maybe fix this up for me so I can move it?' I say, placing the scarf on her lap.

She runs her hands over the fabric, like she's reading braille, and gasps.

'Where did you get this?'

'Some customer gave it to me as a tip or something,' I say. Can't tell her about the Library or any of that on account of Jomo's dad being a psycho.

'Is that right?' she says, playing with the stringy bits at the fringe. 'It reminds me of something I made a long, long time ago, Ropa.'

'Nah, the stitching on this one's horrible. There's no way you could have done a job that sloppy.'

'We all had to start from somewhere,' she says wistfully, handing it back to me.

'No, I don't want it,' I say.

'Take it. If it was a gift offered and you received it of your own free will, then you keep it. There's nothing wrong with this scarf. It's made of good Highland cashmere. You must have really made an impression on this *customer* of yours.'

'Whatever, Gran,' I say, stuffing the damned thing back in my pocket. 'Anyways, I've got to pick Izwi up from school. See you in a bit.'

We're friends again, Izwi and me. Though that kid can hold a grudge, man. Had to deal with the silent treatment and side-eye, until Gran was like, 'Mr Gorbachev, tear down this wall!' Otherwise, who knows how long it'd have gone on for?

I'm hanging out with the mums and dads at the school gate. Sighthill Primary's like Lego blocks glued together – cheap and cheerful. The tallest thing on the site's the chimney from the boiler room, which towers over everything.

The tiny tots come out first, faces beaming seeing their parents waiting for them. Wish Izwi had that too, but all she's got is me. And Gran. Could be worse, I suppose, thinking of Katie. Then again, I also remember a warm house with solid brick walls. Three square meals a day.

It's a good thing Izwi doesn't recall a time before this. She was too young. Amnesia's a blessing, and so is ignorance sometimes. Memory remains in the past while we hurtle ever onward. And as time passes, we have even less power to change what came before. That's why I envy the fact that Izwi doesn't remember some of these things.

The kids' voices are loud and sharp. I don't know how anyone can manage this monkeyish screeching five days a week.

I see her bestie Eddie in the throng and know Izwi can't be that far off.

Mrs Robertson comes out and waves in our direction. Half the parents wave back. So she gestures at me to come over. She looks amicable in the practised way teachers do. But you can never really know what's truly behind the mask of staid professionalism.

I'm thinking cuts and scrapes or some such jazz. Don't let it be anything I have to pay for, please. I wade through the little people going in the opposite direction. Izwi pops up from the throng and hugs me.

'Go wait with Eddie. I have to talk to your teacher.'

Izwi skips away and I know at least she isn't hurt. Mrs Robertson's eyes look massive behind thick bottle-bottom glasses. She's a small woman in her fifties and she exudes the authority of an experienced disciplinarian.

'God save the king,' Mrs Robertson says.

She's holding some glossy brochures in her left hand.

'Long may he reign,' I reply.

'I thought we could have a little chat about Izwi.' I try to look suitably concerned. 'She's been exhibiting some – how do I say this? – challenging behaviour.'

'What's she done? I'll straighten her out.'

'No, no, it's nothing like that.'

'—'

'The thing is, she's being disruptive in class. Not anything serious yet, but I'm seeing the beginning of a trend. Izwi is a very precocious little girl. Top marks all the time. She's advanced far beyond her peers.'

I feel some relief. That's good, right?

'Me and Gran try to stay on top of her books.'

'Yes, and you are doing a very good job. But—' Mrs Robertson purses her lips '—because of this, she gets bored in class and starts distracting the other children. She's not being challenged. The smart ones need to be stretched.'

'Feel free to stretch her – hell, drawn and quartered if you like. We can have her do any extra work you set for her,' I say.

'It's not so simple. I have a classroom with forty pupils, all of whom need my attention. Izwi is gifted, probably at the extreme end of the spectrum, but I've also got children with special needs and others who are not doing as well. And there's also the big chunk of so-so students in the middle. I only have so many hours in the day.' She sounds apologetic and thrusts the brochures my way. 'When I started teaching, there were options for children like your sister, but these days you have to do it yourself. Izwi's started making kekking noises during reading time.'

'Because she's gifted?'

'And she's not paying attention during class like she should be. She's always looking out the window, easily distracted, and I worry she won't get the full benefit of an education. It's not helpful that she's taken to helping others cheat by giving them answers during exercises. Not to mention shouting out answers all the time, and not giving others a chance to participate. Passing tests is one thing, but unless you learn the skills of working hard for your results and socialising properly, you will suffer down the line, eventually.'

I take a look at the colourful brochures. Something about enhanced learning in a safe environment.

'I can't afford this,' I say.

'Give it some thought. I heard you were once just as gifted too. They say you were a walking encyclopaedia,' Mrs Robertson says. A practised smile appears on her face, like a stage curtain closing.

The veiled implication that my little sister might end up just like me if I don't do something grates on me. Blunt truths don't cut cleanly, I guess.

I stuff the papers in my pocket and thank Mrs Robertson for her time and advice. The kids have thinned out now. Just a few stragglers remain, waiting for parents running late. I put my arms over Izwi's and Eddie's shoulders and we head home. That's one more worry to add to my already bustling menu. What am I gonna do with this kid?

XXVI

I've got grease on my hands and clothes after sorting out my bike. The stuff's everywhere, and soap and water don't wash it off too good. It'll come off in its own time; the important thing is, I've fixed my baby now. Means the world's my oyster and I gotta find the pearls. I need to give my bike a spinaroo – make sure everything's as it should be.

I grab my backpack, give my peeps a shout, tell 'em I'm off to see Jomo. Back soon, don't wait up for me, that kind of thing.

I'm not going to see Jomo, though.

I text Priya and tell her I'm going on a recon mission to the house Rooster Rob told us about. The place Katie was taken. Like Uncle Tzu said, you gotta prepare before you meet the enemy on the field of battle. You can't go flying in like some sap. Send scouts out, have a nosey, find out their strengths and weaknesses, and the battle is won before you even take to the field. I'm thinking of listening to an audiobook by von Clausewitz next, 'cause I keep hearing talk about him on my podcasts.

That's the thing about this learning stuff. No sooner have you picked one thing up before you're sent off after another book. Sometimes the guys I listen to say contradictory things and I have to choose for myself who's right and who's wrong. Other times they're both right and it makes no sense to pick one over the other, so you just have to be pragmatic: pick what works now and discard it for something else when the time comes. That's how I like to operate. Can't afford to put myself in some sort of ideological straitjacket. That's for losers.

I get a ping back from Priya saying be careful and not to make a move until she gets back. I ask her how the conference is going, and she says it's a posh wank. Figures. Really shouldn't cycle and text at the same time. I don't need Uncle Tzu to tell me that's dumb.

I veer off the main road and head towards Newington. It's a short walk from here through the Meadows to the university. Used to be posh when folks with dosh lived here. Bourgeois paradise with students from all over the world spicing it up. That was before things went to shit. Back when looking at some punk the wrong way didn't necessarily result in your guts being sliced open, and your entrails poured down the gutter.

Once we got to that level, the rich said sod it and split, going up the East Coast line to hunker down in Gullane and North Berwick. Hell, even Dirleton was a better option them days. That, or they established enclaves of privilege further out from the city centre. It's not as bad as it used to be, though. I've heard the stories of when anarchy reigned supreme and they were thinking of renaming the city Fife 2.0 (the 0 pronounced 'ewww').

The houses and tenements out here are therefore sublet by the absent rich. Families now share rooms with communal kitchens and toilets. The gardens are overgrown and unkempt. Broken windows go unrepaired. Graffiti artists ply their trade without restriction. Suppose it adds a little colour to the gloomy grey.

I pass a skip overflowing with garbage on the corner of Lauder Road, change gear and my chain clunks into place. Short ride from here and I stop on the pavement in front of a grand house. It stands out like a flower growing in a compost heap. The hedges are neatly trimmed back. Driveway cleared of snow. Yep, that's a sore thumb in this neck of the woods.

The gate's open and there's a fountain in the yard, but it's not turned on. Reckon the pipes must be frozen. This is one of them houses with a name in lieu of number for an address. The pillar on the left of the gate says 'ARTHUR' and the one on the right 'LODGE'.

This is it, I think. Can't blame Rob and them for trying to score here. It looks like a good spot to hit. There's no way other operators haven't tried before. This is pretty much an open invitation to burglary. But it's too obvious. I scan the streets and the adjacent houses.

I can't shake the feeling I've been here before. Can't place the when, why or who for, though. There's something off about the place too. I can't quite put a finger to it. It's like them games I played when I was young, the ones that ask you to find the mistake in the pic and you don't quite know what's wrong at first or second glance, until you study the damn thing and see what's what.

This is a house built for this city. Grey stone blocks form formidable walls. They'd have been quarried in Blackford or the Hailes, tying it indelibly to the very earth it stands on. It has that imposing Georgian obsession with classical architecture. Solidity and wealth. Back when they built houses with deep foundations. Wings on either side recede back into the garden. And even as the neighbourhood around it decays, this house seems to stand firm against the buffeting waves of time. If I was to use Callander-speak, I'd say it resists the second law of thermodynamics, turns the arrow the other way. The windows are large. Very large.

I look for a way in. Any lapse in security. Houses are puzzles to be broken into. When I was working for the Rooster, even Santa Claus didn't have anywhere near my level of stealth. In and out. That's how we used to do it. Between the Clan and me, I think we've been in half the homes in the city . . . the nicer ones anyway.

I've seen all I need to see. Not much else for me to do until Priya gets back. At least I've satisfied my itch, seen the place up front. If we can trail where Katie's been, then there's a good chance of finding Ollie – or his body – from there. I shouldn't be thinking like that. Mustn't think of Ollie as dead. If Katie and Mark survived whatever this is, then there's no reason to assume he's gonna be killed. He hasn't passed through the everyThere, so there's hope. Always.

The curtains are open, so I take a final look through a window. There's someone in what must be the drawing room. My vision blurs a bit. I blink and squint to focus, and that's when I see her, standing with her back to the window. She wears a colourful robe whose patterns I can't quite make out. She turns her head one way and then the other, as if searching for something. I recognize the way she's tied her hair in a bun on top of her head – she used to do that at night, so it wouldn't disturb her while she slept. But it's not just her appearance; the essence of her is in that simple gesture of turning, the way she moves her head. She has her back to me and I can't see her face, but I know it's her.

I've searched for so long in every place, and even among the dead, but until today, I could not find her.

'Mama,' I cry.

I wheel my bike through the gate and up the gravel driveway. My eyes are fixed on her. Her long neck. Her back. Her. Her.

It's her. My mother. Tears run down my face. I've found her again. She's been here all along. I don't care where she's been or why she vanished. I don't care about the past, or anything else. All I care about is that I can see her again, when I thought this would never be possible. I've had a lifetime of pushing down memories of her because they hurt too much. Put them in a box in my mind, sealed off from my life. But it overflows sometimes and the memories break out, their sharp hooks piercing every fibre of my being. How I've missed her.

And now she's walking away from the window.

I run faster than I've ever run before, toss my bike on the lawn. Leap over the stairs to the terrace. The door swings open. I run to be with her, and the world opens up beneath me.

XXVII

When you fall so suddenly, and the laws of physics have been suspended, you have no time to scream. Hands flail, clutching at invisible straws. The shock's something else altogether. One minute there was firm earth – now, nothing. I land on my face. Winded.

But I'm okay, like Evel Knievel. That's a relief.

Bugger. Spoke too soon. A hollering pain kicks in. Tsunami of pure agony. Everything hurts so much, I don't even know where to start. Throbbing all over. Oh man. Try to get up, but I can't move. Oh man. This is post level-ten pain where you can't even cry. You just have to ride it – ouch.

'Mffph . . .' What the hell just happened?

I'm lying on something sticky and hard. Wriggle fingers. Once the pain dials down a notch, and I'm in a 3D corporeal body again as opposed to the physical manifestation of agony, I try to get up. Knees hurt like I'm ninety-five. Slowly I rise up. Wow. The left side of my face pulsates. That's gonna swell. And there's goo all over me too. I think I'm bleeding.

Need to scope out the situation. Reach into my pocket and fish out my phone. Screen's cracked, but it's working. I go into my apps and turn on the torch.

Okay.

The light's bright, but the darkness surrounding me is a thick, foggy kind that resists illumination, as though it's trying to throttle the torch's beam. I touch my face and examine my hand to check for blood. I'm okay, just covered in a thick yellow slime of some sort. Don't know whether to be relieved or grossed out right now.

I walk further out into the thick dark.

The walls are a brown lattice of minute honeycombs. Rough to touch, like bone marrow. They're gooey too and exude a foul scent. Rotting flesh? It's not the same odour I smelt coming off Mark and Katie. No, this is something older. It's overpowering, more sinister, layers upon layers of decay. If I had to imagine falling into a mass grave, this is what it would smell like.

I circle the room. Takes everything I've got not to shout out in terror. I need to get out of here. There has to be a door, but I can't find one. The room's barely bigger than our caravan, and there are things that look like massive fatty pustules on the floor. They stand out against the reddish-brown paint of the other surfaces. I complete a full circuit and still don't find the door.

It's freaky as hell. I have to call Priya or Jomo.

No signal.

I wave my phone about to get bars so I can send out an SOS, but there's nothing. Zero reception. We can't be that deep underground or I'd have broken something on my fall. Reckon the house above, with its thick walls, might be enough to stop the signal getting through. Murphy's Law, my old friend – anything that can go wrong will go wrong.

But I saw her through the window. I'm convinced it was

her – though why would she be here, in this place? It seems so unlikely, but I have to find out more anyway. I sensed something was off, deep down in my bowels, but it felt too real to dismiss.

And I miss her so.

Don't cry. Not now. There's nights when I dream about her. A few weeks ago, I saw her sitting in bed in our old place. She opened her arms and I hugged her. I held her so tight, I wasn't going to let go. When I woke up the next morning, my arms were crossed against my chest. She'd slipped out. I'd lost her and I was convinced that if only I'd held on a little bit tighter, she would have stayed.

I miss her so much. Most days I don't even think about her. I don't talk about her. I lock her in a dungeon deep in my mind. I thought I'd thrown away the key, but.

I'd give anything to have my mum back. Even the world itself.

I'm sinking back into that place again. I do everything I can to avoid it. Keep moving like a shark, never stopping, 'cause if you do, the sorrow catches up to you and it's too much to bear. It eats you like a cancer, devouring your entire being from the inside out.

My knees click as I squat down. I need to think. There's some grub in my bag, so I won't starve. I've got a half-litre bottle of water, which ain't much, so I have to ration that. I shine the torch up to the bone marrow ceiling. I fell from up there, meaning that's the way out. Must be a trapdoor of some sort. My dagger might come in handy if I have to scrape out a foothold or wedge it to form a handhold.

I'm still studying the ceiling when scorching light floods the room. I squint, my eyes stinging. The walls of the room take on a sickly yellow hue in the bright light, not the brown I was seeing with my torchlight.

A metal ladder descends and clanks onto the floor.

I take a deep breath and walk towards it. Don't see much save for the ladder and hole in the ceiling. I circle and change my position to see if there's anything else, but the angle's too tight. I'm worried someone might lob something down. But I don't have too many options, as far as I can see. I grab the ladder and give it a shake to make sure it's steady. Then I take out my dagger and bite the blade, holding it in my mouth, and begin the climb. The ladder wobbles a bit under me.

I stick my head out when I reach the top and do a quick sweep. There's a pair of black Clarks and trousers under a kitchen table some way out. I take the last few steps up, push out on my elbows and make it onto the floor.

An old man in a butler's uniform is sat at the table observing me. He takes a sip from the china teacup on the table, all the while watching my struggle.

Kettle, stove, sink. If this is the kitchen, am I now at the back of the house? And if so, how?

'Trespasser. What shall we do with you, hey?' says the butler, still at his tea. His white gloved fingers bend awkwardly round the cup as if the joints are dislocated. He wears a bowtie and looks like a Victorian atavist. Must be pushing eighty, and I can surely take him hand to hand if push comes to shove.

'I saw a woman through the window. I know her. If you show me to her, we can clear this up,' I say.

He sniggers. 'Did you now?'

'She's my mum. Where is she?'

'People see all sorts of things through that window.' He puts the cup down. 'Money. Gold. Sex. Sweeties. Doesn't matter, they keep coming all the same.'

'What?'

'It's not a window. It's a mirror of your innermost desire. I'm sorry to say your mother isn't here. Think of it as a flytrap. Only the ones who don't have the discipline to resist their base desires fall in. And once they are here . . . we teach them a lesson.'

This shit sounds ominous. I have to get out of here and come back with someone who knows what they're doing.

'I don't want no trouble now. Just let me go, okay? I won't say a word to no one,' I say.

'Sure. If you say so,' he replies.

I blink. That was way too easy.

'Really?'

'You're free to go.'

He doesn't need to tell me again. I hastily make my way out of the kitchen, rush through the house to find the front door. Please let it be unlocked. I glance behind and see the butler following at a distance, but he doesn't seem that bothered. So I reach for the doorknob, turn it, and open the door. Freedom. Fresh air. I don't even bother shutting the door and scuttle down the stairs as fast as I can.

There's my bike on the lawn.

I break into a trot.

Owbloodyouch. I'm stabbed in the abdomen. Someone's

driven a sharp blade through me. I cry out and check my belly. It's alright. Take a step forward, but my foot doesn't even land before I feel the knife in my abdomen again. I clutch my stomach and try again. The slightest attempt at going forward brings on an intense supernova of blades and fire. It's as if something's holding me back.

I take a step backwards and immediately feel cool relief. Ice on a sunny day. Sweat drips down my face. I lift my leg, tempted to take a step forward, but I'm shaking. I can't do it.

'Good girl. I could see you're clever.'

The butler's standing in the doorway, arms folded.

'You didn't think he'd let you get away like that, did you? You've invaded his master's home. No, can't allow that, can he now? He lets you go and what next, everyone can just do whatever they like? They can simply come in here when they choose and steal? You think he'd let that happen?' says the butler.

'Let me go. Please, I wasn't here to steal anything. I'm sorry. I didn't mean no harm.'

'They always beg. He's tied you to us now. Tied you by your greedy little insides. From now on, if you exit this door, you can only go as far as the length of your intestines.'

'Who? What are you talking about? *Who's* tied me?' I cry out.

'I am merely a servant's servant. It's not for me to answer your questions.'

The butler holds out his gloved hands and begins to pull, as if reeling in thin air. One hand, then the other. I'm hit by a jolt of pain, my insides rushing towards him. I can't fight it.

It'll slice me in two if I do. His hands draw on the invisible spool like he's bringing a kite home. It doesn't take him much effort, but I'm drawn back like carp reeled from a loch. The butler walks backwards. There's nothing I can do but follow. Back into the house we go, into this evil place. The door slams itself shut behind me and the lock clicks.

Okay, I screwed up.

Bigly.

Broke every rule I know and rushed in like a fool. Now I'm shitting myself. The mocking smile on the butler's face freezes the blood in my veins. A sick, sadistic pleasure radiates from him. He runs a hand over the bald patch on his head and regards me as a cat would a mouse squirming in its claws.

'Yes, of course, yes, you're right. I should properly introduce myself to her,' he says to nobody visible, cocking his head to the side. He simultaneously raises his shoulder and rubs his ear with it. It looks really weird. 'I am Wilson.'

'Look, mister, I don't want no trouble. My friends will come looking for me,' I say. 'Let me go and we can call it evens.'

'Let them come,' Wilson replies. 'He wants to know your name.'

I stay schtum. Clan code from when I was burgling: never give up your name to the man.

'I don't think she wants to tell us . . . I agree, that's rude. Yes, yes, of course. As you wish.' Wilson's ear-rubbing with the shoulder thing is clearly a tic. It's freaking me out. 'I'll have to name you then. You'll be Sunshine from now on. Do you like that?'

A dark shadow moves in the corner of my eye. But when I check, there's nothing there. We're in the lobby. Stairs lead up to the first floor and I see marble flooring with oriental carpets. A chandelier on the ceiling. Statues on plinths. This is rich pickings, a cloying ostentatiousness. Something out of time and place.

'Of course, the work must never stop. With your permission, I'll give her one small task to perform before sending her to bed . . . Yes, I know you have plans for them all. Of course. The bicycle will be cleared by me personally tonight.' Wilson stretches his thin lips into what should be a smile, but is more bared teeth and black gums. 'I have a little job for you, Sunshine.'

He takes me back to the kitchen. There's a trail of slime on the floor from my footprints when I tried to bail. Wilson retrieves a bucket and mop. He goes to the sink, pours some water in and adds a squirt of soap.

'Don't worry. A bit of clean-up, that's all we ask of you,' he says, handing me the bucket.

Right now, I figure, 'conceal your dispositions and your condition will remain secret', like Sun Tzu said. So I take the mop and bucket.

'Excellent. He likes you to be obedient.' Wilson chuckles. 'He also wants you to put your weapons on the counter. We wouldn't want you hurting yourself.'

I put my dagger and katty on the black granite countertop. Give up my ammo too. The clasp on my sheath's come undone and I clip it back on. This sucks ass, royally. Wilson doesn't bother searching me. He's confident as anyone could be if they knew they could rip your guts out in an instant. The shadow appears again in the corner of my eye, near what looks like a pantry.

'There's a good girl,' Wilson says, as I start mopping up my footprints. The kitchen floor's wood-effect tiles. I scrub hard because the substance is sticky and turning black. 'I'm going outside to collect your bicycle. I'll store it in the shed out back. We wouldn't want anybody stealing it, would we? We respect other people's property, don't we?' says Wilson slowly, as if he's talking to a child. 'You stay here and clean it all up. Yes, you're right. We needed the help. Thank you.'

Wilson walks out the kitchen door. I wanna sneak off, but I remember the razor blades in my belly. They say if you keep a dog chained up long enough in one spot, until its spirit is broken, when you remove the chain it won't dare move further than it was allowed before. It gets used to captivity. That's mega messed up. Still, I can't risk making another move. I felt the power of this thing. I need a new plan.

By the time I'm done mopping, Wilson's back.

'Good job,' he says. 'Well done, Sunshine.'

Go screw yourself, I'm thinking, but I keep that to myself. Bite my tongue so hard, all I taste is copper.

'It's getting late. Time for bed. We have an early start tomorrow – the Milkman is coming.'

Wilson takes me to the back of the house, somewhere on the ground floor. I'm still trying to get my bearings. Part of me wants to take him on, but I've seen the shadow trailing us in the corner of my eye. Its dreadful gaze penetrates every pore on the back of my neck, filling me with a cold dread. Hard to describe. This thing feels ancient. Jurassic. Older than anything I've encountered, older than this city. Something really bad – and not of this realm.

Wilson opens the door to a small room and orders me in. There's two bunk beds against the walls on either side. A small sink near the door. A chest of drawers rests against the wall on the far side – on top of which sits a carafe. Someone's sleeping on the bottom bunk of the bed to the left. Their head's covered with a blanket. A pair of black wellies sits on the floor at the foot of the bed, pungent in the windowless room. A little girl on the top bunk sits up as we enter. She looks at me, unbridled fear in her large blue eyes.

'You've done well today. Don't let the bedbugs bite,' Wilson says, shutting us in.

I press my ear to the door and listen until his footsteps recede. I reach for the doorknob, and as I turn it, a samurai sword slices through my guts. I double over, take a step back, and am immediately rewarded with relief. The lights go out. I think I hear something creeping up the wall. I rub my stomach with both hands, feeling nauseous.

'Don't, you'll only make it worse,' the little girl says, when I reach for the door once more.

XXVIII

Her name's Grace, from Prestonfield. She was going home from a play date when she saw a cute teddy waving at her from the window. The poor thing doesn't know how long she's been here for. She's scared and wants to go back to her mum and dad. I imagine this is the same room Katie would have found herself in. How she must have been so, so afraid, trapped in here.

'I need to ask you something very important, Grace, okay?'

'Okay,' she replies.

'Have you seen a little boy called Ollie, or Oliver?'

She shakes her head.

'Are you sure? I can show you a picture, if you like.'

'I haven't seen any little boys here. It's you, me, Wilson and him sleeping below me. But he's not little.'

It was worth a shot, I guess. Eliminating what is not true is just as important as knowing what is true. Something I came across on a science podcast: we learn as much from failed experiments as we do from successful ones. But I wasn't supposed to *become* the experiment. Then again, there is no 'outside' of the experiment. The observer has a bearing on the outcome and is therefore always part of the process, whether they know it or not. I think that's how it goes . . .

A faint wail comes through the wall. It conjures up the anguished sound of slowly rending sails. I press my ear against the wall and hear several muffled voices.

'Can you hear that, Grace?' I ask.

'Hear what?'

'Nothing,' I say. 'Go to sleep.'

'I'm scared. Can I come sleep with you?' she says in a tiny voice.

'Sure, if you want to,' I say, budging over.

Don't want to alarm her with the terrors I hear weeping through the fabric of the walls. Grace climbs down the bunk and curls up in the sheets beside me. Soon enough, she's fast asleep. I try my phone again, but still can't get a signal. I write a message for Priya and Jomo anyway, in the hope it might slip through.

The door clicks open, and light from the corridor pierces the darkness. I don't recall falling asleep. I'm groggy as hell. Grace wakes with a start. She sits up, rubbing her eyes. Wilson walks in and places a bundle he's carrying on top of the chest of drawers.

'You are to get dressed in the appropriate attire,' he says and leaves us.

Give me strength: black dress of dubious fabric, white apron, little cap and *clogs*. The hell? The fabric's old and there are patches where it's been mended. The black's so faded it's become grey. Grace has one too and she looks like a little French maid in it. I slip the dress on. It's at least three sizes too big and hangs off my frame. I keep my trousers on. No way I'm taking those off. And I don't do clogs either. Apron, maybe . . . Okay then, yes. I don't even know what I'm supposed to do with the cap. I throw it on my head askew. I don't care.

Wilson comes back and we follow him to the kitchen. Through the window, there's a male figure in overalls shovelling snow in the back garden. Each shovel load apparently has to be taken all the way to the back fence where he's building a pile. The clouds outside have broken and patches of blue appear in the gloom. It'd have been easier to let the snow lie until it melted. My dagger's stuck along with some knives on a magnetic strip on the wall.

'I'll teach you to make the master's breakfast. Weekdays he takes a bowl of oats, two slices of toast, one boiled egg and a cup of black tea with two sugars,' says Wilson. 'Afterwards, he'll have grapefruit or mandarin. Understood?'

I nod.

The morning's hazy, like I'm in a strangemare. It's all so surreal. Gran must've been worried when I didn't come home last night.

On Wilson's nod, I start making the porridge. Luckily Gran showed me how. But why am I cooking porridge in this strange house?

When will I wake?

He turns to Grace, who is taciturn, but she follows Wilson's instructions on sweeping the floor to the letter. Her little hands tremble as she works. Breaks my heart; Izwi's nearly her age and I would never have allowed her to endure this.

Wilson then sets out a silver tray with a teapot – smells like

Earl Grey – a tea cup with gold trim and a sugar basin. This is also silver. He's clumsy; uses both hands to pick up each object as though he's a child with small fingers. He works with concentration, but now and again checks to make sure I'm following.

Soft rays of sunlight stream in, whitened by lace curtains, grazing my tired face like a gentle hand.

In the daylight an umbilical cord from my belly becomes visible. It's a ghostly thing made of grotesque curls, like an old telephone handset cord, running all the way down to the floor. It's so faint that it's no wonder I missed it in the dark. It trails along the floor towards the hole I fell into last night and disappears.

What kind of sorcery is this? Grace has one too. And so does Wilson, though his cord is thicker, denser and darker than ours.

I tug at my stomach to see if I can remove it, but that doesn't work. Totally freaks me out seeing this thing going through my navel to my insides. I curse Callander for not helping with all that book knowledge of his, when I told him about the children. Why didn't I stick to delivering messages? It was a nice little gig, but there I went, trying to stick my beak in the big league. Look where it got me, trying to be some kind of hero.

The porridge's done now and Wilson passes me a bowl. 'One tablespoon of sugar,' he instructs. I add it and stir. And then we set the breakfast on a table in the conservatory. After we're done, Wilson makes us throw everything in the bin – because the person we're making breakfast for isn't there. It's such a waste, and also like digging a hole and filling it up again. I find I'm annoyed more than anything and I refuse the scraps of food Wilson offers afterwards. I've read enough fairy tales to know you don't accept the food. I'll get by on what's in my backpack. The hunger starts to bite, though, when he sets us to deep cleaning the kitchen. Grace and me have to take everything out of the drawers and wipe the place down, floor to ceiling. It's back-breaking work and I spend every second plotting my escape.

Late that night, the doorbell rings. I shudder at the gleeful look on Wilson's mug as he goes to open the door. We're finishing off the cleaning and my phone says it's just struck twelve – midnight – when Wilson returns. He's carefully carrying an old-fashioned glass milk bottle with both hands. He keeps it close to his chest. There's a milky fluid in it, swirling like a turbulent cloud. It has a strange glow, a kind of effervescence coursing through it.

A big man's behind Wilson. He has a thick beard and looks like a mountain man dressed in a crisp white uniform. He wears a white cap with a black brim, and a bowtie completes the look. His arms are hairy in that short-sleeved shirt and his eyes are hidden behind dark sunglasses. He carries a brown sack in one hand.

'Say hello to the Midnight Milkman, children. He's come to collect his prize,' Wilson says with relish. 'Which one of these two pretty little things would you like?'

Grace hides behind me, seeking protection. She holds

onto my dress. I take off the rubber gloves I'm wearing and throw them onto the floor.

The Milkman takes his time, looking at me from behind the dark glasses. Then he points down at Grace and beckons her with his finger.

'No!' I say. Something spikes in me, real indignation. I'm not letting this child out of my sight.

'Stay in your lane, Sunshine. You're alright. Nothing to worry your pretty little head over,' says Wilson, rubbing his hands. 'He likes them young, you see. Older bodies have nothing to give – that succulent youth is what he needs. Come on, Grace, do as you're told. It's rude to keep grown-ups waiting.'

'She's not going anywhere,' I declare, and clench my fists.

Wilson reaches out with both hands and yanks hard. I'm wrenched by something in my stomach and fall to the floor in agony. Grace screams and kneels next to me, gripping my arm so tightly her fingernails dig in. I try to get up, but I'm pinned to the floor. All I can see is the Milkman's spit-polished shoes walking towards me.

'Don't do this, Wilson,' I say, gasping with pain.

'You have a lot to learn, Sunshine,' he smirks. 'The work cannot be stopped now. Things are in motion. The Midnight Milkman cannot be denied, not when the house owes him for his nectar.'

The Milkman yanks Grace up by her hair and throws her onto the floor next to me. He takes a zip tie from his pocket and uses it to bind her hands behind her back. She wriggles and fights, but the Milkman's too strong. It's not a fair match and is terrible to watch. I try to stop him, but he stamps on my hand, and I cry out. He slaps duct tape over Grace's mouth. Then he lifts her, dumps her in the sack and ties it up.

'Let her go,' I scream helplessly.

The big man lifts the sack easily, like there's nothing but air in there. He slings it over his shoulder and heads for the exit. I push up to my knees. The thing pulling my string's eased off. I follow him and Wilson through the corridors to the front door.

This is not a fight I can win, but I beg them to let Grace go. I feel weak and defeated and can only watch helplessly as the Milkman throws Grace in the back of his milk float, like she's a sack of potatoes.

The float's an electric three-wheeler. Its white paint has been defaced by hand-drawn pictures of flowers, poorly drawn impressions that could only have been done by a child.

I'm too weak to stop them – I can't fight the pain in my guts. The Milkman climbs into the cab and drives slowly back down the driveway. Rage swells up inside of me. There's nothing I can do.

'Hang in there, Grace. I'll find you,' I shout. 'I'm coming to get you.'

Wilson shuts the door. I don't see which way the milk float goes. And I can't even imagine what they're planning to do to that little girl. The terror in her large eyes haunts me. I feel like I've failed. But if this isn't where Ollie is, at least now I know who took him.

'Come on, Sunshine. It's over and done with now. No one ever comes back from the farm,' says Wilson. He grabs the back of my neck and pushes me towards the kitchen. 'It's time to feed the house.'

He takes the milk bottle from the countertop and shuffles to the trapdoor in the kitchen floor.

'Don't just stand there, open it,' he says. I do as asked, he unscrews the lid and then slowly pours the white liquid down the dark hole. 'I want you to watch very carefully. You've got to eyeball it . . . half a bottle should do for now.'

The 'milk' floats down slowly, more gas than liquid, swirling as it does. I can feel the floor move underneath my feet, an urgent motion, and I imagine the lips of a hungry baby suckling. The whole thing is disgusting somehow, but I have no choice except to watch.

'There you go,' says Wilson in a syrupy tone. 'You look after us, we look after you. Drink the nectar.' He pours a final drop then stops and closes the bottle.

I hear a sigh of disappointment from the walls around us.

'I know, I know . . . There'll be more next week,' Wilson coos.

The house burps, a foul odour escaping from the hole into our faces. I close the damn trapdoor in a hurry.

XXIX

The snow sparkles like diamonds strewn on the earth. It's bright and pure. The back garden is hidden from view by tall hedges on all three sides, a shed and a cottage – right at the bottom – is surrounded by bushes. This is the sort of place a child might call their secret garden and see magic in the world for the first time. But I doubt any kids have been allowed to play here in a while.

The gardener's carrying a bucket. He waddles from side to side as if his balance isn't great. There's a dark cord running over the snow, tying him to the house, and he's lost in his tasks. It's almost as though he's in a trance. But that head, the nose, the hair . . .

It can't be. Surely not?

I couldn't sleep at all – kept hearing Grace's cries over and over in my mind. I'll not spend another night in this godforsaken place. There has to be a way out. That dark cord running from my belly is a rein of sorts. A rider may hold the reins, but the horse can still throw them off. The rider's power is nothing but an illusion. All the horse has to do is realize its power to shake itself free. The prison of the mind is greater than any real actual prison. Or so I hope.

'You will need a proper tour, so you know where to go
when I send you on errands. Yesterday I had you scrubbing
down the kitchen because in time it will become your personal
fiefdom. He wants you to get used to it,' Wilson says after I'm
done with the dishes. 'There'll be lots of cleaning for you. Not
a speck of dust must be seen when the master returns.
Laundry too. Cooking, naturally. You're a servant now and
you'll be kept busy; idle hands are the Devil's workshop. I'm
proud of you so far, but I must warn you of the consequences
if you disobey him or fail to execute his instructions to the
letter.'

I don't recall applying for this job, man. Like, this guy
expects me to stay here permanently? No way. I ain't cut out
for no servanting.

Wilson removes his left glove and puts it on the table.
Then he takes off the right, watching me for a reaction. The
corners of his lips pull back, a mocking smile.

'I used to be just like you once: young, foolish, thought I
knew it all. He soon took care of that, showed me the right
way,' he says, wriggling the stumps of his fingers. He holds
them up to my face for show. 'Take a good look, Sunshine.' He
has thumbs sure enough, but all his other fingers are neatly
amputated at the second knuckle, leaving him with just the
first stub to work with. The scar tissue is red and angry.

Once he's satisfied I've got the message, he puts the gloves
back on. I remain impassive. My heart's thumping, but I'm
not giving him anything to feed on. Bullies love fear – you
might still take a licking, but it's in your power to deny them
that.

'I deserve every one that got hacked off. I take responsibility,' Wilson says ruefully. 'He takes them with no anaesthetic. Cuts them clean off and expects you to get back to work. I was lucky. I've seen him take eyes, noses and ears over the years. If it can be hacked, he'll have it – till you come to heel . . .' He jerks up and twitches, rubs his ear against his shoulder. 'Yes, I'm telling her. You're right, she has to know. I don't think we'll have any problems with her. The tour? Right away.'

In broad daylight it's easier to see the shadow behind him. I try not to show that I've caught on. It sways like a cobra, whispering all manner of evil into Wilson's ear.

A sickness akin to jet lag hits me. The house warps space and time into a mutant form. It's an architectural Frankenstein's monster, like one of them trees grafted with branches from other trees, so you have oranges, lemons, limes and grapefruit all growing off the same trunk. I walk through a door whose wooden frame's a classical knock-off, complete with triangular lintel.

'The house was designed by occultist extraordinaire Thomas Hamilton,' says Wilson, beaming with pride. 'There isn't another like it anywhere in the world. Famous people have stayed here: earls, counts and marquises, performers of all sorts too. And now you will be looking after it. You are privileged to become part of a great tradition.'

He makes a show of pointing out fine details such as the elaborate cornices with his stubby fingers.

One moment you're in a wood-panelled room, the dark wood glistening with oil polish, antique clocks on the wall, Victorian chaises longues, bureaus, oval framed paintings of fair-faced aristocrats, and the next you're violently jerked across time into a 'Napoleonic bedroom'. The dining room has a barrel-vaulted ceiling with a mural depicting what Wilson calls 'The Apotheosis of Lord Byron', which is some Greek-style thing with chiselled men and butts and penises floating up in the clouds. Naked guys with ruddy pink flesh are pulling a chariot for a man in a red toga with a laurel wreath on his head like he's a champion of some sort. How anyone could dine under that is beyond me. The rich move in mysterious ways.

The rooms that aren't wood-panelled have the most hideous wallpaper. The only thing this place has going for it is its size. I'll take my cosy cara any day.

'See, Hamilton's greatest triumph was summoning a house spirit from the land of the Fae. He was seeded in the earth here, bedded in with the foundations,' says Wilson. 'He's a Brounie unlike any other and he keeps this property safe. This Fae has served all the lords of this house, including the one who shall return. Everyone who buys or inherits this property receives, along with the keys, the title of lord. It's the smallest estate on these isles that comes with such a grand title. Things are in motion, Sunshine. Once the work is completed, the Tall Man, the last lord, will return—'

Wilson cries out and falls to his knees. The cord that binds him has been yanked hard, like the reins of a cantering horse brought to a quick halt.

'No, that's not what I meant to do . . . She's a good one.

You'll be safe, the house is safe. I didn't think . . . Yes, it was too soon. I agree . . . No, please, not another! I've been good. I was only trying to help!'

He's dragged across the floor. Flung this way first, then the other. Legs and arms flailing, as if some invisible beast has set upon him. The attack is ferocious and sustained, dragging him from one corner of the room to the next, violently bashing him against the walls.

I'm frozen, not knowing what to do. My legs tremble and threaten to give way under me.

'I would never betray the master,' says Wilson, sobbing bitterly. 'I meant no harm.'

He is dragged back to the floor near my feet and pinned there. An anguished cry rises from the back of his throat. I step back. He jerks like he's having a fit, his body jolted by some unseen electric force. It goes on and on, freaking me out. Then, suddenly, he falls limp. His breathing slows. Eyes wide open, like he's seen Death with the sickle right in front of him.

'Wilson?' I say.

'Shut up, whore! It's all your fault . . . Yes. I've learnt my lesson. It won't happen again. Yes, of course. We'll proceed exactly as you planned from now on. I am sorry.'

'You okay?' I say, ignoring his invective.

He gets up slowly, a small pool of blood where his face had lain. I take him by the shoulder and help him up. He holds his hand over his left ear and the white glove is stained with blood. Bright crimson blossoms until the glove's empty fingers sag under the weight of the flow.

'How bad is it?' he says, turning to show me.

'Your earlobe's gone,' I say. It's neatly sliced off below the cartilage.

'Just a little nick, that's all. He's kind, the great spirit, may he be praised,' says Wilson, covering his ear again. He has the beatific look of a martyr. 'This is what happens when you cross him. You'd better learn quick.'

I feel a slight tug on my dark umbilical cord. It elicits just enough pain to make me see this was all for show. It's a lesson from the shadow to me.

I take Wilson to the bathroom, decorated with garish oxblood-coloured wallpaper, with mounted horsemen and trees and stuff on it. He sits on the edge of the bathtub while I find bandages and Savlon in the cabinet. Wilson winces. I can only imagine what he's been through in the years he's been here. My heart softens towards him a little. We're all what we are because of circumstances larger than we are. Example: if I was rich, I'd never have been about breaking into people's houses.

I wet some gauze and use it to clean the blood round his ear. It's clotting and I take care not to disturb the wound.

'This is gonna hurt,' I say and spray the antiseptic on it. Can't risk an infection, even if the floor was fairly clean. And I need Wilson. He's the only thing standing between me and the Brounie. If he dies, it turns its full attention on me.

'Bugger,' Wilson yells. I knew it'd burn, but at his age an infection would croak him for sure.

I dress the wound with multiple plasters, making sure the whole thing's covered up. Psycho Brounie sure did a number on him, with this and the fingers. Damned if this shit's gonna happen to me too.

'Thank you, Sunshine,' says Wilson. 'I knew you were a good one. She's a good one, you see. She'll take over after I'm gone. I'll train her up, teach her everything I know. She won't be like the last one . . .'

Don't like the sound of that one bit. If this is the frying pan, I don't wanna know where Grace has been taken.

It's hard to get blood from a cream carpet. That's the whacko thing about this place – why carpet the bathroom in the first place? I'm on my knees, blotting so I don't smear it and end up with a larger patch. Job's not going great and I really don't want trouble from the man about this. He seems like a clean-freak from what Wilson has to say. It's moved from ketchupy to rusty, and I wonder what I have to do to get it all out. I have it looking half decent before I wipe the bloody handprint off the side of the tub. The great thing about living in a caravan is that the rooms are much smaller when it comes to cleaning up. I get up and inspect my labour. The Brounie's watching me again. I can feel its eyes on the nape of my neck.

As far as probationary periods go, this has to rank as the worst gig ever.

I return to the drawing room where the incident happened, and clean up the floor there too. Not sure what to do with the remaining earlobe. If medical care was an option, maybe it could be reattached. I end up throwing it into my bucket. The blood's easy to get off this floor because the laminates are well waxed.

The gardener walks past the window and I look up. I knew I recognized him. It's Willie Matthews from the hood! He's zombified, moving in some sort of shuffle. That's been him sleeping on the lower bunk all along.

'Hey Willie,' I call out.

He looks at me, but there's no hint of emotion in his face. I open the window and cool air rushes in. Willie doesn't move or anything. He just stands there.

'It's me, remember me from Hermiston? Home ring a bell? Hello?' I say.

There's nothing inside him. The empty vastness of the desert at night. He's lost an awful lot of weight. I remember how we used to call him the Michelin Man, roly-poly and all that. Now he's skin and bone. Didn't even pay attention when I heard he'd gone missing. That's the nature of life at HMS. Folks come and go. Lads head down south to seek their fortune. More often than not they don't come back. But it's Willie alright. Though there's no one home now inside of them blank eyes.

'It's me, Willie.'

'He's not your concern,' Wilson says from behind me. 'On your way, Willie. You have work to do. There's a good lad.'

Without question, Willie shuffles away. He does what he's told. Is that what it's going to be like from now on? Nah, this ain't for me. No freaking way.

There's blood on my white apron.

'Close that window. *He* doesn't like them open,' says Wilson.

The longer I stay in this place, the worse things will get –

and Gran's definitely got to be worried by now. I remember listening to a podcast about the Second World War, something about Chamberlain's policy of appeasement. Didn't work then, doesn't work now for bullies or tyrants. Things always get worse. Wilson's here, trying his best to serve this thing, and the only thanks he gets is having bits hacked off his body.

Stuff that. I've got places to be. And now I know what I must do.

XXX

I sometimes wonder about slaves back in the day. How does it happen a free woman's taken and broken until she accepts servitude as a natural condition? If the true nature of woman is to yearn for freedom, then how come everywhere she's in chains? Always seemed hypothetical, the kind of shit that went down in other places, other eras. Serfs. Indentured servants. Bondsmen. What makes one person bend at the waist before the other? Feel like I get it a bit better, lying here in the bottom bunk. The only currency more powerful than money in this world is the violence of man.

Willie's in the bed next to me. Four nights in and he's still not talking. Head under the covers, balled up all foetal. Gets suffocating in here without windows. It smells of old chemicals snagged into the paint. The walls weep around me. Forlorn wailing of destitution and despair. It's so hopeless it threatens to break the spirit.

But I won't break.

Never.

I'm gonna have to take this slimeball head-on. I might lose. But if it comes to that, I'm still gonna make sure I land the mortal blow. If I'm going down, this house is coming with me. Every single brick and layer of mortar. At least that way, no one else need ever go through this bullcrap.

In the face of overwhelming odds, I'm left with only one option: I'm gonna have to magic the shit out of this. I take out my copy of *Foundational Aspects of Scientific Magic* from my bag. Slide under the duvet and turn on my torch. Been moving so much doing the tasks Wilson's set me that my battery's almost full. I could have the light on all night if I need to. I skip the introductory shit and go straight to the fire spell. Reckon I'll burn this place to the ground. But I've gotta be able to create a spark first. Though I'm gonna need a bonfire after that.

During the Cold War, the Russians had a fully automated system called 'dead hand' set up. If the system sensed a nuclear attack on Russian soil, by seismic activity or radiation or some such, it would send a signal to their silos, unleashing a retaliatory volley of nukes at the Americans, even if the Russian leadership had been decimated. Mutually assured destruction was the doctrine of the age: if you take us out, we'll make sure you're coming straight to hell with us.

Let's see what Montague and Chandrasekar have to say about all this. The upside of reading them is that, compared to Thomson, they're more modern and easier to understand. They don't use five sentences when one will do. And reading up on this will take enough time as it is. I get to it.

These two recommend different incantations depending on 'mood'. Fire has many uses – to warm, to incinerate, to light, for work, and so on. So the idea seems to be that a softer incantation might be suitable for a fire whose purpose is to light a candle at a romantic dinner. Whereas one meant to arson the shit out of a house of horrors will need something heavy. I skip the soft shit because I need full-on pyrokinesis on an industrial arson scale here. I want any fire I start to be a MIRV intercontinental ballistic missile – targeting all the rooms at once, so there's no chance of saving this place. I feel myself getting angry as I think about the house, but calm myself so I can focus.

So you got this thing called 'yield', the power a spell can produce, which Montague and Chandrasekar go on about for a bit. Seems once a practitioner masters the fire spell, they can control the rate of the burn and even the temperature too. There are limits, though, and these limits are governed by the energy available within the area covered by the spell. So if it's a fire spell, we're talking about the amount of wood available for burning, the amount of oxygen in the air et cetera. Roger that. This is shown by the Somerville equation. Gotta don my math goggles and get super scholarly here. I take in the equation on the page.

$$y = w(c + a - N)/t$$

y – Yield
w – Practitioner's potential
c – Combustible material
a – Agitative threshold
N – Natural resistance
t – Time

Kind of a drag when your math is all letters and symbols and not even any numbers, but hey ho. These theory guys are like, this is one of the finest achievements in magical theory. Before this, incantations for fire were well known and their effects widely observed. But Somerville was the first to provide a mathematical *proof*, giving the logical backbone to these incantations. This made pyromagic predictable and quantifiable in ways it had not been before. Then in 1833 the American Rosenberg-Taylor backed up the equation, confirming it was accurate with experimental evidence.

I flip to the next page, see what's there . . . Hmm. Looks kinda heavy, but I have no choice – if I want to use magic, I have to suck it up.

So nowadays, the Somerville equation is mainly used as a way of deriving w – or the practitioner's magical potential – in magic schools around the world. New students are taught fire incantations, and then rigorously tested to find their personal 'w'. This is the benchmark method of measuring a magician's power. Before that, it was commonly assumed the chap with the longest, greyest beard in the room was the most powerful. Not really what I'm interested in now, though . . . I just need to *get my fire going*. Problem with this magic stuff is it's not like in the films where the hero sees a couple of tricks – and before you know it they're off casting spells. You actually have to *understand* what it is you're doing before you can do it. I sigh and turn back to the page.

It seems Montague and Chandrasekar agree with Thomson that the basic spell has three parts to it, known as the AAA. The first 'A' is the Approach, according to Thomson. But Montague and Chandrasekar prefer to call this initial stage – the channelling of the practitioner's will – 'Supplication'.

The easiest Supplications, according to our two guys, have religious overtones. This is because religious practice encourages the type of mental state that is also necessary for magic . . . The 'right state' being where an individual's will can somehow connect with the external universe in order to prompt a change. Lucky for me, you don't need to be religious to do magic, it seems. But earlier 'proto-scientific' practitioners invariably had religious leanings.

So, the spell then flows seamlessly into the 'Anchor' part of its formula – the second 'A' of AAA. This is supposed to be a word or trigger image, something that the practitioner associates with what they want to do – i.e. the intended outcome of the spell. The trigger could be related directly to the outcome or, in the case of more poetic incantations, tangentially. For example, through use of metaphor or hidden meanings.

I pause for a moment to let that sink in.

Apparently hidden meanings were important for medieval practitioners. They worked in secret and didn't want their spells falling into the hands of commoners, which was potentially dangerous. It wasn't thought proper for ordinary folks to know this stuff back then . . . Though I don't think it's much different nowadays. The book says secrecy also safeguarded the practitioners, by disguising their craft in poetry and song. This is why a lot of medieval spells sound like gibberish when compared to modern or post-Enlightenment spells. In those days, the more abstruse the incantation, the better it was thought to be . . . Well, that and the fact that the Scots they spoke back then's a wee bit different from ours today.

When the 'Anchor' successfully encapsulates the intended outcome, the incantation moves into the 'Accelerant' stage of the spell. This is the final stage of that AAA mnemonic, and in some ways it's the trickiest to follow at first. The Accelerant, as the name suggests, functions as a catalyst. It adds a boost to the spell, so the desired result happens faster. From there, I can easily map out for myself that if the spell works more quickly, its impact is greater. Or looking at that equation, if 't' (or time spent) is a small number, the 'y' (yield or effect of the spell) over that short time is high. Okay, think I'm heading somewhere useful now. Though this stuff is *dense*.

Finally on that last A, the term 'Accelerant' is a reminder to the novice. It's a nod to the fact that the spell speeds up something (though they call the something 'an entropic shift') that was going to happen anyway, given enough time.

There's then an interesting digression, to me anyway, into the local peculiarities of N – the Natural Resistance of a given area to magic. It would have been way more interesting if I had more time for this stuff. N is in the equation because some places in the world are more receptive to magical practice than others. And, in those areas, it is easier for a practitioner to work a spell. These locations are often ritual sites where generations of practitioners have gathered to do magic, and certain naturally occurring locations qualify too. For example, areas where ley lines meet – or transdimensional zones. Maybe they'll explain those later. I figure this house must be good for it then, since there's already a Brounie in residence.

Conversely, it goes on to say, there are some rare spaces where only the most skilled practitioners can practise. That's because this Natural Resistance is too high. If the N is too great, the spell simply doesn't work – because that equation produces a negative magical yield. However, apparently some scholars claim something else is happening here. That negative Ns result in the spell merely taking place in a different dimension. They point to incidences of spontaneous combustion as an example. Seems these are not that spontaneous, but a case of luckless people being fried to a crisp by mistake – because practitioners are doing magic elsewhere, in a parallel universe.

Montague and Chandrasekar say that these claims, while fascinating, are impossible to prove. They are therefore set aside as interesting speculations, but not taken seriously by the mainstream scientific community. I chuckle to myself. Could I use 'parallel-world magic use' as an excuse, next time I burn the bacon in our cara?

I skim through the 'Agitative Threshold' malarkey. That's 'cause it's kinda similar to N, though a bit different, and I'm fine with N. The important thing now is that I've got that theoretical know-how pinned down. And I know a *lot* more about this shit than last time, when Priya tried to get me to do magical stuff in front of her. Necessity is the mother of invention and all that.

I lie under the covers and memorize a spell these guys say is pretty damn powerful. I'm finally getting what they're arguing. And – coupled with the learnings from Thomson's book – I think I know what I'm doing. The spell's not that long and the words are easy to recall. Once I'm done memorising, I'm gonna be ready to rain down fire and brimstone on this place.

And I've *got it*. I'm now a certifiable, badass magician.

XXXI

It's about four in the morning, and the house creaks and groans. The woodwork pops at its arthritic joints, making disconcerting sounds. The walls thrum with fretful wails. This is what it's like inside the belly of the leviathan. I've done my swotting – now it's time for action.

I close my eyes and brace myself. Ignore my thoughts and focus on being. Flow with my breathing. In. Out. Oneness with the breath of the universe. I relax my toes and work my way up my body. Let the relaxation wash over me, primed to 'travel' but staying inside my physical form for now. And then I open my eyes and stand, feeling light as a burn flowing through open fields. I try the door handle and it gives way with no resistance. There are no locked doors here. I can move around the house, but once outside I can only go as far as the length of my intestines. Wilson grossed me out with *that* when I first got here. That means there's only one way out of here. The shadows outside play like forest leaves caught in a breeze. The cold floor under my feet ripples away in waves. The walls sway as a cornfield would.

This place isn't nearly as solid as it looks.

Something's masking that truth.

As I continue to the front door, the shadows grow darker and the wood of the house howls.

I'm not afraid. I know magic now. I can feel it, just at the tip of my fingers, a power forged in the heart of a burning star. I hold my hands out to the side and begin to recite the spell that will burn this place to ash, once and for all.

'Fiery flame from Prometheus's torch, blaze and raze. Boil sea and hill, wood and home. Now is the time for your wrath to feed!' I shout. My voice rings out through the empty halls.

I look around but see neither spark nor flame. I said all the right words. I did the spell. So why isn't it working?

The floor tiles ripple angrily, throwing me off balance, and I hold the wall for support. The chandelier above sways, crystals clinking, lights flickering on and off. The Brounie emerges from the shadows, creeping up on the walls. It sways like a cobra dancing to a flute, waiting for the perfect moment to strike. Malicious intent written clear in its every hypnotic motion.

Screw this book magic. I switch to plan B.

It yanks my cord and my body falls, but I remain standing. I've cast off my physical form as spiny mice shed their skin to outwit predators. Casting off an appendage to survive – this is how I regain my autonomy.

Seeing me in astral form makes the Brounie hesitate. Must be 'cause this world is mine. Why else are we able to exorcise spirits – because on this plane people like me have Authority. And visitors here do not.

The Brounie's legless torso is still attached to the walls of the house, and this stretches up to a small, neckless head. It has neither eyes nor nose, only a mouth that extends across the whole width of its face. Its reptilian hands have three long fingers.

'You have no right to be here,' I say, making my move. 'I cast you out, back to the depths from whence you came, Brounie.'

But nothing happens.

Well, that should do something. I mean, it usually works. As I said, I have Authority here.

'I remove your ties to this plane and cast you out into darkness,' I shout.

It crackles and laughs, sending vibrations through the fabric of the house. Windows shake. The chandelier swings, crystals clinking in a maniacal melody. An antique case on the table drops to the floor and shatters. The Brounie rears up, drawing strength from some awful place that I can't sense. Oh no. This is not good. Shit. Don't panic, not now, I need to keep a clear head.

'Stupid child! My master, more powerful than you could ever dream to be, conjured me here. I've bested souls stronger than you for two hundred years, and you think you can cast me out as easy as that?' Its voice is disconcertingly shrill.

Stuff plan B. I'm gonna have to wing it.

It flexes its hands and swings, whole body arching like a whirlwind and striking me with such force I'm thrown through the wall into the living room. A painting falls from the wall and shatters. Before I can recover, the Brounie throws another blow. I roll just in time, under a low table and out the other end. The floor ripples violently and I'm flung into the air by a concussive blow from some unseen force. Have to shake out the ringing in my ears, and reorient myself in the astral plane.

'I knew there was something off about you,' it says. 'Wilson will be punished for this mistake. But first I'll deal with you – and you'll be just another fly I've swatted.' It's now circling the room, still connected to the house's walls.

I'm waaaaay out of my league.

Best form of defence – I rush it, fist clenched, and catch it square in the jaw. The Brounie grunts and recoils, but manages to grab and hold me. We soar through the ceiling with its blue and white St Andrew's-inspired paintwork as I struggle in its grasp. Then, suddenly, it slams me back down onto the floor. I gasp in pain – I felt that one.

The Brounie's still got me. I try to wriggle away, but its grip is true, powerful hands crushing me.

I feel dizzy. Can't breathe.

This home is its base. And it draws its strength from the ley of the structure where Hamilton seeded it. As much as I struggle, I might as well be under a hydraulic press, crushed by gigatons of power.

So tired. It would be so easy to stop fighting. To let it take me.

But what would Gran do here?

I stop struggling and put my arms around the Brounie, embrace it and suck it down with me. Deep. Down. Across. To a sullen grey place with neither up nor down – the colour of ash.

If I'm going down, I'm taking it with me. M.A.D., bitch. I'm up for Mutually Assured Destruction – if that's what it takes.

'I am going to destroy you,' the Brounie shouts.

It squeezes harder. As I'm engulfed, a ball of relentless pain, I lie limp and embrace sweet death. The oppressive grey around us is a heavy fog. There's a stench of stagnant marsh and the cold ash smell of a long dead fire. The departed wander aimlessly in the void, uncaring of our presence. I've played my last card as darkness hovers over me. I just hope it bloody works.

We're in the everyThere.

While I'm locked in this deadly embrace, the dead shuffle on around me. The Brounie squeezes tighter and tighter, until a blurring of my vision begins to turn to darkness. I know the score. Die here, die out there.

Izwi.

Gran.

Izwi.

I hold on, knowing they won't know where I am. They will never find peace, not if I'm missing. It seems I've only succeeded in worsening a losing hand. I . . .

A pair of black talons appears in the fog. Sharp claws slicing through the murky air. Then I see its monstrous horse's head, with carnivorous teeth. Blazing white eyes. Horrible shrieks emerge from its throat. The claws grip one side of the Brounie's long torso. Something snaps.

The Brounie yells out in pain, but it's too late. The sky's turned black with a murmuration of voykor, who descend like black comets. The Brounie releases me to face this deadly new onslaught, but I remain limp. Dead as can be.

The Brounie howls, throwing the first voykor to one side as

its talons tear at my tormentor's ribs. It sees the danger coming from every conceivable direction and tries to run, but the dead zone is no place for speed, not for an outsider. The voykor approach screeching, their hunger driving them to feed.

In 'Vengeance', episode 22– the finale of *Mortal Kombat: Conquest* – there's a mighty battle. Shao Kahn, evil emperor of Outworld, faces off against Raiden, god of thunder and protector of Earth Realm. (They are both played by the same actor, the mesmerising Jeffrey Meek.) Shao Kahn had rallied his army against Earth's defenders. But in the final battle, the god of thunder proves too skilful and defeats him in one-to-one kombat. The god orders the vanquished emperor of Outworld to return to his realm. Shao Kahn just bursts out in an evil, mocking laugh and announces, 'You're already in Outworld.' Raiden tries to summon lightning bolts at that point, but gets nothing but static. He's shocked to see his powers no longer work. While they were fighting, Shao Kahn had transported Raiden to the Outworld – where the god had no powers. He changed the rules of the game and so secured victory.

Cold-ass move, same one I played tonight. While the Brounie was crushing me, I brought us to the everyThere, the home of death. Here, where immortal beings like him aren't meant to be.

The Brounie screams and fights the voykor, who have fallen upon it with gnashing teeth, their steel claws like reapers' scythes. They make horrible noises of greedy glee as they feed on the flesh of immortal Fae – they so seldom see its kind here.

Amidst the feeding frenzy, I slip away slowly, quietly, as if through lace curtains. I imagine laundry smelling of fabric conditioner hanging in sunlight and my Gran waiting for me. I set sail and slip away over the threshold, back into my world.

XXXII

I slip back into my body, like a hand fits into a glove. Son of a . . . Got a cut on my brow. Stings like Frazier gave me a good licking. I get up slowly. Nothing broken as far as I can tell. Dental situation: A-okay. Not a bad result, given the circumstances. I check my navel and see the cursed cord chaining me's disappeared. Freedom, baby.

There's a rumbling in the bowels of the house.

I hear the creak of beams buckling. Smatterings of plaster rain down from the ceiling. Thin hairline fractures spread through the wall. There's a moan, sounds like something from the pit of hell itself. Not that I would know. There's a tempest tearing through the house now, ripping pictures from the wall, rocking furniture. And from outside I hear what sounds like breaking tree trunks and falling roof slates. Metallic screeching. Glass shattering. The floor also ripples in the storm.

Voices in the walls weep and exalt in jubilation. There's a cacophony of sound amidst the destruction.

I'm about to hit the door and bail from this bitch, when I remember Willie's still inside. I make a mad dash, racing through the crumbling house like I'm Jesse Owens with A.H.

watching in the terraces. Skid at a corner 'cause the floor's polished like a mirror. I'm going one way, feet going the other, yet somehow we meet in the middle and jam on it through the corridor to the bedroom.

There's the crash of a chandelier hitting the ground.

An earthquake's going on in this house, as it resists its destruction with a convulsion-filled death rattle.

Willie's sat up in bed. Poor git looks blank and doesn't know what to do with himself. No time to explain, I haul him out of bed.

Oh man. Brounie cut off all his toes. I order Willie to put his wellies on, while I grab my backpack and throw a jacket on him. We bail, back into the long corridor. Massive bit of plaster drops in front of me. Not today! I'm getting out of this hell-hole. Skid into the kitchen. 'Come on, Willie, we gotta go.' Cupboard doors have been thrown open. Cutlery flying like confetti through the air. A half-empty bottle of that weird milk is edging towards oblivion. I catch it just as it falls from the countertop, ram it in my bag.

'Get out,' I tell Willie, as I swipe my katty. I'd seen Wilson stash it in a cupboard. And I grab my dagger from the magnetic strip on the wall.

We make it through the back door, just in time to see the roof caving in on this motherfucker. A cloud of dust rushes outwards and upwards. The Brounie's cries echo from the everyThere, transmitted through the crumbling walls. I feel a massive relief at hitting the relative safety of the snowy back garden. Not a moment too soon. The house itself looks like it's being devoured by the voykor, as though each bite they take of the Brounie's flesh is transposed onto the brickwork of the house. Hamilton must have tied the two into one being.

With each crack, a soul escapes from them wicked walls and rushes into space. Soon enough I see a mass of dead people from across the ages who this house took to paper over its cracks. Their cries of relief move me. At last their shackles are broken and they can rest in peace.

I check for Oliver, but he's not there.

'Murderer!' old man Wilson screams out, deranged. He hobbles towards us from the cottage at the back. His face's beetroot red, eyes bulging, veins pulsating in his temples. 'What have you done?'

'Saved your arse, man,' I say, and nod at Willie. 'His too. You're free now.'

'We took you in. Gave you a roof over your head. We gave you higher purpose, a reason to live.'

Wilson falls to his knees in front of me. He's much diminished in his nightgown and cap à la Scrooge. He trembles and weeps bitterly, tugging at his remaining hair in grief. Something in him moves me. Maybe he can't imagine life outside Arthur Lodge. I don't even know how long he's been here for – and maybe he's got nothing left to go back to in the world outside. He's a douche alright, but still . . .

'You've ruined everything . . . That noble spirit, the Brounie, only lived to serve the Tall Man. All it wanted was for you to serve alongside it, don't you see? Now you've murdered it. What's to become of the *work*?'

I try to restrain myself as he makes a feeble rush for me. No. Don't do it. Okay, can't help myself. I sock him good in the speaker and send him flat on his butt. That shuts him up.

'You're welcome,' I say. 'Now tell me where the Milkman is. He has Grace.'

Wilson puts his hand on his bust lip and spits blood onto the white snow.

'I don't know. He just comes in the middle of the night and leaves a gift for the spirit of the house. We give him fish in return, now and again.'

'Wrong answer.'

I raise my foot to stomp on his shin, but the way he shrinks away like an abused animal stays me. This isn't how it's done. I wanna get my licks in, but that's just not who I am. I won't lose myself the way this cursed house wanted me to.

'I don't know. Honest. Only the great Brounie knew the full arrangement, and you've killed it.' He weeps, tears mingling with blood dripping down his chin. This is a man used to doing what he's told unthinkingly. That makes him less man, more beast in my eyes. He's no good to me or himself.

'Have a nice life, dickwad,' I say.

He laughs and sobs as I make to walk away. 'You have no idea what you've just started. The others will be after you now.'

Wish I could say he'll have a load on his conscience – for the things he's done and the things he's been made to do. But he's too far gone for that. His maniacal laugh crackles through the night, amidst the broken sounds of the house coming down.

Knapfery. I get my bike from the shed and wheel it past

Wilson, now sobbing uncontrollably on the ground as if the greatest tragedy's befallen him. Methinks this is an uppercase example of Stockholm Syndrome. But I don't give a flying rat's arse. He's getting off easy. Collaborators like him deserve to be strung up in a public square; because evil doesn't happen because good men do nothing. It happens because they get sucked in, they participate. There are no neutral observers in this world, Old Albert E. showed us that already.

We're all in the game, whether we like it or not.

I trample through the flowerbeds.

The moon breaking through the clouds reveals the house for what it really is now the illusion has been shattered. I see a ruin out of time with crumbling walls. Even the furniture's gone to shit, with foam spilling out of sofas. Rent curtains flutter in broken window frames. And rotting timbers are exposed to the air, next to fallen stones.

Arthur Lodge is no more.

Willie and me walk down the driveway he would have cleared of snow as a slave. Past broken gates hanging off rusted hinges that can't hold anything anymore. Something's not right inside of Willie, though. He just does what I tell him without question or complaint. It's like they broke the light inside of him. All I can do now is take him home, back to his people.

I take one last look at the window where I saw my mother, just to make sure the damned thing's smashed for good.

XXXIII

Dawn's breaking over Hermiston Slum. The sun's behind the hills, colouring the horizon gold. The new day's a treasure chest, ready for the taking. I've come from dropping Willie off at his parents' trailer. Didn't wait to explain nothing to no one about Willie, though – he can tell his own story when he's good and ready. His cara sits in a field by Union Canal, near a bridge marked with a commemorative brass plaque. It celebrates the only notable thing about our hood I can think of: here John Scott Russell discovered the solitary wave, which transformed shipbuilding way back in the day.

The snow's melting now across the fields dotted with our temporary-looking homes. Puddles appear with thin crusts of ice floating in them. The brown earth sits in clumps, as though it remembers what it was to be ploughed over back when McAlister was still tilling the land. I can still see furrows running through it in neat lines. Folks just built their homes atop it, or parked their caras here, and hoped for the best. I'm kinda dazed. A bit numb. Here but not quite. Not all of me anyway.

The bare trees wait for spring, looking as lifeless as I feel. Spindly branches reach for the sky in supplication, begging for the thaw to come.

I put my bike under the caravan and River steps out. She comes over and licks my hand with her warm tongue. I kneel and throw my arms round her neck, give her a big hug.

Then it hits me.

I'm home. My battered Mark 1 peels off and clatters to the ground, as I shed my backpack and, finally, start to feel safe. I cry into River's thick red fur.

By and by, I pick myself up. What else can you do?

I leave River and she whimpers after me. My hands are shaking. Wipe my eyes, try to clean up my face. I tear the weird apron off and dump it on the ground. Swear that's the last time I'm ever wearing one. I also lift up the damned dress and ditch the bonnet too. It's cold and I'm in my bra and trousers. God, that feels good. The cool air. Light. Freedom.

Don't wanna look like a perv, so I pick my bag up off the ground, open the door and step into my home.

'Ropa, is that you?' says Gran, sitting up in her bunk. Curtains are closed, and it's dim in here.

'Morning, Gran.' I try to sound cheery.

She gasps and swings her feet onto the floor. I swear there's ten times more lines etched on her face than when I left. I kick off my boots and take my trousers off too, so I'm barefoot in my undies.

'I've looked everywhere for you. On every plane, but I couldn't find you. Come here, child.'

I give her a hug. She sniffs and I see tears glisten on her cheeks. I'm all out of waterworks and am trying to maintain my front here, but I break down again into small, small pieces and melt into her warm flesh. I love the scent of sleep coming off her body. Talc, old age and love. I soak it all up, then I glance at Izwi fast asleep on her bunk.

'Where were you? What happened to your clothes?' Gran says.

'I took them off when I came in. I was at the library with Jomo. It's open 24/7.'

'The library?' There's incredulity and also anger in Gran's voice. 'You should have called to tell me. I tried your number so many times and it went straight to voicemail every single time.'

'It's an old building with poor reception. I'm sorry I was so thoughtless,' I say.

'It's not like you to do this. Your sister and I were worried sick . . . I searched for you in all the planes, but you were hidden from me.'

'I know. I'm really sorry, Gran. I won't let it happen again.'

She holds me tighter. It feels so good.

'People go missing all the time . . .' She chokes on her words.

Them few days I was away feel like centuries. It's as if I'm that astronaut from *Planet of the Apes* who got home and everything was changed. Only I think it's not the world but me who's not quite the same. It hits me that I might never have seen them again. Might have been trapped in that place for years, bits of me getting hacked off for minor infractions. That I could take, but not seeing Gran and Izwi again? Nah, I couldn't live with that. I tell Gran it's okay, I'm fine, I should have said. I lost track of time.

'Izwi's got to get ready for school,' I say, deflecting any other questions.

I let go of Gran and shake Izwi awake. Kid turns away, so I reach in under the covers and poke her. She writhes, trying to hold onto sleep, until she can't take it.

'Alright, alright, I'm awake,' Izwi says. She yawns, opens her eyes, sees me and squeals. 'Ropa! Gran, it's Ropa. She's back. Yay.'

I feel pain in my side as I lift her out of bed and give her a cuddle. The night's activities have left their mark. Izwi wraps her bony legs around me and I'm, like, this kind of squeezing I can take. But, oh God, can she yak. Think she wants to give me a crash debrief on what I missed. Okay, so there was a fight at school over a pencil case. She's a princess. And who's got a boyfriend now? It's all too much to take in at once.

Man, I love that little voice.

'What happened to your face?' Izwi asks.

'Nothing, I just slipped and fell on some black ice.'

'Are you okay?' Gran asks.

'It's nothing major, seriously,' I say with a laugh. 'Just a small bruise, that's all.'

'You really sound tired from all that studying. Get some rest, my child. I'll make breakfast today. Marie's taking the kids to school. She's been really good to us the last few days.'

Gran gets up and the room shrinks. That's what happens when the three of us are all up. I kneel on my berth and flop down sideways. Gran throws her quilt over me. I lie flat without a pillow. It feels so good.

Izwi's in the way, busy disturbing Gran, who's trying to get breakfast sorted. I wish I had all that energy. I close my eyes, but open them quickly when I find myself back in that stupid house, as if this is a dream and I'm really still there. Arthur Lodge is stencilled to my eyelids. That dreadful wallpaper. Those tacky statues. The sinister mirrors. The caravan feels like paradise after all that. But I'm not quite back yet.

Good things continue to feel like dreams. My sister's frizzy hair. Gran's slow bulk at the far end of the caravan. That's a good dream you can have with your eyes wide open.

Izwi has her jumper on the wrong way round. Should correct her, but I don't. Instead . . . I relax into the movement of shadow and light and colour. The scent of Gran's mealie meal porridge wafting from the hob. A firm berth with nice cushions. I'm home. I punch out and hand the wheel to Hypnos.

Can't move. I'm trying. Using all my strength to get up. Stuck. I can't. Heavy bastard's sat on my chest. I just need to. Can't breathe. It's like a python's coiled round me, crushing. Long shadows on walls. I have to fight back. Pushing with all my might. My body's a useless sack of weight. I'm trapped in darkness. I just . . . .

Open my eyes.

Okay, breathe. You're good. It's nothing, just a freaking nightmare.

Goddamn.

Gran's stroking my hair. There's sweat all over my face. The duvet's drenched too. Piss quantities of sweat. Gran's face hovers over mine. The gentle motion of her hand stroking through my hair is all I can feel now.

'Bad dream?' she asks.

'What time is it?'

'You need to rest. I came to sit here earlier; you were tossing and turning so much I was worried you might fall and hurt yourself.'

'I'm okay, Gran. Just had a long night, that's all.'

'Is there something you're not telling me?'

'Of course not.'

I sit up and put my feet on the floor. The air feels heavy around me. I open the curtain and daylight pours in. Looks like late afternoon. A bead of sweat trickles down my neck. Feels like insects crawling on my skin. I stink. I need a shower.

'What's this foul stuff you've got?'

'It's nothing, just a chemistry experiment I'm running. Applied science.' I stand up and stretch.

'Is that so?' Gran says. She reaches up and touches my hip. 'You know you can tell me anything, right?'

'Uh-huh. Need a shower now.'

I escape to the bathroom. The door's jammed and needs a bit of a shove. The room's smaller than a closet, and coated in vinyl top to bottom. Mould's forming on the ceiling too. That'll need cleaning. Can't have the spores making us sick. I stick my head out and reach into the drawer opposite to retrieve my towel before getting undressed.

I turn the knob and brace myself. In the shower, the water starts out freezing cold, but usually warms up soon after. Thank goodness. Though it's always pot luck as to whether the heating element works. Once I'm wet enough, I close the tap and lather up. I want every speck of dirt from that messed-up place off my body.

As the water runs over me, it's the greatest feeling in the world.

I turn round so my front can have a blast too. Stings where I have cuts and bruises, especially my face. I'm in the shower until the flow slows to the last few drops and nothing but air belches out of the pipes. The tank's real small, so if you let the water run continuously there might be nothing left by the time you're through.

I'll have to fetch water to refill the tank. But it was worth it.

I dry and wrap myself in the towel. There are dark bruises on my arms that weren't there last time I looked. Knapf. The most painful thing's the lump on my noggin. It feels hot and pulses against my skin.

Wasn't a smart move to finish all the water 'cause I gotta brush my teeth now. Mouth feels like I have a ton of plaque in it. Will have to make do with Gran's Corsodyl for now. I take a mouthful, gargle and swish like my life depends on it. I spit and let the drain swallow it.

Feel half human already.

I step out of the bathroom and grab some fresh clothes, combat pants and a tan vest. I'm in a hurry as the sun don't wait for no one. Things to do or things do you. I check my phone and get a gazillion messages from Priya, something from Jomo, missed calls from Gran.

'There's leftovers in the fridge,' Gran says. 'You should eat.'

I'm not hungry. I know I should eat something, but I can't

bring myself to do it. Not while Grace and Ollie are still out there. Don't quite know where 'out there' is, but I'll figure something out. At least I have more info now.

I zip open my bag and look at the bottle. Its sickly glow illuminates the lining of the bag. There isn't a label on it. I flip it, hoping for script on the bottom, but nothing there either.

There's maybe a quintillion farms around Lothian. Assuming the Milkman came from one of them, and he's not just some nut who happens to roll in a float, can I suppose Grace and Ollie are at one of them? Get my Sherlock hat on. Milk bottle and milk float equals farm. How many of said farms are dairies? I know a man who knows everything there is to know about this kind of thing. Problem is I owe him quite a bit of rent. I'll have to link up with Priya, see what she thinks about all this.

XXXIV

Izwi comes back from school with Eddie and Marie. She heads straight for me and hugs my legs, so I can't move. It's like she's tying me down, like she knows I'm going back out onto them streets again. I feel guilty. There's no way I can stay here all evening, all nice and cosy, when I know something terrible's happening to children out there. I have no choice now but to act.

'Hello stranger,' Marie says. 'When did you get back?'

'This morning,' I say.

'She was in town with Jomo,' says Gran.

'Great. Had us all worried there for a bit. Hey, you hear Willie Matthews came back this morning?'

'How very strange,' says Gran.

'His parents say they heard him knocking on the trailer door before daybreak. He's in rough shape. Won't say where he's been or who's done things to him. The city's full of bullies and pederasts now. That's why I don't let Eddie out of my sight.'

'I have to get more water for the tank. Nice seeing you, Marie,' I say, freeing myself from Izwi's embrace and leaving the cara. I'm almost surprised I can do that. Just walk out at will. Go where I wanna go. That's real magic if I've ever seen any.

The Matthews' trailer is at the furthest edge of the slum.

HMS started on one field, but it's grown over time, following the M8. The fields this side of the canal don't drain too well because of the contour of the land. And there's stubble from last year's harvest in the field. Broken stalks of barley poke out here and there, amidst spaces between the newer settlements. Farmer McAlister's house's just opposite the Matthews' trailer, on the other side of the canal. It sits on four acres, with trees growing in its large front garden. The troll's house stands between two bridges, insulated from us.

The reason there's so many bridges along the canal is because its length cuts the farmers off from their fields. The older stone bridges that cross it are barely wide enough for a horse-drawn wagon to pass.

Voices filter out from the Matthews' trailer. Some feral toddlers run between the lanes of caras, down towards the motorway. Their clothes are caked with mud, and they howl and shriek like banshees.

Ron Matthews, Willie's dad, is outside, having a fag. He's got a crumpled hankie in one hand. He coughs and hocks phlegm in it. His face is all lines, bad teeth and sunken cheeks. Even from steps away, I can hear the rattle of his breathing, like something's bubbling through his chest. Whatever he's got, there ain't no cure for it, so he might as well keep on smoking.

'We can't afford none of your telegrams,' Ron says, and attempts to laugh, which sets him off coughing some more. He flicks ash to the ground.

'I'm here to see Willie. We heard he was back,' I say.

'Aye, that he is. Most of him anyway.' Ron stops to catch his breath. No sign he knows anything about my involvement in his son's return. 'Best you come back in a few days. He's still a bit shook up.'

'It's important. There's something I need to ask him.'

'They cut his bloody tongue out! Who does that?' Ron says, shaking. He's a father and I take pity in his impotent rage.

Lorna, his wife, comes out. She gives me a stern look and says, 'I think you should come back another time, Ropa.'

Ron flicks his fag away and goes inside, and Lorna follows, shutting the door in my face.

'Pathetic how people we've not seen since Willie disappeared are all of a sudden taking an interest. Where were they when he was missing and we were going out of our minds asking after him?' Lorna says, her voice muffled behind the cara walls.

'Busybodies,' Ron replies. 'Pay them no heed.'

It's all good, I feel their pain. Can't even begin to imagine what they've been through – what they're still going through. I feel sorry for Willie, but if there's anything I've learnt it's that the world don't stop for nothing. He's got to find his own way back from that horror show.

The sky's turned blood red as the sun sets. This time of year, it happens quick. To the west's a yellow strip of cloud, vivid like a sweltering vat in a forge. From there, the red-orange spills out like brushstrokes going north to south until the paint runs out at the purple fringes of the sky. Maybe this is what hell looks like and it's beautiful.

I'm leaving the field when something moves in the water.

I'll be. A lone mallard makes its way up the canal towards the city. Rich green head, yellow beak, lush brown and black feathers. There's something composed about its approach. Without thinking, I have the katty loaded up and ready in my hands. I've got a clear shot lined up.

I can make this quick and painless.

The bird doesn't seem bothered by me. It carries on paddling, coming closer, making my shot a dead cert. I follow it. Does it feel death in the air?

I can end its life, right here, right now. Done this a thousand times before. Why am I even thinking about this? Dinner, five feet away. There aren't too many easy kills like this left out there.

I just can't seem to do it.

The duck calmly swims past. Pure gangster. I ease off the katty, take my rock and put it back in my pocket. I'm saving this slug for someone else.

This time of the day, HMS is a cacophony of voices and noise. Salesmen wander through the narrow lanes of trailers hawking pilfered wares. Could be a radio here, a tyre there, books, leggings. Everyone's trying to squeeze out a few extra dukes before dark. The speakeasy's blaring indie from its sound system, sending bass vibrations through the soil to the heart of Midlothian.

An electric scooter honks and I make way.

It rolls past and I follow the rut it leaves all the way back to our caravan. I forgot to get water for the tank. Forgot that was the reason I came out in the first place – caught up in thoughts of Willie. We've got bottled water in the fridge, so at least we have drinking water. That'll have to do for now – I can worry about the shower later. I wait out in the fading light and check

Priya's reply to my message, asking to meet at the Library tonight. That's cool 'cause I can see Jomo too. Two birds, one stone, whatever.

I tell Gran I have messages to deliver, a few deados I have to see at the pits before sunrise. I kiss her too. Kinda my sayonara, just in case things go south.

'You've barely been back, and now you're off again this late?' Gran says.

'I have commitments, Gran. Sorry,' I reply.

'You can unmake those. You don't have to go out. Stay.'

I'm so tempted. There's nothing I'd like more than to chill with her and chew this cud. To watch Rumpole on a case, in an old-style court – or listen to Thomas Mapfumo, the Lion of Zimbabwe, play Chimurenga music. But I have my obligations, duties I can't shirk.

'I can't. I have to go,' I say. 'Sorry.'

Gran touches my cheeks with both her hands and says nothing. Keeps me there for a few moments before she lets go.

'Thanks Gran,' I say awkwardly, making my way out.

'It's cold out there. Make sure you wear your scarf. Be safe,' she replies.

I keep on because if I stop, I won't be able to do this thing. Have to harden myself. The nippy air helps. I grab my bike, get on it and head back into the big, bad city.

XXXV

I'm deep in the bowels of the underHume in a lab Priya indicated by text. Keep checking my phone 'cause I ain't too enamoured of places with dodgy mobile reception at the mo. Or dark places that want to stay hidden from the bright sunlight of ordinary life. My imagination's running wild and I'm pretty jumpy. Keep checking my navel just to make sure I ain't got some dark umbilical cord bursting out of my gut. My face's still throbbing and the bump on my brow's on fire.

'That was a right nippleskimpel that,' Priya says, once she's arrived and I'm done telling her my story. 'I mean, the Brounie would have had to be super powerful to pull off anything like that. On a basic level, you need consent and compliance to perform magic on someone – and the human body is the most resistant thing there is to magic. That's because it is a vessel of will, so to pull off a spell like that would be quite a feat. I suspect the Brounie induced some sort of psychosomatic suggestion, as opposed to any real binding of your intestines by a magical umbilical cord. The Fae are known for their use of glamour. Suggestion is more likely to succeed than brute magic on a person.'

'You make it sound really abstract. Trust me – it was way

more alarming than that. But I got something out of there. A clue to where the kids might have been taken. I'm going after them.'

'You really shouldn't go charging in on your own like that. I'm just getting to like you; don't die stupidly on me now.'

'I second that motion,' says Jomo.

'Let me show you the shit I found. What do you make of this?'

I take out the milk bottle and place it on the table. It casts the dull glow of the morning star on the table around it. It's giving off a sort of radiance, white tinged with silver, and the fluid swirls in the bottle in the most playful dance. It's as though the Milky Way was spinning, captured in one small container.

'You wanna get us nicked, pal?' Priya says, quickly wheeling to the door and locking it. 'Next time, warning please. I'm having a heart attack the noo.'

'What's that?' Jomo asks.

The lab's bigger than the practice room Priya brought me to before, when we tried making fire. It's filled with glass beakers, pipettes, Bunsen burners and weird metallic implements, orbs and rods, plates and filings. Some of the stuff looks proper old and is made of copper, like gear from a medieval alchemy lab. There's a strange burnt smell, some kind of residue lingering in the air. Molten candle wax sits on the worktops, evidence of magicians who must have worked here recently. The shelves spanning the walls display coloured bottles filled with exotic liquids, and they are something in themselves. But nothing is as strange as the fluid dancing in the bottle I've brought.

'What is this?' says Jomo, holding up the bottle and closing one eye to examine it more closely. He opens it and takes a sniff. Milky fluid rushes up his nostrils and he crinkles his nose and pulls back.

'Watch it,' Priya says, grabbing the bottle. 'You're even dumber than you look.'

'Steady,' says Jomo.

'What do you think?' I ask.

'We should run a full spectrographic analysis.'

'Only we're not on the Starship *Enterprise*,' I say.

'Okay, smarty-pants. It's not something I can do in this pit. We don't have a gas chromatograph or mass spectrometer here, so I need to take this stuff to the biomed lab at my clinic and suss it out from there. Also, we need to be really careful, keep this between just us. You stole it from a dark place. Who knows who's involved with this or what it can do.'

'Everything's so biiiiiiiiiig,' Jomo says, holding his hands out in front of him. 'It's like in *Gulliver's Travels*, man. I've landed in Brobdingnag . . . this is insane.'

He giggles maniacally and Priya raises her eyebrows. Jomo leaps off the stool and claps his hands with glee as soon as his feet touch the ground. Unadulterated mirth and mischief radiate from his face. He reaches out towards Priya's hair, strokes her purple fringe, and she swats him away. Jomo's eyes open wide, he blinks a bit, and the corners of his mouth stretch out in what I first think is a yawn, but turns into a wail of frustration.

'What the hell?' I say.

'You okay, Jomo?' Priya asks.

He folds his arms angrily and stomps away from her. His gait is unsteady, and he sways from side to side, using his arms to hold onto the shelves and lab benches for balance every time he totters. Then his attention's caught by the colourful glass bottles on top of a wooden cabinet. He grabs one and smashes it to the ground. Picks up another one and raises it.

'Oy, put that back – right now,' Priya says sternly.

Jomo hesitates, looking at the bottle, then at her face. Finally, he puts the bottle back, leaps over the broken glass and starts to run round the room, pausing now and again to open a cupboard and inspect what's in it. There's a frantic, unrestrained energy about him. No sooner has one thing intrigued him than he loses interest and moves on to the next. Priya watches with undisguised fascination, as though his every move only serves to confirm some diagnosis brewing up in her mind.

'What's wrong with him?' I ask. I'm weirded out by Jomo's shenanigans.

'I suspected as soon as I saw the bottle, but I couldn't be a hundred percent,' she says.

'Would you like to play hide and seek with me?' Jomo says, ducking behind one of the workstations.

'Come here, Jomo,' Priya says.

He pops out from under the workstation and comes to us on all fours, avoiding the broken glass. He seems to be really enjoying crawling about like that. It's as if he's rediscovering his body, enjoying all the primitive things it can do. He crouches before Priya and looks up at her with big, innocent eyes.

'It's called yang-yang. I've caught a few cases like this at the clinic. Wears off in a couple of hours, depending on the dosage.'

'I don't get it.'

'It's a new drug; big hit on the rave scene these days.'

'I've been walking around with a backpack full of drugs?'

'Naughty naughty. They sell this in 5ml vials, and here you are with a half-pint of the stuff. You've been a bad girl, Ropa Moyo.'

Jomo leaps up and jogs on the spot for a bit. He's super-fidgety, as if he's desperate to burn all this pent-up energy inside him. A sly smile appears on his face, and he's away again, ducking behind another workstation.

'Looks like we're stuck with babysitting duties until the yang-yang leaves his system,' Priya says. 'You've heard of the jingle scene that's taken over underground raves? Mostly electropop remixes of popular nursery rhymes and jazzed-up cartoon soundtracks. Yang-yang's what the ravers take to make a night of it. I've got mates who've tried it and they say it's like nothing else. You feel uninhibited, full of energy. Time stretches out and expands so five minutes feels like an hour, and everything, the world around you, is vivid and large and new. You experience an incredible feeling of euphoria and warmth.'

Jomo pops up again and shouts something about being hungry. He's being a big kid and it's pretty annoying. I'm fighting the urge to slap it out of him.

'Looks like the Midnight Milkman's the one supplying this stuff all over town. He had a float filled with it,' I say.

'And to find him, we have to find one of his dealers. It just so happens, I know a guy who pushes this sort of stuff,' Priya replies.

XXXVI

After waiting a couple of hours for him to work it off, we leave Jomo the man-child in a somewhat more normal state, with instructions to drink lots of water to flush the yang-yang out of his system. Jomo's pretty embarrassed by the whole situation and stripping naked in front of us definitely ranked high on the uncool chart. I tried to console him that others too had made asses of themselves in the service of science, but that didn't help much.

Left my bike at the Library and am out with Priya, making our way across North Bridge. It's nearly midnight. The city lights flicker from the inconsistent power supply. And the waters of the new loch extend out into the distance, swallowing up what were once buildings and roads. The full moon above the castle is reflected as white ripples on the water's still surface.

'By the way, nice scarf, pal,' Priya says.

'This old thing?'

'Vintage is all the rage these days. I think it's pretty dope.'

'Cheers,' I say.

Past the Tron, we plunge down Blair Street into the murky depths of the flesh market. Priya tilts back in her chair, and there's a slight squeak as she brakes because the slope down is steep. There's ice on the pavements and I step carefully behind her, so I don't slip. We make it to the bottom and find ourselves mingling with a crowd of revellers, out on the town. This late at night, this part of town comes to life with its own rhythm and blues.

A boy bumps into me and I check my pockets. Can't be too careful here; the slightest contact with anyone means either your pocket's been liberated, or you just got a healthy dose of antibiotic-resistant STI.

Good thing about moving with Priya is that she navigates a straight line and folks get out of her way. I savour the warmth as we pass one of the burning bins and braziers that line the road. The smoke drifting through the streets paints a grey haze in the air. Hawkers pass by, shouting out their late-night wares. Pimps are easily recognized too, by their severe looks as they keep an eye on the rent boys and working women strutting along the street in revealing outfits, oblivious to the weather. Their cheap perfumes indicate the main business of this area, as does the smell of sweat and sex lingering in the atmosphere.

There's dung and chippy wrappers on the trampled snow. And used condoms. The hum of voices haggling back and forth in the flesh market extends throughout the old Cowgate, all the way to the Grassmarket up ahead. Clubs blare loud music, and bouncers stand out in the cold, watching the chaos on the street. The noise of voices and music echoes and rumbles down the narrow, built-up lane, loud and incoherent. This whole patch of town is a mess of painted walls, broken windows, faded posters, narrow lanes and stairs. Makes this place feel claustrophobic. It's as if at any moment the walls will come tumbling down and bury us.

We pass under an arch, its old bricks stained with black soot and white limescale. A shirtless boy in leather pants and a leather jacket accosts us.

'Shilling for a willy, lassies. Make it a night to remember,' he says, bending down to favour Priya with a flash of perfect white teeth. I'm hit by the scent of his cologne. 'I can do both of you at the same time, if you like.'

'Not tonight, Romeo. We're looking for something else,' Priya replies, giving him a flirtatious smile.

'If it's a girl you want, my sister's right here. You can call her Juliet,' he replies.

'She's very pretty, but not what I'm after,' says Priya.

'If it's the best of both worlds you're after, I can dress up for you. I can be anything you want me to be,' he replies, charming smile dialled to ten.

'See that man in the Savile Row crap? He's more what you're after tonight,' Priya says, pushing on.

All around are familiar faces. Even if they're not the people I remember from my time at Camelot, they're all the same in this town. Those lean, hungry looks, the barely masked guile of people trying to earn a living off the only thing they actually own and possess. If you can't trade your labour, all you have to offer is your body. And in this city, anything can be bought and sold for a price.

'Keep an eye out for Paul, will you?' says Priya.

'I don't know who that is, let alone what he looks like,' I reply.

'Blue hair, lanky, dresses like a punkstar.'

Needle in a haystack in this place, where half the people are wearing glow necklaces, bracelets or luminescent bits in their hair. Moving advertisements for our hedonistic delectation. This hood is alive, but the vibe is dialled down a bit as we move into the old Grassmarket. If the Cowgate is mostly brothels and massage parlours, this side is more titty bars and pubs. Now and again, I catch a glimpse of some deados weaving in among the living. Mostly old ghouls with whom I have no business. The Grassmarket used to be the place for a good hanging, back in the really old days. And a few who met the gallows are still lingering for a refund or something. A lot of people were offed here for reasons that don't quite hold up nowadays. Three hundred years later, the dread is still stencilled on some of these old ghosts' faces.

'Over there,' says Priya.

We turn up onto West Bow, which leads up to Victoria Street, then up onto the bridge we passed under before. Priya wheels over the granite setts, which replaced the tarmac in many of these streets, towards a youngish guy. He's leaning against the fountain, watching the crowds go by with a keen eye. There's no cops patrolling this part of town. They only come here when the sun's up to collect bodies – if there's any abandoned after the night's excesses. It's a strange unwritten pact they have with the patrons of these parts that, though the townies hate the fuzz, they'll tolerate their presence for that service at least.

'You'll like Paul,' says Priya. 'He's from my ends.'

'If he's got the info we need, or knows more about that milk stuff, he'll be my best pal for life,' I say.

The geezer's wearing vintage pilot goggles and a leather aviator hat, so I wouldn't have been able to make out his blue hair anyway.

'If you want it, I got it,' he says, not looking at Priya. Always, he keeps his eyes on the moving crowd.

'Something special,' she says.

'Got your Uncle Charlie. You know him, a bit pervy, won't let you sleep. Must be Molly, she's got the love bug, makes you all warm and fuzzy inside. No? Or maybe you going old school and you wanna hang out with the Virgin Mary full of grace . . .'

I haven't got a bloody clue what he's talking about, but Priya nods like she understands. 'Next level.'

'Damn, you wanna put a horse to bed, is that it?'

'Do I look like a vet to you?'

'You need to graduate from college before you can call your Aunt Hazel, or maybe I can get lovely Tina for you. Do you wanna go up, down, or sideways? Fly like Superman, or float like a butterfly? It's up to you because I pack a sting in my pack.'

'I need something with a jingle like Santa's sliding down my chimney.'

'Get out of here, you can't handle it. They say that stuff makes getting laid feel like it's your first time.'

'Who wants to shag a virgin? It's overrated. I'm good for what I'm asking, you know that.'

'You I trust. What's up with her, though?'

I realize the gravity of the situation; if Paul's already getting cold feet about pushing this product, then it must be wow. He gives me another quick once-over and goes back to scanning the crowds. There was talk some time ago of undercover cops coming in at night and then lifting folks in the day on hearsay. The pushers bear the brunt of that, 'cause even if you ain't got nothing on you, the boys at the local will still give you a licking to show their hospitality.

'She's with me and that makes her good,' Priya says. 'Tonight is actually your night, Paul. You've hit the jackpot.' She turns to me and adds, 'Show him what's in your bag.'

'You hogging my spot and that ain't good for business,' Paul replies.

I remove my backpack, place it on Priya's lap and open it. Paul takes a look inside, sees the starlight glow and whistles. He looks at me and then at Priya, and I know we've got his attention now. I close the bag as soon as he reaches for it, slinging it over my shoulder.

'How much you want?' he says, scratching his nose.

'It's more *who* we want than how much . . . I need a link to your plug, Paul. Fellow who goes by the Midnight Milkman – he's into cosplay, so I hear.'

Paul laughs and wags his finger.

'You got a screw loose or something? This guy's got eyes round every corner these ends, so don't stick your chebs in the hornets' nest, girls,' he says, anxiously rubbing his neck. 'And don't waste a good opportunity by asking questions either. I can move this pronto for you pretty little ladies, but if this is his juice you're peddling, no one within a ten-mile radius is gonna push it. I say we take this to a quiet little alley to do some business. Half now, the rest when I finish selling.' He opens his jacket to reveal a wad of cash.

'For what this is worth, I think I can find someone willing to cut the deal I want,' Priya replies, moving her chair back a fraction.

He frowns, scanning the heaving crowd all around us.

'Look, any one of these faces, any idiot on a mobile, absolutely anyone could be making a call to the man right now. You don't know what you're messing with here.'

'This pussy's a waste of time,' I say to Priya, trying to sound hard.

Paul grins. But there's hunger in his eyes, a desperation to get his hands on what's in my bag. I casually rest my hand on the hilt of my dagger and make sure he sees that, just in case he's getting ideas. He shakes his head and looks at Priya.

'This is stupid, but what the hell? It's your funeral not mine,' he says, thrusting his pelvis like Elvis. 'Okay, okay. I don't know where he's based, but I can tell you where we meet him – on his runs. How about that?'

Priya gives me a look, seeking confirmation. I figure we'll be at least a step closer if we know where the Milkman hangs out. From there, we can follow him back to his base, or wherever he's holding Grace – and maybe Ollie too. It isn't much progress, but it will do, so I give Priya the nod.

'Deal,' she says.

Paul desperately fights to mask a smile. Shows that he thinks he's getting a bargain and a half.

'Alright then. But don't say my name or associate me with any of this,' he says.

Just then, an old ghoul bursts through the mass of people and comes straight for me, booga-woogaring. Startled, I step back, stumbling into Priya's chair. These old ones don't usually need the likes of me.

'Hey,' Priya says.

But her voice is immediately drowned out by screams and curses. I catch the rumble of tyres against the street's flattened cobbles. As the ghoul flies towards me, shrieking, Priya points up the road. Two blinding headlights roar towards us. A milk float. I dive out of the way, shoving Priya back.

There's the scratch of metal against stone, and then a gasp of sheer horror erupts from onlookers as the vehicle misses us by a whisker and careens into Paul. He's thrown back and crushed against the fountain. His blood runs warm onto the slush and he looks at us, eyes wide with shock behind his goggles. The air wheezes out of his crushed chest once, twice.

XXXVII

If it wasn't for that ghost booga-woogaring, we'd be toast. Now, despite the sinister presence of the milk float, I'm tits deep in this surreal dissociative state. It's like everything's gone slo-mo and I'm checking it out from inside a bell jar 'cause everything's coming through all muffled. Words aren't making too much sense right now; everyone around me might as well be booga-woogaring.

Then my mind turns to Paul. Oh god . . . He tried to warn us this was dangerous and we didn't listen. We just kept pushing him for more information, and now he's . . .

My job's dealing with the dead, it's simple and clean. I see them after the fact, so I'm not really used to seeing crushed bodies, the vomit and piss and blood that leaks out – and it's as if Paul was a bag of meat.

We were just talking to him, and now there's no *him* to speak of. He even tried to warn us there were spies or some such around. But who? And where?

Am I bombed?

The ghost that saved my arse has melted into the crowds. Didn't even get a proper chance to say thanks. An angry mob forms around the fountain. Men in various stages of intoxication come to suss out the strange situation. The noise was such that people peek out of the windows of the tenements above the establishments.

'Gadgie arsewipe drove straight into the laddie,' a drunken voice slurs.

'Hit him like he were a sitting duck.'

'There ain't nothing for it now,' a man says, doffing his cap.

But there's a tone of menace in the voices that rise above the discontented throng. A young man raps on the side window of the milk float. The float's electric motors whirr as it suddenly reverses, causing Paul's body to slump and fall like a sack of tatties. It twitches as his last remaining life force leaks out into the ether.

A bunch of bampots surrounds the milk float, going ultra-radge and rocking it back and forth, demanding satisfaction. Then there's a whizz; two fine jets of water spray across the blood-covered windscreen, obscuring the driver. The wipers come on, arcing from side to side. Some of the lads step back, angered even more by the splattering of blood and water. But I have other things to worry about as the windscreen clears up and I see a familiar menacing face staring at me from behind dark sunglasses.

'It's the—' I start to say.

'Yeah, I figured. Let's get out of here,' Priya cuts in, already wheeling her chair through the crowd. We fight past a mass of bodies, as those coming to view the spectacle slow us down.

'Out of the bloody way,' I shout.

I turn at the sound of tyres screeching. The milk float jerks free of the men rocking it, sending some sprawling. The air erupts with curses and indignation, but anger soon turns to terror as the float barrels down towards me and Priya, knocking people out of the way like bowling pins. They leap left and right to get away as it skids onto tarmac, then all the way to the opposite pavement, before lurching forward again. He's coming for us.

'Move!' Priya shouts as we race over the roundabout, back into the Cowgate.

The milk float is gaining on us, its motor straining with a high electric whirr.

I'm running my damned fastest, but Priya is moving even faster down the slight slope. I turn and see a volley of beer bottles flying through the air – courtesy of pissed-off patrons watching as shit hits the fan. A few land on the float's roof; others hit bystanders or smash onto the pavement. From the noise, it's easy to tell a riot's about to break out because folks are at each other's throats already. My heart's racing, feet pounding against ice and asphalt as we go under the bridge, with the Milkman in hot pursuit. For a microsecond I allow myself to reflect on the fine irony that we were the ones supposed to be chasing him. But, as Iron Mike Tyson once said, 'Everyone has a plan till they get punched in the mouth.'

'Hop on,' Priya yells.

'You crazy or something?' I say.

'Do it,' she says, grabbing my arm.

I fall into her chair, which wheelies to the left side. But Priya leans hard right, bringing the wheel to the ground. I scream my lungs out, feet dangling one side of the chair and my head over the other. The ground rushes below us, and the angry-looking lights of the milk float glow red. It looks like a beast seeking to devour prey. And it's gaining.

'Sit properly,' Priya shouts.

'Sorry, I've never shared a wheelchair before,' I yell.

'I have a good mind to toss you out,' she replies. 'Abraxas and Therbeeo, bringers of dawn, I beg you pull my chair as you would Helios's chariot. Charge!' The air around the chair takes on a limey glow as she finishes her incantation.

I'm upright, half sitting on Priya's lap, my legs still dangling over one arm of the chair. We hurtle downhill faster than seems possible, past the open fires and street sellers and working boys and women. This road could take us all the way down to Parliament. And from there, we can cut across the park to Camelot, where I'm sure we can get reinforcements. I'm about to relay this splendid plan to Priya when a horse catches fright in front of us. It rears up, tossing the rider and blocking our way forward.

'Hold tight,' Priya says.

She leans left and the wheelchair skids across the road at an incredible angle, taking us into the Old Fish Market Close by a whisker or less. Before you can say hillbilly cheese, Priya has us racing up the road, past the displays of thighs and butts and bellies and boobs for sale at the sides of the lane.

'Watch yersels, yer twally-washers,' a man shouts, waving his fist.

'Sorry!'

Old Fish Market Close is on a pretty steep incline, and, great chariots of fire, I have no idea how Priya's even steering this chair properly at this speed. Then there's a screech and a crash as the milk float flies into the lane and hits the wall opposite. There's an eardrum-bursting screech as it backs up, then drives towards us. Sparks fly as its side drags along the wall of the block. The sound of metal against stone grates against my skull.

It must be some kind of souped-up milk float because these things just ain't meant to go that fast. Soon it's bounding along the setts again, headed straight for us. I reach into my pocket and grab my katty.

'Stop tickling my belly,' Priya protests, as I search my other pocket for ammo.

Got it. No chance for a comeback as we scoot past the ancient buildings, the lane getting narrower and narrower. I reach round the back of the chair to take aim and let fly. My stone moves true through the icy air and catches the windscreen. It wasn't hit hard enough to break, but a bloody spiderweb spreads out, and the Milkman zigzags. Despite that, he's still gaining on us as we zip into the narrow pedestrianized arch that leads onto the Royal Mile.

'You smell nice,' says Priya.

'Parfum naturel, baby,' I reply.

'Brace yourself.'

I catch a glimpse of the Milkman's hideous face through the cracked windscreen, just before the float rams us in the alleyway. I'm gripping the armrests, and the force of the impact throws us up and forward, and we jolt onto the Royal Mile, the wheels clattering even more roughly against the setts as we bounce side to side, with Priya furiously trying to regain control. I'm thinking the metal bollards in the alleyway will stop the Milkman, but his float blasts through them as though they were matchsticks. We narrowly miss a rickshaw, but the rider ain't so lucky. The float barrels straight into him, throwing both bike and rider to the side.

'Get out of the way,' Priya shouts at the late-night strollers on the Mile, as we turn down the slope, heading for Holyrood at the bottom.

He's hot on our tail – and as fast as Priya can make this thing go, we're no match for his float. We fly past restaurants and pubs and tobacconists and newsagents, past buskers with acoustic guitars serenading drunks.

'He's gonna hit us again,' I say.

'We've got to shake him. Hold tight,' Priya yells.

She makes a hard left into a tiny alleyway, one too tight for the float to follow, as it was made for pedestrians. It also turns into stairs partway down, another vehicle deterrent. My legs were sticking out over one armrest but I tuck them in quickly, as two people can barely walk abreast here. It's easy to stumble upon these little closes in the Old Town. I can still hear the whine of the float's motor as we judder down a staircase and past doorways. I'm pretty much wheelchair-sick right now, everything in my stomach flowing the wrong way as Priya tries to steady our descent.

A couple kissing at the bottom of the stairs hear our racket and leap out of the way just in time as we fly onto Cockburn Street. And we are screwed six ways from Sunday because the end of the street is flooded with water from the loch, cutting off our escape. And from the other end of the street, the milk float is barrelling towards us.

I'm hollering my head off, but Priya already has a plan, because in the hair's breadth before it hits us, we bound onto the opposite pavement and fly down the stairs of Fleshmarket Close towards Market Street. We cannon down several flights of stairs before hitting the ground with such impact that the left wheel flies off and I lose my grip. As when Phaethon's carriage was struck by Zeus's thunderbolt, we're thrown into the void.

Legs flying one way, arms flailing the other, we fall. I get an impression of thick grey walls, dark windows and moonlight. The chair is hurtling somewhere above us.

Priya's chanting some wild stuff. I don't quite catch it over my own screams of terror, but she yells something like 'Anemoi'. A green light flashes in the air. I feel static all around, a drastic entropic shift, the scent of air before the rains. I then hear the noisy rush of air whirling around us. We are falling still at a rate that seems potentially fatal. The ground is coming to meet us and in the blur I catch sight of something that looks like a cloud hovering below. Then I slam straight into what feels like a damp airbag. There's a loud pop as it bursts into nothing on impact, but it's enough to give me a relatively gentle landing.

Before I can scramble away, Priya falls near me, smashing hard into the concrete, too late to be helped by the airbag cloud she conjured up. She lands with a groan and a sickening thud. Her left arm is at a horrible angle.

'Hey, you okay?' I say, reaching for her.

She's breathing, but not responding.

There's a clang followed by a loud splash as the chair falls into the loch below.

'Priya, wake up. We've got to go,' I yell, but get nothing back.

I put her into the recovery position, for lack of any better ideas. Try to get my bearings. I'm a bit dizzy and the world is wobbling around me like a spinning top. Close my eyes for a bit and open them again. Shake my head to try and reboot. Shining red lights loom at the top of the stairs where the Midnight Milkman's parked his float, blocking the only way out. The stairs below us lead right to the new loch – and had Priya been conscious, I'd have staked everything on us swimming across. No way that's possible now. I'm a half decent swimmer but I couldn't take her with me – especially when unconscious.

The battered door of the milk float opens and the Milkman steps out. He stands at the top of the stairs and watches for a few seconds. He looks grim in the bloody headlights as he descends, tall shadow reaching us long before he does.

We've flown past the Jinglin' Geordie Bar and are on the landing close to the water's edge, near the Halfway House. It's a quaint pub, with garish paint and a brass tankard dangling off its sign. But the doors are firmly shut. I bang on them, hoping someone is inside. The Milkman is slow coming down the stairs. He takes great care on the ice, and I'm praying he tumbles and breaks his neck.

'Open up, please,' I beg, but the Halfway House is dead inside.

If I'd picked the field, I'd have chosen higher ground. Instead, here I am on a lower elevation and cut off. The Milkman's got this – game, set and match. We're square in a kill box with no way out. I'm shitting myself, thinking of what he did to Paul, what he's going to do to us. My hands are shaking and I take a deep breath. Panic will get you killed sooner than anything else. He's already made it to the first landing by the Jinglin' Geordie.

I've still got my katty and I hunt through my pockets for more ammo. Only got one good stone left. I can't keep my hands steady, not with his towering figure coming at me like this. His white uniform is starched and pressed, immaculate like a sailor's outfit. I load up and take aim, but with my hands shaking so much, I daren't let fly – even from this range. He keeps coming, casual like it's Sunday morning, dark sunglasses blanking his expression.

I step over Priya, keeping my eye trained on the Milkman, controlling my breathing as best I can. He's so close now, but I finally feel my heart settling into a normal rhythm, my arm taking over like I'm David and he's Goliath. I just need to step a little bit mo—

Knapf, I slip on the ice and fire off balance. The shot goes wide and hits the wall behind my target.

He turns and observes the rock clatter onto the stairs.

The first time we met, the Milkman looked past me, like I was nothing. But this time he recognizes me and I'm not liking the attention. He'll have gone to Arthur Lodge, seen what happened to it and put two and two together, so he'll know I'm a threat.

Can't say I feel much like a threat now, though.

As things stand, I reckon offence is the best form of defence. I swing one at his crotch as he comes down the last set of stairs. I hit something, but it don't matter none. The Milkman reaches down, grabs me by the throat and lifts me clean off the ground. He bashes me against the wall and holds me there with one hand, while he inspects Priya – still lying prone on the ground. I feel the raw might of his hand, fingers squeezing into the muscles of my neck. I grab for my dagger. But before I can make a cut, he grabs my knife hand and slams it against the wall. I'm forced to drop the knife and it falls to the ground.

The Milkman looks at me through his dark shades. There's no shred of emotion or humanity emanating from him, as he brings his other hand to my throat and starts to squeeze. I gag. Can't take in any air. Feet flailing through the air like a condemned man dancing at the gallows. My face swells from the pressure and my chest burns. I can't scream, can't call for help. The colours of the world meld into one, dripping like something's melting.

Everything's turning into a blur . . . then the two ends of my scarf float up in the air. They turn and bow inwards, then wind around the Milkman's wrists, and start pulling. His hands tremble and he grits his teeth as I feel his grip loosen a little. I inhale. That first sweet, painful breath slices my throat. I cough and almost choke as I suck in more air. The scarf finally prises the Milkman's hands right off my neck, continuing to pull on his wrists until they are far apart and my face is close to his. Sonofabitch, now I'm hanging in a noose created by my own scarf! I gotta fight for my life, bring the Milkman down before I pass out.

I hit him again and again, give him everything I've got. His sunglasses fall off and I see horrifyingly empty eye sockets. Dark, malevolent holes where his eyes should be. I keep swinging. Even though the scarf has his hands, he moves in and headbutts me. My nose bleeds and I taste copper. Screw my fists – I jab my fingers right into them empty eye holes.

The big man screams like Cerberus set loose on a winter's night. I catch a quick movement below us, as Priya sweeps his feet from under him with a swipe of her good arm. The Milkman's howling must have brought her to. We tumble and fall side by side, and I hear a sickly snap, like plastic cracking, as his head nails the sharp edge of the step. He goes limp.

I back away from him and gasp. I can still feel those strong hands digging into my neck. The air tastes sweet and sour to me. I'm not minding the auld reekie right now though, in fact, I'll have seconds. He doesn't move, just lies there with them blank holes staring out at me. I struggle upright, step over the Milkman and go over to Priya, who's sat herself up against the door of the Halfway House. She's cradling her left hand in her right.

'Neat scarf,' she says, wincing.

'You were passed out. I didn't know what to do,' I say. 'You okay?'

'My head hurts a little and my arm's wrecked, but apart from that, I've never been better.' Priya gives me a half-smile, but it's clear she's in a lot of pain. 'Hey, you seen my chair by any chance?'

I point to the loch and she starts to laugh but stops to groan in pain instead.

'Is he dead?' I ask.

'We need to get out of here,' she says.

I look up the stairs and realize it's gonna be a long climb up, with Priya on my back. Least I can do for the girl who saved my life, though it's not gonna be easy. I pick up my dagger, sheathe it and get to work.

XXXVIII

I don't like going to the hospital, 'cause folks say it's just as like to make you sick as well. Who knows what you can catch out here? Things are desperate, though, and Priya's arm is looking wow. It's all swollen and bruised up. Looks more like a floppy elephant trunk than a normal limb from where I'm sat.

'How you feeling?' I say.

'Eyes on the road,' Priya replies. 'The hand's tingling a bit. I don't feel that great, thanks for asking.'

'Hang on, we're almost there,' I say, straightening up the wheel. We were zigzagging all over the show when I first took the milk float, but after I kicked the busted windscreen out, I could see better.

I swing us awkwardly through the gates of Little France. Odd name for a place bordered by the oh-so-Scottish Danderhall and Moredun on one side, Niddrie and Craigmillar on the other. Throw in Liberton too if you fancy, but Edinburgh ain't got a Chinatown, so we have to make do with Little France. Not too many French people here now, 'cept for if you look in the gene pool. The story goes, Mary, Queen of Scots, for whom we all still weep, rolled up there – coming back from France sometime in the 1500s. She brought a ton of servants and courtiers and such, and some of them settled there. They called it Petty France, a corruption of Petite France, and then the locals got tired of all the pretentiousness and so Little France it became. Can't see why they didn't go for Wee France instead, but who cares? There's a long history of the French coming over here doing Frenchy things too; there was that whole Catholic–Protestant malarkey . . . But anyway, that's where the Royal Infirmary is, and I park up in an empty bay near A&E.

I find one of them cheap, hard-backed wheelchairs near the entrance, and help Priya in. It's got these small shopping trolley wheels on it, the ones made with vulcanized rubber – and it shudders over the tarmac, causing Priya to wince. We make it in and the place smells of that cloying sick scent merged with bleach. Makes me crinkle my nose. There's tons of people waiting, all in varying stages of distress. On some days it can mean a twelve-hour wait before the nurses even touch you, but luckily, this late at night it's bad, but not so bad.

'Take me to the desk, I've got insurance,' Priya says.

Posh girl, hey. I'd do the same if I had dosh and I was in pain. They say back in the day all this was free. I struggle to believe it myself, but yeah, you could just waltz into any hospital on this here island and they'd mend you, put you back on your feet, and you could say sayonara without paying spit. It's true. Don't quite work like that now – and I remember Gran stressing about the bill we got after Gramps died. I mean, they couldn't save the guy, which means they screwed up, but they still expected us to pay for all of that. Anyways, if you have plain old cash, or a Platinum Star insurance card like

Priya, you right at the front of the queue. And today I'm right there with her.

The triage nurse's face lights up, recognising Priya, and she rushes over.

'I wasn't expecting to see you this side of the health service,' the nurse says.

'It's been a wild night,' Priya replies.

'It's all fun and games until someone breaks an arm,' the nurse says, looking at Priya's arm.

'You got that right.'

'Your friend doesn't look to be in great shape either. Have you girls been in an accident or something?'

'I'll tell you all about it if you throw in an ampoule of morphine,' says Priya.

I excuse myself and step outside. Need to voice note Gran to let her know I'm gonna be late again. Also gotta call Jomo and let him know the score. Staring out into the car park at the battered milk float, I get how bad it looks. We've been driving around town in a stolen, bloodstained wreck. Good thing it still moves, though, and I know where to shift it for a few bob.

The problem I have right now is that, despite catching up with our man, or rather him catching us, I'm still no closer to finding Ollie and Grace. It's like, I've come into contact with people linked to this whole applesauce and I've got nothing out of it. Wasn't exactly going to get anything out of an unconscious man at the bottom of the stairs. I've seen too much tonight and this sort of rodeo ain't my cuppa.

I shiver and wrap my scarf around me more tightly – then I wave it about to see if it'll do the ninja thing again, but it stays limp. I tap it against one of the pillars next to me and still nothing. So I adjust it to cover the bruises on my neck and tuck the ends inside my jacket.

By the time I get back inside, Priya's been whisked off to have X-rays. I follow the signs on the walls till I find the right department, and see her sitting out in a corridor waiting to be zapped. She's in one of them hospital gowns, the ones that show your butt to the world.

'The doctor thinks my fib's broken too,' she says solemnly, looking down at her leg. 'I can't feel anything down there anyway, so I didn't know. And they think I have a concussion too.'

'I'm really sorry. I shouldn't have got you into this,' I reply, touching her arm.

'Are you *kidding*? I haven't had this much fun in ages.'

'You really did take a knock on the head, didn't you?'

She taps her temple with her good hand. I think she's an adrenaline junkie. Like, I swear I saw her grinning a couple of times as we were being chased through the flesh market.

'Don't take this the wrong way,' I say, 'but you're a healer and everything, so why don't you just magically, you know, sort it?'

Priya laughs. 'You've been watching way too many movies. Healing a fracture involves a complex and sequential set of processes involving inflammation, repair and remodelling to heal the bone – and I'm not even dealing with proximal soft tissue damage yet. First the haematoma forms, so that the haematopoietic—'

'Okay, I get it, it's complicated.'

'Very, but once they set the bones and fix me up with a cast or two, there's things I can do to speed up the process. I'll be fighting fit in two, three weeks tops. It's much easier to mend injuries in children. You can heal their bones in a matter of days, because they don't yet have a fully developed sense of self. Their will isn't as great an impediment. I can handle the wait; what sucks is I have to stay in for twenty-four hours because of the concussion thing.'

'You've earned the rest,' I say.

Only two weeks' recovery is great, but Priya's out of action now. I can't risk taking her out there again. She's already saved my arse twice; it would be rude to ask for a third helping. But with the Midnight Milkman out of action, wherever the kids are being held, they'll starve to death. Or worse, they might die of thirst even earlier. That means the clock's ticking for me. I have to find them and fast.

XXXIX

After leaving Priya with the professionals, I take the float and head out to Camelot. Taking the back road that goes past Craigmillar Castle, I follow it all the way to Duddingston Village. And from there I'm up on Arthur's Seat in no time. Bit of a hustle getting the float up the snow-capped hill, on account of the icy road not being gritted, but I make it in the end. Had to loop round the Salisbury Crags end of the hill, which are these dark dolerite spurs jutting up at sharp angles against the gentler slopes.

I get to Camelot atop the hill and arrange with the Rooster to discreetly shift the float for a 50/50 split. There was a few bottles of yang-yang on it and I made sure to get 'em before handing it over. I'll have to figure out what to do with them later. I fetch my bike from the Library and cycle out of the city. I've had enough of it for one day.

Something's bugging me along the way. See, I know the Milkman's got a gang of distributors pushing yang-yang in the city, but if he's moving all this stuff and managing them, he can't be making it too, right? He's got to be working with someone on the production side. That makes him the middleman. No way it's just him at the top of the chain either.

He's way too visible. In fact, if he's going about assaulting people and the like, he's even more likely to be the muscle and not the brains. If I'm right, then I ain't liking the implications of this one iota. But it's late and I'm frazzled, I can't figure it all out now. So as soon as I get home, I dump myself on my berth and it's lights out for me.

It's pouring outside when I wake up. Rain makes a patter-patter on the roof of the caravan and cascades down the windows, so you can hardly see outside. I try to sit up, but my entire body aches. Head to toe. There's a duvet on top of me and a pillow under my head. Must have been Gran or Izwi, 'cause I went straight to sleep. Didn't have no energy to faff about – I was well zonked.

'Good morning, angel,' Gran says, putting her knitting to the side. 'Another long night?'

'It was a bit mad. What time is it anyway?' I yawn.

'After ten. I just listened to the news. Would you like a cup of tea?'

'I'm starving.'

'Don't get up. I'll warm up a plate for you and put the kettle on. You know, Izwi doesn't like it when you stay out late. She worries about you and so do I.'

'Sorry, Gran.'

'Hmm,' she says, getting up to fix me some breakfast.

My mind's only on one thing now and it's finding the kids. I don't like having her and Izwi worry about me, but I couldn't live with myself if I didn't try. I've already wasted a couple of hours sleeping. Once I have grub in my belly, I'll have to get back on it.

Everything hurts as I sit up. Feels like I've gone twelve rounds with the champ and my ribs don't like it. Gran gives me a bowl of tatties and peas. Lean times, but it fills the belly nicely. I wash it down with a cuppa and listen to the radio drama she's got on. It's some period play about a young lady who wants more from life than is permitted by the suffocating Victorian society in which she lives. Don't we all?

I get a message from Priya saying she's bored in hospital. She sends me a neat pic of her cast and asks if I'll sign it. Tell her I'll think about it and send her a kissy kiss. I sure could use her now. Kinda wondering if there isn't, like, a magic tracking device I could use to hunt people down. I remember watching some movie, ages ago, about a witch who'd wave a pendant over a map and it'd find people for her. Kinda like a dowsing rod for finding water, only more high tech 'cause you're not tramping over arid land searching.

'I need to go on a walkabout, Gran,' I say.

'What for? The everyThere is not a playground for you to prance around in, child. You're out late most nights too. *Please* tell me what's going on.'

'That person I told you about, back when. Nicola. I'm still trying to help her, and I have to question a new soul before it crosses over. There's info I need that can help. It's hard to explain, Gran, but I don't have a lot of time on this.'

'Hmm.'

Gran turns back to knitting that rainbow-coloured cardigan she's been working on. All she's gotta do is set the sleeves in. There isn't much else I can say, and the worried expression on her face seals that for me. If I tell her the full extent of this thing, she'll shut it down and give me some yak about having to look after myself and stuff like that. I totally get why she would, but still, there's no way I can just sit on my hands and leave them kids to starve out there. I have to go everyThere and see if I can find Paul the dealer or even the Milkman . . . If he's, you know . . . Though that thought fills me with dread; I prefer doing business in my own plane. Maybe I can strike a deal of some sort with one or both in exchange for more info. It would have to be a great deal, though, on account that I had a hand directly or indirectly in their untimely demises. They might be a bit miffed about that. But for some people, death has a way of opening up new perspectives, a kind of enlightenment.

'Whatever it is you're up to, don't forget to watch out for yourself.'

'I won't,' I say. That's the cool thing about Gran. She reads you and doesn't push you too hard if there's stuff you wanna keep to yourself. She'll prod, then back off, until you're good and ready to come to her yourself.

I lie back on the bunk, relax my body from head to toe, put my mind in the zone and slip out of my body like pulling a hand out of a glove. I leave the world and thread myself into the grey gloom of the everyThere. Shuffling with forlorn spirits, I search for the faces I want to find. It's not easy in this press with people walking above, below and beside me, like we're atoms jostling in a lattice of some dense element. I walk carefully past a voykor and it totally ignores me. Its teeth don't chatter with unceasing hunger or anything. It seems placid and content, well fed – even happy, if that word could ever be used to describe anything in this plane. Must still be full from the Brounie.

Among the new souls I see, none has the signature of either the Midnight Milkman or Paul. There are many of them here, more joining the press all the time. But not the people I'm looking for.

'Fancy seeing you here,' Mr Chowdhury says, appearing on my flank.

'Oh, hi. I'm just looking for someone. New guy, goes by the name of Paul, or another weirdo, calls himself the Milkman,' I say. 'They'd have come in sometime last night.'

'Well, it's good to see you have time for that, especially since you don't bother delivering our messages anymore.'

'It's not like that at all, Mr Chowdhury. I've just been really busy.'

'Busy means doing your job, young lady. I was on my feet every day, working in a shop for fifty years. Never missed a day off sick. You think I enjoyed that?' he says, wagging a finger in my face.

'I'm sorry.'

'You should be, because I'm taking my business elsewhere. There's a great clairvoyant working off Great Junction Street. Nice music when you walk in, candles, incense, the works. Open 9pm to 5am, Friday to Tuesday. Regular, predictable hours. Five-star reviews all round. She even offers discounts and a loyalty scheme. That's how sorted she is.'

'Please don't. Honestly, I'll get back to work soon and

things will be back to normal. I promise. I need to finish something first.'

'Oh, it's too late for that. You should have thought about it before you started stiffing your loyal customers. I wish I'd discovered her sooner instead of you. We're having family consultations, the lot of us, group mediation too, and it's going very well, thanks. We're close to a breakthrough and as soon as that's done, I'm out of this dreary plane. Going to Svarga.'

He walks off in a huff, and before I can reach him, I'm surrounded by more of the dead. Sucks arse big time, 'cause he was my cash cow. There's no business like repeat business. But that's okay, one big withdrawal don't break the bank. I'll be back to work soon and everything'll be hunky-dory.

'Hey Nicola,' I say when she appears in front of me.

'Any news?' she asks, the desperation evident in her voice.

'I'm really close, but I need some help. There's a guy, goes by the moniker Midnight Milkman. I think he might have taken Ollie and a whole bunch of other kids. He KO-ed before I could find out where he was holding them . . . Well, I don't know if he's dead or not so I had to check. I really need to find him so he can tell me where they are.'

'I haven't seen or heard of anyone who looks like a milkman here . . .'

'Please ask around for me. If he's here, it's very important,' I say.

Nicola agrees, happy to do anything to help her Ollie, and I figure it's better to let the dead find the dead. The voykor might be chilled out today, but I don't wanna push it by staying too long. Best to get out while the going's good, and if my visit has filled one person in this horrible place with a sense of purpose – that gets me one step closer to my goal – then I've done alright. I let myself fall up, out of here, back into the world of light.

When I return to full wakefulness, Izwi's lying on top of me. She's already out of her uniform and dressed in her PJs. I'm a bit surprised by how late it must be, but those distortions happen in the everyThere, a place where there is no time, versus our world, where time reigns over everything. This time of the year, darkness sets in early too, making it hard to tell the time, so there we go. I put my arms around Izwi and she sighs.

'You were gone a while,' says Gran.

'Yeah, but you know what it's like out there,' I reply, and the sound of my voice rouses Izwi. 'Hey Sis.'

'Can I have your phone? I want to play,' she says.

'It's nice to see you too,' I reply, digging into my pocket and giving it to her.

'The screen is cracked.'

'It still works. Play to your heart's content, kiddo.'

'When I grow up, I'm gonna have my own phone.'

'Trust me, I can't wait.'

She gets off me and moves to her bunk to play some game with a lot of blips and boings. Missing her warmth already, I get up. But my mind's on one thing only. I need to find them kids. Some part of me feels guilty just for being here, while Susan and Niall are out there, pining for their grandson Ollie.

So I apply my mind – and some principles from a crime podcast. According to Mr Holmes, the science of deduction demands that I look at everything I've seen so far, whisk that round in a centrifuge, and wait for the truth to come out on top. Elementary, really. To be fair, Arthur Conan Doyle might have got this wrong because that methodology is kinda something else, not strictly deduction, 'cause the way deduction works is a bit different. You say something general, e.g. all foxes are Scottish. Then you can conclude River is a fox, so she must be from Scotland. Clearly that wouldn't help Sherlock solve his crimes. At the other end of the lens, you have induction. Here you start with an individual case, or a few bits of evidence, and draw generalized conclusions from them. So you kinda go from saying River's fur is red, therefore I can inductively reason that all foxes are red. Deduction is more certain – and induction is kinda probabilistic.

But I'm even further away from those two methods. I'm chancing it. Or to use more fancy terminology, this is where you have abductive reasoning, where you can't even guarantee a conclusion. It's kinda more creative and you pool the info you have, the things you've seen, you've heard, your gut, whatever. You mash it all up and see what kind of smoothie you get out of it. I guess I'm mastering the science of abduction then.

Deep in the mix of whatever's going on is or was this dude called the Milkman – and he dresses like one and drives a milk float. So . . . I can infer that he's probably from or works on a farm since that's where the dairy game's played. Wilson did say no one comes back from 'the farm' during one of his rants. And this means the kids are likely to be held at some kind of farming operation. There's tons of farms round the Lothians, so I have to narrow this thing down further. Since the Milkman did his rounds in an electric float, then I need to find out how far he could get on it both ways, to and fro.

'Izwi, can you get off that game and Google the standard range for an electric milk float?'

'What? But I'm playing.'

'Pretty please, with cherries on top.'

It takes a few secs but the blips on the game fall silent.

'They can go sixty to eighty miles,' she says.

'At what speed?'

'Twenty miles per hour. Weirdo. Can I play now?'

'Hold on.'

So, I'm thinking, this float's souped-up and it can go much faster than that. Increase the speed on those things, you decrease the range. It's like the difference between a sprinter and a long-distance runner: to go very fast you burn lots of energy so you don't go very far, but if you take it easy, you can go much further on the same calories. Factor in the fact that the float has to stop and start during deliveries and I reckon I'm looking at a thirty-mile possible daily range tops. But the float also has to go out, do deliveries and come back home. So I can confidently halve that to a fifteen-mile radius between the farm and the city centre, where the Midnight Milkman delivers his yang-yang. Ergo, I'm looking at any farm between the city centre and Livingston. Or from the centre to Penicuik, then arcing round to Haddington. That's quite a stretch of land out there. How many dairy businesses are in that radius, that's the biggie . . . There's quite a few that drop off milk in various neighbourhoods around the city. Not our slum, obviously. If I can find that out, then I can eliminate the proper farms, depots, et cetera, and see if there's anything dodgy going on with the others. Reckon that's my best shot right there.

The bleeping starts again and I know my little sister is back on her silly game, but this is much, much more important.

'Izwi, can you look up dairy farms near Edinburgh?'

'Gorgie Farm.'

'Don't be stupid. I mean actual working farms – not show farms for city kids to stare at the animals.'

'It's still a farm, though.'

'No it isn't.'

'Is too,' she says absentmindedly, too busy on her game to pay real attention to what I'm saying.

I'm about to give her a rollicking when the light bulb comes on. I jump up from my berth, kneel in front of her and give her an almighty smacker full on the lips.

'You're a genius, Sis!'

'Get off me. Now you've got me killed,' Izwi moans, pushing me away with her elbows and turning the other way, so she can restart her game. I don't let her get away with it. Just pounce on her and tickle her little armpits, making her squirm, until she relents and kisses me back.

XL

Long after night has swallowed the sun, I settle Izwi in bed. I get my gear, backpack minus books so it's much lighter. Make sure I have enough ammo in my pockets to take over a small island nation. Dagger – check. Katty at the ready. Phone. Scarf – never leave home without it. Got everything I need. Sun Tzu taught us, 'The general who wins the battle makes many calculations in his temple ere the battle is fought.' He had fancy ways of telling simple truths.

The downpour's eased off to a fine smirr when I step outside the cara.

I grab my bike just as River pokes out of her burrow. Her eyes glint in the dark as she rubs herself against my legs. She's coming with me tonight. I figure her nose might help if the kids are in some sort of basement or something. I'm hoping that with the Milkman out of the picture, the risk factor is dialled right down. But you never know.

Jomo and me catch up on the starfish junction where Gorgie meets Dalry, with Merchiston to one side.

'Jesus, you look awful,' he says. 'Get into a fight?'

'You should see the other guy. Hasn't even got any eyes,' I reply.

If Jomo's dropping quips like that, then I'm certain the yang-yang's fully out of his system. So he made an arse of himself – who hasn't? He gets off his skateboard to walk, 'cause it's a hard slope up Ardmillan Terrace. River walks between us. There's B&Bs to our left and the old Springwell House medical place on our right. It's boarded up now, but it had been converted into a block of flats. Although the whole place burned down years ago, in a gas explosion round about the time I was born. Only charred stone and empty hallways remain. The gates at North Merchiston Cemetery are chained up and locked when we get there, so we bear right onto Slateford Road.

St Michael's Church is a hulking mass across the road. Its stained-glass windows are covered by wire mesh to protect them from vandals and it has a great square bell tower that rises high up. The sheer bulk of it reminds me of a tanker making its way to port on calm seas. Its endurance is somehow reassuring, though it still doesn't feel entirely stationary either. As we walk by, it seems to be moving through time – just much more slowly than its surroundings.

A man passes us, heading for Fountainbridge. 'God save the king,' he says, and we give him the 'Long may he reign' spiel back.

The wall around the cemetery is a head taller than me. I toss my bike over, lift River up and lob her in. She yelps in protest and doesn't take the whole affair kindly. Jomo goes down on one knee, cups his hands and gives me a boost up.

The top of the wall's concave and icy, so it's tricky finding my perch. In the end, I sit cowgirl astride it, my tooshie getting soaked, while I give Jomo a hand over with his skateboard. I hop in after him and land on someone's grave.

The silhouettes of trees reach into the sky above us. It's so peaceful here, you might think you've found yourself in woodland far from the city.

This cemetery's from the 1800s and they were burying people here till the 1990s. I haven't had too many customers from here, though. The folks I deal with tend to be the ones in newer cemeteries or unconsecrated council ground. There, you get a turnover of occupants because the plots are rented. Final resting places ain't so final, it seems.

I walk past a headless angel. Neo-Nazis have done in some of the beautiful sculptures, and most of the tombstones lie flat on the ground. The council tips them over when they get loose – too expensive to repair but too unsafe to leave standing. They lie slowly crumbling in the grass; time wins over posterity any day. But holly thrives here, among the dead.

'It's proper dark and spooky in here,' says Jomo.

'Much worse for me, pal, I actually see the ghosty bastards,' I reply.

'Are there any about? Like, right now?'

'What do you think?'

We trample dead leaves underfoot, our boots squelching in the mud. The terrain's uneven and mounds of earth are heaped up here and there. Ivy and other climbers grow on the trees. Flower pots have been placed on graves here and there, but they have weeds growing in them now.

We follow the dirt track looping round the place. I'm pushing my bike and Jomo's got his skateboard under his arm. The nearby Caledonian Brewery is visible over the cemetery walls and is well lit tonight, revealing red brick and a tall chimney that competes with the church bell tower for supremacy. The scent of hops is strong.

A ghoul in First World War uniform walks right through me, making me jump. It has the form of a Lee-Enfield rifle slung on its shoulder, a metal helmet on its head and a gas mask covering its face. It ambles with the forlorn walk of a shell-shocked veteran.

'This is the dead centre of Edinburgh,' Jomo says, attempting a joke. He looks nervous as heck.

'You think they have a library under here somewhere too?' I try to distract him.

'I honestly haven't a clue.'

One section of the far wall's crumbled. It reveals the rail track and tenements on the Gorgie side of the cemetery. In the distance, well lit up, are the white struts of Murrayfield Stadium. We remain in the cemetery, following the breach in the wall until the railway line veers north to run around the boundary of Gorgie City Farm.

Kinda weird having a farm smack bang in the middle of a city, but hey ho. Edinburgh couldn't expand any further north because of the sea, so she marched south, chowing up farmland and turning it into new neighbourhoods. That's all except for this last holdout against progress – Gorgie Farm. Well, it was more of a show farm – so city people can see what pigs look like – than a *farm* farm. In a sense there's some kind of

292

weird reversal going on. These days it's more profitable to farm human beings than it is to work the land honestly, like in the olden days. In *this* age, people are the livestock, they're sheep. You can make a hell of a lot more fleecing them than you would shearing sheep.

It was the drawings on the milk float that did it for me. I knew I'd seen them someplace before. Some place kids adored, where we were taken in primary school to learn about agriculture – before I lived on a kinda farm myself. I now remember that I'd sat in the cab of that very float when I was little, and pictures were taken of me playing with the steering wheel. Izwi's been here too; it was once practically a rite of passage for every kid in town. But it's been shut down for years and I'd forgotten all about it.

Jomo moves over a mound to stand on some graves. I wince despite myself.

'I can see over the wall here, but I can't see down into the farm,' he says. 'The angle's wrong'.

'We have to go over. No one will see us from this side.'

'What about your bike?'

'I'll leave it in these bushes. We'll pick it up when we're done.'

Can't exactly knock on the front door – as Old Tzu says, 'He will conquer who has learnt the artifice of deviation.' So I figure we'll come in through the rear, just in case. That's how we did it when I was burgling with Rob. Seldom went in the front unless we had to. Too many eyes on the street to worry about. We weren't exactly Jehovah's Witnesses bearing good news. The wall between the farm and the neighbouring Springwell House is too tall to scale without equipment. And the left side is protected by the railway line, making this the only other option.

I climb up on one of the tombstones further along, one that backs right onto the wall itself, so I can see over too. I stick my head over the parapet and have more luck than Jomo. The farm is below us.

'You sure about this?' Jomo whispers. In the still air, his voice carries.

'Don't even think about chickening out now.'

'Your faith in me is inspiring, Ropa. But can I just say maybe we should get adults involved?'

'Who? Your dad? Callander? Like they'd believe us.'

Settles it then.

All the same, I feel kinda hesitant myself. My gut's going all funny now. Makes me feel a bit sick. It's hard to focus on what's in front of me, almost like there's something making me not want to look directly at the farm. Some sort of subtle, repulsive enchantment, I reckon. I fight it and warn Jomo he might be hit by it too.

'What do you see?' he asks.

There are solar panels lined up on the roof of the main building. On the far side of the yard, near the railway line, is the building they called the Pet Lodge. It all comes back to me now, from when I visited as a child. This place went bust a few years ago and stopped giving tours. They said they couldn't afford stock feed and veterinary care anymore. The owners didn't have the heart to send the animals to the slaughter-house, so they gave away the ones they could and left the rest to fend for themselves.

To call Gorgie Farm a true 'farm' stretches the meaning of the word. The size alone puts the claim under quite a bit of stress. The fields below me are tiny in scale. Small enclosures for grazing animals, overgrown now because the livestock has moved on. There's the old sheep pen made of wooden slats, with a flat roof. It's still standing and in good nick. Then there's the cow pen, right at the far end, where I first saw a woolly highland cow.

I don't see anyone about 'cept for two scarecrows out in the yard.

'All clear,' I say to Jomo.

'You sure? Maybe we should give it a few more minutes.'

'I'm going in. Once I'm down, help River over and I'll grab her.'

I pull myself up until my torso's over the wall, gripping with both hands. It's slippery, but I have my arms close together, a narrow base for support. I swing my leg over the top, and that's when one of the stones gives way underneath my fingers. I find myself gripping thin air, tumble over and land hard.

Jomo's head pops over the wall. Hit by the farm's 'revulsion field', as I call it in my head, he fights the unnatural urge to turn away from me until he can look at me square. I give him the thumbs up.

River jumps up beside him and, with the grace of an Olympic gymnast, she vaults the wall and lands – scoring a perfect 10. She saunters down the embankment, comes up to me and licks my face. I'm sure I can detect a hint of vulpine arrogance. She sniffs the air excitedly.

Jomo clambers over without incident and hurries down to squat beside me.

'You okay?'

'Not a scratch.'

'Where to?'

'Keep quiet and follow me.'

It's exposed where we are, so I make a beeline past the raised flowerbeds to stand in the shadow of the farmhouse. The lime-coloured door nearby is padlocked shut. It's the only entrance at the back of the farmhouse. I signal to Jomo and we creep past a bench in the direction of the woodshed, which still has a few logs in situ outside.

Something smells off in the barns. Even in this city of olfactory tragedy, this scent's more pungent and desperate than anything I've encountered before.

I pause to make sure we're alone.

After what feels like an eternity, but is probably a few seconds, we creep on. We're going to have to make it round to the front. I move into the shadow of an old shipping container, the others close behind. Below it, there's a drop to some vegetable beds and disused greenhouses. One of these is a newer model, resembling an arched plastic tunnel. It sits next to a more traditional angular glass structure. Beyond are the chicken coops: open cage installations.

Some of the lights are coming on in the windows of the flats, the ones over on Gorgie Road. I wonder if anyone there's looked down here before and seen anything strange. More likely than not they'd have been hit by the overwhelming urge to look away, as I was earlier. Wouldn't they have been surprised, though, if they found themselves no longer enjoying the view all the way down to St Michael's Church?

The front part of the farmhouse is illuminated by a security light. It's a simple building, with a whitewashed bottom half and a pebbledash finish on the top half. That's where the offices used to be, when the farm was open for business. The building is glued onto the barn, as it were.

'You two stay here. I'm going to scout ahead,' I say.

Jomo seems relieved to wait. He's smart like that. Overkeen and thoughtless doesn't do it for me. River follows his lead, lying belly flat to the floor, ears pricked and twitching. I scurry past the horse trailer, the yellow skip, go by the pens and hide behind a blue recycling bin. My rustling clothes sound mega-amplified here. The slightest noise carries far into the night.

I crouch, making myself as small as possible, and then head for the barn.

There are two wheelbarrows leaning against the wall. A stepladder. Torn bags of rotten grain.

The door's bolted and padlocked.

But through the cracks in the woodwork, I catch movement. There's someone inside. I give the padlock a gentle tug. It's shiny and new. Too new for this place where everything else is going to rust, rot and ruin.

Seconds stretch out into aeons. And I'm caught in the light cast from the windows of the nearby tenements, exposed.

Sometimes locks designed to keep animals in aren't engineered to keep people out. You need something a lot more sophisticated to deter the determined intruder. But this one looks pretty damn functional. The sliding bolt is screwed into the wood of the door and the slot is on the door frame. They're fixed in place with crosshead screws. No way could I break it. I could lever the bolt's lock out of the door, but that's a sure way to make a racket this time of the night.

I take my dagger out and work the screws holding the part that secures the bolt. My blade slips out of the grooves a couple of times, but that's no problem. I work them screws until they're out, then the part securing the mechanism drops to the ground too. I don't even need to deal with the main bolt on the door itself.

Jomo and River peek out from behind the container. I signal for Jomo to hold their position.

I carefully inch open the door into that bleak, dank place, and I see two little girls and a boy lying huddled together in the hay. It's Baltic in here and all they have is the clothes on their backs, the hay and each other for warmth. This ain't no manger and I'm no wise man bearing gifts, so what the hell is going on? I grip my dagger tighter, hit by a spike of rage that runs like fire down every nerve. I notice that their clothes are soiled. And there is food – but the boiled potatoes, peas and carrots have been left in the trough as if for animals.

I stand there in a state of shock, until I'm jolted back to reality by some primitive sense of self-preservation.

I whisper, 'Grace?'

The kids stir. One of the girls turns to face me and I see an aged, weathered face – something no child should have. It isn't Grace, but like Katie and Mark there's nothing in her eyes, no spark of light or vitality. A husk of corn after the grain's been devoured by weevils. I sheathe my blade so as not to spook her.

The pens inside the barn are made of treated wood with metal bars on the doors. At a glance it resembles a jail in a Western. Timber trusses support the roof and there are bare light bulbs hanging down. Only one is working, and that's so messed up that it flickers insistently. The pens run all the way to the far end, where another door leads directly to the offices in the main house.

Wheelie bins and some grain stores sit against the right-hand wall.

An older boy, head around eighty, body maybe seven or eight, lies alone in a pile of hay in the next pen. I've seen two kids gollumed out before, but this one's the worst. There's hints of Nicola in his face too. The nose. That chin.

'Oliver?'

Oh no. No, no, no. What have they done to him? I'm too late. Kicking myself for ever turning Nicola down when she first came to me for help. I take a deep breath and shut my eyes for a sec before opening them again.

He looks at me meekly like a lamb, then lays his head down without making a sound. In the next pen, labelled 'four' in orange paint, sit two girls who might be twelve or so. One of them is blonde with wispy hair and she comes to the gate when she sees me. There are crow's feet around her eyes, but she's nowhere near as wrecked as Ollie or the other girl with her in the pen.

'Help us,' she half whispers.

'I will. I promise. But first tell me, have you seen a girl

about this tall, curly brown hair, big ears? She's been here a couple of days.' I indicate Grace's height with my hand.

'She was in that pen next to mine, but they took her inside.'

I unbolt the door to the blonde girl's cell, and pick up her companion. She's unconscious and I have to swing both her arms over my shoulders and piggy-drag her outside.

'She's just come back from the milking,' the blonde explains.

From the *what-now?*

I point to Ollie's pen next, and she opens it. We get him to follow. Then Jomo spots us and comes to help. Between us we manage to get the three kids out of the barn and find cover behind the container.

'We need to get them over the wall, man,' I say.

Jomo shakes his head. 'No way we can do that. Look how sick they are too. There's a hole in the fence – up front where it meets the wall. I've seen it lots of times on my way to town. Now we know there aren't sentries here, we can get them out through there.'

'You sure they can fit?'

'Easily.'

'Get them out now. I have three more to come. Not including Grace. Hurry.'

He puts the limp child across his shoulder as I did, and leads the others down the stairs, through the veg patch and on to the fence. I shoo at River to make her go with them, just in case.

I dash back to the barn. And I'm halfway there when something bleats to high heaven. The noise cuts through the quiet air like an alarm. The bleating goes on and on, crazed and loud. There's still a goat on the property it seems. I'm guessing goat sees fox and goes ape.

I run into the barn, get the other three kids out of their pen. They start wailing, that anguished inhuman cry I heard from both Mark and Katie.

'It's okay, I'm here to help you,' I say.

Out in the yard we go. Jomo's on his way back to me now and I hand over the kids to him.

'Is that it?' he says.

'Just Grace left. Wait for me at the church. I'll be with you guys soon,' I reply. One to go. I can do it. But where is she? And what the hell is this milking malarkey? I grit my teeth, turn back to the farm and head for hell.

XLI

I stand in the yard, in front of the main farmhouse building. An orange fibreglass calf, life-size, with large black eyes and a donation slit on its back stands begging at the office door. The city farm was always free, and ran on the generosity of the public and grants, until the squeeze hit. There are some bike racks near the wall and further along is a red rust-eaten Massey Ferguson tractor.

I cautiously go to open the front door, which is unlocked – rather to my surprise. Then I enter a room with walls covered in noticeboards from ages ago, displaying yellowed rotas, veterinary charts and posters. Filing cabinets fill up one corner and paperwork rests on countertops.

Something dreadful hangs in the air too. I'm struck by a strong sense of unease; this place reeks of torture and violation. An agonized cry comes from upstairs. I tense up. It's Grace, I know it, but she sounds less child and more primate. It's as if something truly has thrust her right back to basic instincts. I load up my katty and palm an extra rock for a quick reload.

I follow the anguished cries up the stairs, creeping past old photos of farm workers and happy children feeding animals with hay. I make sure I step as lightly as I can so as not to make a sound. The screams hit a crescendo so dreadful that I feel them in my bones, then suddenly, ominously, they fall silent. The hush that follows is even more unbearable.

The cries came from the room just up ahead, and I push open the door.

A woman in a long purple crimplene dress stands with her back to me, next to Grace, who is unconscious, slumped on a dentist's chair in the middle of the room. As I watch, the woman gestures towards Grace with her left hand, while the right clutches an ornate silver and crystal lab flask. A thread of bright white, effervescent fluid appears in the air and arcs down into the container.

I fire, aiming for the back of the woman's head, but the stone veers away, travelling in an unnatural arc around her, and flies through the window. It punches straight through the glass.

'Little girl with green hair, we meet again,' says a familiar voice. 'I knew from the first time I saw you that there was something special there, but I couldn't put my finger on it.'

That voice, the poise, the grace in her movements – everything about her is unreal. I reload with the stone I'd palmed. The woman turns to fully face me now, her dress flowing with her movements.

'Siobhan?' I gasp.

Her luscious hair flows with every gesture she makes, a plastic smile on her face. I take a step back, confused. Like, what the actual . . . This is me and Gran's favourite TV person-ality, so I'm pretty stumped. The Siobhan Kavanagh we all know and love wouldn't be caught dead doing anything like this. She's a freaking national treasure.

That white fluid, the very essence of Grace's youth, hangs in the air like an ectoplasmic discharge.

'Seriously, who brings a catapult to a duel? I like your style,' Siobhan says with a laugh. Her lips are painted purple with glossy lipstick. There's a false freshness to her face, something cherubic masking her real age. There's a cabinet next to her, near the wall and on top of it is a fluid-filled jar. The Midnight Milkman's eyeless head stares back at me and I swallow down my dread, wondering how I'd failed to missed it before. 'I had to say goodbye to him,' Siobhan says.

'Let the kid go, now,' I say. My fingers strain against the katty, rubber stretched to the max. I wanna stick one in her pretty grey eyes.

'Who, her? She's nobody.'

'Her name's Grace, and she has a mum and dad who can't sleep at night because she's missing. She *is* somebody.'

'You know, you remind me of myself when I was your age. Young, poor, seeing everything in black and white. Those were hard times, but I learnt that you have to be willing to do whatever it takes if you want to get ahead. You like helping people, don't you? You even did me a favour, without knowing it. The Milkman, he was stealing from me. Not much – a bottle here, a bottle there, selling off the elixir to undeserving junkies in the street. I suspected it, especially when he came back here battered, without his float. And then some little watchers of mine said he'd killed a 'yang-yang' dealer, and I asked around. That confirmed things for me. Simplified matters. I can't be doing with this – and sisters like us have to do it for ourselves. Do you know how much all this is *worth*?' Siobhan gestures towards a massive shelf stacked with full milk bottles, the silvery contents writhing and twisting. 'The rich want to look young forever. They'll try anything: Botox, plastic surgery, foreskin facials. Parapsychological enhancements for those in the arts business. Renewed vigour for those in ill health. What's wrong with that, I ask you? Some people just want to get high in ways only youth's essence can supply. And youth is out there in abundance. There's nothing a child's potential can't do for you. Ever heard the expression "youth is wasted on the young"? I'm correcting that, and making money. Join me and you can have your share of it too.'

Sounds to me like there's a whole network of buyers behind this racket. Siobhan holds the lab flask aloft. It glows with Grace's freshly stolen essence, the crystal pulsating like a star. Then she sets it on the cabinet next to her.

'Screw you,' I reply.

'Then you choose death. Such a waste,' Siobhan says. And the words sound so strange, coming as they do from this beloved star of the small screen. But before I can take them in, a wave of her hand sends a vase rocketing my way.

I duck just in time and fire towards the wall, deliberately missing to avoid the force field thing that protects her. The stone ricochets and grazes her cheek, drawing ruby-red blood. Siobhan puts her hand to her face, sees the blood and slowly licks it off her fingers – rage coming off her in waves as she glares at me. There's something papery about her skin, the way it dangles off her face from that small cut. And that face is what she sells on telly.

Grace slides down the dentist's chair and collapses onto the ground.

I put the katty in my pocket and draw my dagger. There's no such thing as a fair fight. Once it's on, anything goes. I have a firm grip on the knife, pointy end ready to stab. If it's good enough for rabbits and squirrels, it's good enough for celebrities.

I charge her, slashing this way and that. But she moves out of the way, nimble and quick like a young person. I can't give her time to think, to speak, now I know she can use magic. We circle the room, her eyes locked on mine, filled with malice. It's a calculating look, but this ain't my first rodeo. She waves her hand and a picture frame rips from the wall, careening towards me. I duck, but it swings right back. I block it with my arm, which goes numb as it hits me then crashes to the ground.

Siobhan whispers something and a brass sculpture of a bull rises in the air.

I'm like, fuck me. I need to get up close and personal. Can't win this at range.

She waves a hand and a stool rises up. Then with a flick of her fingers both stool and bull blur towards me. I leap and dodge. The bull flies past my head – but the stool crashes into my shoulder and throws me to the floor, winded. My dagger clatters down beside me. I hurt like hell too. I grab for my dagger as I scramble to my feet. But it whips into the air where it hovers unsteadily, pointing at me. I step back, but it follows me, vibrating rapidly as it does.

Siobhan keeps her hand raised, directing the dagger's movements.

'I could end this right now if I wanted to, but I like you. You've got spunk, and I respect that,' she says. 'You can come work for me and make a shit-ton of money. Think about how much better your life could be. Or you can die right here, right now.'

I stand there bruised, my own dagger aimed at me. Been skint my whole life and here she is offering me a winning scratch card with a few bob on it. No more worrying about rent, or Gran's medication, or Izwi's schooling. The possibility of getting a proper place to live. All that. I also see Grace's tiny body lying on the floor.

'Choose now, I haven't got all night,' Siobhan says. 'You could have beautiful clothes, good food, anything you want. I can make you very rich.'

I exhale and look at the knife, then at her.

'Eat my vag, Siobhan. You can't afford me.'

I dash to the shelf holding Siobhan's precious elixirs, and pull it to the floor. The bottles smash, then milky fluid floats across the room. Siobhan roars, her whole body shaking with rage. Her gracious TV poise has vanished. She flicks her wrist and the knife comes for me. But in a flash, the arm of my scarf reaches out and grabs it from the air – just as the sharp point pricks my breast, above my heart.

I'm like, ninja scarf, where you been all night?

'Die!' Siobhan shouts with a gesture. The air around her takes on a deep purple shimmer.

She tries to thrust the point deeper, but the scarf holds the dagger fast, then pulls it away. Siobhan launches the brass bull and the other end of my scarf grabs it. The scarf chucks it back, forcing her to duck this time.

'Clever,' she says, 'but let's see you stop *this*.'

The air around us fills with mist from the children's essence. I reclaim my dagger and the ends of my scarf whirl around me, ready for action. I'm grateful for the help.

I hear a sharp clinking like crystal. Siobhan raises her arms high, a vein bulging on her forehead. Her lips move furiously as she whispers a spell that lifts the broken glass into the air. Hundreds of pieces, sharp and deadly. I can't outrun them and the scarf can't catch them all. I'm about to be mincemeat.

But my fear turns to rage. Something electric sparks through my entire being. If I'm going down tonight, I'm going down swinging. I think of the children she's hurt, of Paul, of Priya, but most of all, I think of Gran and Izwi waiting at home for me. And I am filled with the anguish of a Titan whose liver was pecked out by a great Caucasian eagle. My tongue loosens, and I cry out:

'PROMETHEUS.'

The room flashes white as a million sparks ignite – it's like a massive old-fashioned chemical flash, the sort paparazzi used to take their pictures. It's blinding, intense, and the room's bathed in searing light. Siobhan covers her face with her hands. I squeeze my eyes shut. The light pierces my closed eyelids, and I can still see dark shapes, outlines, as if I'm seeing with X-ray vision. I hear the glass shards clatter back to the ground. And an acrid chemical smell makes me choke. The air in the room gets so hot I feel like I'm being baked in an oven. Something fast rushes in and leaps onto Siobhan. It's River, and from the wail, I know her sharp teeth have dug into something fleshy.

'Get off me!' Siobhan shouts, wrestling with River.

I run full tilt into Siobhan and shove her straight through the window pane. It breaks and she screams in horror, trying to to grab me – but she's already falling through the air, and she hits the ground a floor below with a sickening thud. All around the farm, in the quiet night air, thousands of sparkling magnesium flames burn like incandescent snowflakes, reflected in the mass of broken glass surrounding Siobhan.

The sparks rain down on the ground. They seek wood and cloth and hay, erupting into vicious white fires that burn with fury. The flames don't roar – they sizzle along the ground like a lit fuse, lighting everything they touch. Around us, the room burns fiercely too. I cough from the smoke.

'Come on, River, let's get out of here,' I say.

I rush to Grace and pick her up, grab the lab flask, and carry both out through the burning flames. It's so bright it's hard to see and the heat makes the air in here hard to breathe. I'm wincing 'cause my shoulder's sore, but I ain't got time to listen to pain. We make it down the burning staircase and out into the burning courtyard. Still the sparks fly and fall around us as though we're inside a firework display. Damn, did I do all this?

Siobhan's lying on hard concrete, neck bent at an inhuman angle. She's shrivelled into a horrifying old crone of a thing, teeth scattered around her like pills. And the wrinkles on her face resemble nothing so much as the cracked surface of a dry pond. Her purple dress spreads round her, more of a shroud than a garment now. Although, insanely, she's still alive.

She twitches, her gaze filled with loathing. She jerks, an anguished laugh escaping as a stream of blood runs out of her mouth. River growls at her.

'You dare think you can stop the work? This is bigger than you know, stupid girl.' She coughs, splatters blood onto the melting snow. 'You think you've won? I've glimpsed your death in my own. You'll die at the hands of the Tall Man. He will get you and I shall live again!'

Siobhan's face contorts and she moans as her body shudders, more blood leaking out of her onto the ground. My guess is the damage is more than the elixir can repair, and she's wilted back to her natural state. Ding-dong, the darkness comes over her at last. She sighs and finally stops moving. But her dead eyes still project unbridled malice. I'm glad me holding Grace is the last thing she sees.

River barks.

'Come on, girl, we're finished here,' I say. I'm done. Ain't got nothing left in the tank. Everything bloody hurts like I'm a hundred and three.

The barns burn. As does the woodshed. The Pet Lodge. Even the trees and shrubs have caught fire.

Let the whole cursed place burn. Burn to ash.

XLII

I'm unsteady on my feet when I get to the church where we agreed to meet. Jomo runs out to help and takes Grace off my hands. My head feels strange, like my thoughts don't stitch up too well 'cause I inhaled some of that dreadful elixir. Colours seem brighter, time stretches out and slows to a crawl. I try to shake it off, clear my head. Smoke's sunk into my clothes and I can smell it on River's fur.

'Give her that,' I say, handing over the lab flask to Jomo.

The children shrink back at the sight of that evil thing. 'It's okay, no one's going to hurt you.'

He puts the ectoplasm under Grace's nose, and it rises like gas and shoots up her nostrils. She wakes with a start, like she's had smelling salts, and starts screaming. I go over to her, show her my face and tell her it's okay.

'I found you. You're safe now,' I say. 'You all are, and tomorrow we'll find your parents and take you home. I promise.'

Breaks my heart to see the children's ruined faces. The things that have been done to them ain't right at all. The things the mighty do to the weak. They'll need help after this, but I'm so, so tired right now. Put my hand on Grace's forehead. It's sweaty and clammy, but I'm sure the kid's going to be okay.

Ollie, on the other hand. The length of time he's been here. The things they've done to him. He's the worst of the lot. Utterly wrecked, spaced out. But all the children are pale, shaken and sickly. Have to get them someplace warm soon.

I send a text to Rob and warn him to prepare for incoming. I can take Ollie to his nan and grandpa, but I figure the other kids can stay at Camelot till we find their people. Not much else any of us can do this time of night.

Rob texts back immediately: 'Stay there. I'll bring the float to pick them up.'

I ping him: 'No. Bring horses and a cart instead. Some blankets too.'

'Understood.'

I don't want the kids seeing that damned float ever again if I can help it. It would spook them out too much.

'Your bike's back there. I got it for you,' says Jomo.

'Cheers,' I say. 'My pal Rob's coming to get you and the kids. Stay put till he arrives. If he's not here within an hour, call me, okay?'

'Are you alright?' Jomo asks.

I shake my head. But it's no use explaining Siobhan's death, the effects of the elixir. The circus has been to town and gone.

'The rest of you stay here with Jomo. He's gonna look after you,' I say. 'Come on, River, we have a long walk back.'

Can't afford to do another night out or Gran will front. And my needle's gone into the red. I walk up to Ollie, take his hand

and collect my bike, which is resting against the church wall. I take off my jacket and put it round Ollie's shoulders, put him on the seat of my bike and wheel it out. It's gonna be a long walk home. The handlebars are wet with dew and the chill nips my fingers. Smoke's rising high up into the sky a short distance away.

What feels a long, long time later, I say goodnight to River as she crawls into her hole under the cara. My girl's done right by me tonight and she deserves a juicy rabbit or something. We'll have to go hunting soon, her and me.

I take off my muddy boots and tiptoe into the caravan, taking Ollie with me. The kid hasn't said one word to me all night. He's bottled up someplace deep inside of himself. It'll take some work to find him and bring him back out into the light again.

Gran's still up, sat in the dark.

'Who's that with you?' she says. 'I see two shadows.' Her eyes are poor in the day and worse in the dark.

'That ghost you asked me to help. This is her missing son,' I say.

'Bring him to me.'

I take Ollie over to Gran and she pats her hand along his body until she finds his face and strokes it. She places both hands on his cheeks for a few seconds and her brow creases with worry. Then she places one hand on his back, the other on his forehead, and whispers, 'Zorora hako, muzukuru.' Ollie slumps, and she rises and eases him onto my bunk. She covers him with a duvet, looks to me and pats the seat next to her.

Bright lights dance inside my eyelids. But I can hear the two people I love most in the world breathing right beside me. I curl up on Gran's bunk, lie down on my good shoulder, place my head on her thigh and soon I'm in New Zzzland.

XLIII

I'm jolted awake by violent banging on the door. I instinctively reach for my dagger before I return to my senses. My whole body aches. Crick in my neck. Oh man . . . I touch my swollen cheek. Shoulder – forget it. Everything hurts, but I get up. Must have got through last night on pure adrenaline. Something smells nice in the kitchen. Gran's spoon-feeding Ollie, and the wee man looks like he's enjoying the broth she's made. He makes gurgling noises with each spoonful he takes.

'Ah ken yous in there, Ropa Moyo,' the troll yells from outside.

'Hold your zebras, I'm coming already,' I say, stifling a yawn.

'Want me to talk to him?' Gran asks. 'I have a little money saved up from my knitting.'

'No, you alright, Gran. I'll take care of it.' I'm just so tired of this crap. Like, give me a break already.

At least it's not the fuzz. I'm in the kitchen before I notice flakes of blood on my hands. Nothing in the tap, so I take a bottle from the fridge and wash up. Shit was real last night. Farmer McAlister doesn't relent with the knocking and I catch his enormous fist when I open the door. Push him backwards

T. L. HUCHU

and shut the door behind me, so Gran doesn't have to put up with his drivel.

'Where's my rent, yer wee snookersmot?'

'I'm sorting it out. I just need a little more time.'

'Aye, same thing you says tae me last time. What you been up tae?'

'Saving the world.'

'Disnae pay my rent now, does it? See, I've been more than reasonable, but you've crossed the line. One more week or you're oot,' the troll says in a huff.

'Okay.'

'I mean it.'

'Good morning to you too,' I say, going back inside and slamming the door in his face.

Two millennia ago, Uncle Tzu wrote in *The Art of War* that the most important thing to do before you set off for conflict is to 'first count the cost'. Emperors and kings have been ruined by marching their men off to battle before they checked it was kosher with the treasury. I went off and did this thing without first making sure I could afford to, and now I have to deal with the consequences. Every minute I spent chasing Siobhan and the Milkman was a minute I didn't spend delivering messages, making money, and it's come to bite me in the arse.

I stand at the sink and wash my face with the rest of the water in the bottle. It soothes the throbbing pain from the swelling there. Take my scarf off and wipe down my neck too. I don't even want to look in the mirror. The frozen peas in the icebox come in handy now. I take the pack and hold it to my cheek.

316

'Come sit with me,' says Gran, patting the spot beside her. She's still feeding Ollie, 'cause even though he likes the grub, he eats super-slow.

I chill next to her and rest against her shoulder.

'What did he say?'

'You know the troll, always moaning about one thing or the other. Nothing new there.'

'Let me help.'

'We need that money for your meds, Gran. The rent's my thing and I'm taking care of it.'

'You can't hold the weight of the world on your shoulders alone, child.'

'I know, Gran, but I have a mighty big lever.'

She puts her arm round me and I sink into her tenderness. The scent of her, the fabric of her dress against my skin. Stuff the rent, this is a good day. My phone rings and I let it be. I'm gonna chill for now, then tonight I'll put my nose back to the grindstone.

XLIV

The long shadows creep across the pits, my base of operations, the old quarry where I run my business. I've rung Jomo and Rob, put them on the case about getting the kids back to their people. The Clan's working pro bono, but Rob's not liking the possible implication of Camelot in this whole mess, in case the pigs get involved at some stage. Best I could do was tell him to keep it hush. File under classified, as in: torch the damned file, shoot everyone involved, and put the gat to your temple level of classified. He got the message.

River's close by and I feel plenty safe knowing she can handle things. I figure once I make a bit of cash, I'm getting her a nice collar – like a medal to say thanks. Nah, she won't go for that. Gran says she's a free spirit. A juicy steak, proper Angus beef, medium rare, sounds more like her sort of thing.

I've brought Ollie to the pits. He's in the new rainbow-coloured cardigan Gran's just finished knitting. It's the right size and fits him perfectly. I'm gonna take the kid to his grandparents later, but first he has to say goodbye to his mum. What's a few more hours after everything that's happened? Slip my backpack off my shoulders and place it on the ground next to River. I open it and get the three bottles of elixir I stashed. Their celestial luminosity brightens the night around me.

Ollie stares at me with large, vacant eyes. Funny thing is, he seemed a bit livelier when he was with Gran. I'm trying to find something of him inside, but the door's closed.

'I need you to lie down here on this nice grass,' I say.

I gently guide him down and use my bag for his pillow. He stares up somewhere past the orange clouds. I pop open the bottle of juice and put it under his nose. The fluid rises up and enters him. His chest expands as if he's being pumped up. Then I get the second and third bottle into him too. He jerks around like a rag doll for a few seconds then stops. His old-looking face, man. The elixir barely made a dent. It's like I tried to blow up a flat tyre with my own lips. I put something in there, but nowhere near what he needs. Damn it.

The effort feels wasted. Maybe I should have saved the bottles for some other kid who was less affected. Grace recovered pretty well once I stuck the stuff back inside of her, maybe 'cause she'd only been at the farm a couple of days.

I sit Ollie up and he makes a sound in his throat. It's not a word, more of a stutter, the precursor to speech. Keep trying, kid. The bastards haven't beaten you, after all. Keep on swinging. I stroke his hair and that's when Nicola appears in front of me. I've never seen her brighter. She's so fully formed that every detail – from the pimples on her forehead to the nails on her hands – is distinctly drawn. She hovers, unsure of what to do, a sorrowful frown on her face.

'What have they done to my baby?' she says, reaching out to touch Ollie's cheek. But her hand passes right through him.

'I'm so very sorry. We just didn't catch him in time,' I say. 'My nan says he'll be okay, in time, given enough care. He needs plenty of TLC, and I know his grandparents will give him that. Kids are strong. He'll bounce back.'

Even in death, a mother's love cannot die. There are bonds that bind us tighter than time and matter and this is one of them. It's elemental, fundamental, woven into the fabric not only of the universe, but of existence itself. It makes death seem so small and petty in comparison to its unalterable grandeur. I see it there in Nicola's face. The way she reaches out across the dimensions to hold her son, even if he cannot consciously know it. But there's something inside of him that must feel it, a surge in his atoms, a profound connection his young mind's incapable of comprehending. But it's there nevertheless.

I kneel there for a few minutes. Nicola's transfixed. She sees nothing but her son, and I guess she's taking it all in, holding it inside, because once again the river of time has begun to flow through her. She must sense its relentless rush, the flitting nature of our material being in the face of something bigger than ourselves.

'He's alive, that's all that matters. Where there's life, there's hope – more so for the dead,' Nicola says at last. 'Thank you.'

'Just doing my job. I'll take him to your folks after.'

'I'm sorry I can't repay you for all you've done for us.'

'Your fee's already been paid in full by an anonymous benefactor,' I say, stroking my scarf.

'That's alright then?'

'Square like a melon.'

'Please tell whoever it is I said thanks from the bottom of my heart. You've done more than I could ever ask for. Ollie is my everything.'

I put my arm around Ollie. Nicola draws back. Not for a second has she taken her eyes off the boy. But now she lets go and turns her eyes to the rapidly darkening sky as night falls. The winter air fills with the scent of jasmine. Then Nicola bursts into white petals that colour the gloom, drifting high up into the night. She's going to the place with long grass, where the hurts of this world cannot salt her mahewu.

This job's done, as far as I'm concerned. I reach over and pat River. Good feeling in my bones, positive vibrations in the air after Nicola's fireworks. The only way's up from here, I reckon. I need to have an intense week. Double my deliveries. Give the troll part-payment to shut him up. Happy days. Should be a boom in business tonight 'cause it's been a while. Messages will be piling up – I hope. That should get me back on track nicely, and with the bike back, I can do double the number of stops and stretch my range. Yep, good vibes. Now all I've got to do is wait for my other customers to show up, then I'll take Ollie home.

Watching the fringes of the pits for the deados to appear, I take out my phone and check the time. It's getting on. Where is everybody? I sit down on the swing. River's pacing about, getting impatient. Can't blame her. Where *are* they?

A reddish light somewhere in the treeline. Here we go. This never gets old. It does the weird ghost dance, appearing nearby then far away. River pricks up her ears. Twinkle, twinkle, little ghost. It comes closer and I get up to say hello.

Gutted. It's only Kenny from Clermiston. Doesn't seem to have worked out his form either. Still looks like a misshapen gummy bear. Kenny's booga-woogaring and gesticulating while he's at it too. The things I must endure. Anyway, gotta keep it pro. I take my mbira, twang it to get the harmonics sorted for him. He has a different wavelength to Nicola's. On a night like this, I reckon I'll hit him with 'Nhemamusasa', the 1972 Mhuri yekwaRwizi rendition. Requires an accompanying leg rattle instrument to get the full effect. But for talking, you only need the mbira. In my head, I can even hear Hakurotwi Mude chanting to the beat.

'Hey, Kenny,' I say. 'Look, I'm hoping you're not wasting my time – and you've got dosh sorted for any messages you want sent through.'

'That's disrespectful,' he replies.

'Actually, it's called business.'

'And it's booming, right?' he says, sweeping round in the darkness. 'Where is everyone?'

Strange, they really should be here by now. I've been expecting more lights to show up in the void for the last hour, but there's nothing.

'I'll tell you where they are,' he says. 'They got tired of your crummy service. "Oh, I can't be arsed showing up till whenever. Hold those messages until my royal behind is good and ready." You're unreliable.'

'What you on about?'

'Everyone's gone off to find a new medium or clairvoyant. You're not the only game in town, you know.'

Sinking feeling in my stomach right now. Deados from this end of town are going all the way down to Leith for this clairvoyant I heard about? River senses something's amiss and cocks her head. I'm trying to absorb all of this. I look in the distance and see nothing but shadows. Check the time on my phone again. No one's coming out tonight, save for this strawberry jam knobhead.

'You're so done. But I can help you with the departed community,' says Kenny. There's an annoying arrogance about him. He's enjoying this a little too much for my liking. 'Do a couple of messages for me for free, and I'll spread the word, tell them you're back and better than ever. I'll even start a campaign on your behalf. You do that for me and I could be your hype man. It's a win-win.'

I have to give him points for taking the initiative. Sweet deal for him: free service in exchange for some word of mouth. Problem is, I need cold cash now-now. No one survives on clicks and likes these days. Butter, cheddar, guap, that's what it's about.

I'm so screwed. Took my eyes off the prize. Slept at the wheel. I know the score.

Stop playing my mbira and pack it in my bag. I call River and tell her it's time to go. Kenny's booga-woogaring, waving his arms about, pleading, but I don't pay him no mind. All I can do now is to take Ollie home.

XLV

I'm kinda stressed out this afternoon, body aching all over, but I still meet up with Priya in the coffee shop on Elm Row for a wee debrief. Since I'm skint, insolvent, broke, indigent, she's paying. I order a mocha with marshmallows sprinkled on top to get my kick. Priya's looking dapper with her leg and arm casts. Says she has bruised ribs too. For some reason, though, Priya's all energized, like she's got a buzz out of the whole thing. Her eyes are bright and full of mischief.

'I wish I'd been there,' she says, after I tell her about Gorgie Farm, Siobhan, the kids, what Siobhan said about the Tall Man, all of it.

'No, you really don't,' I say. 'Anyway, what do you think I should do with this?'

I bring out the accursed lab flask from my bag and place it on the table. It looks beautiful and ordinary now, without its vile contents. But part of me is repulsed, because I know what it's been used for. It's a reminder of what has been done to innocent little children. I don't find the scattering light passing through the crystal seductive at all.

'You shall form a fellowship and travel east to Mordor, and

324

there cast it into the fires of Mount Doom where it was forged,' Priya faux-quotes in a fake baritone voice and laughs.

'Hilarious,' I say, keeping a straight face.

'Come on, finish your drink. We're meeting Jomo on Calton Hill. He'll come out when he's finished his shift,' she says.

I push my bike, walking beside Priya in a new wheelchair. It's an electric one, and she tells me she's had it for ages, but seldom uses it because it's not great for exercise. She prefers a manual chair but is forced to use this one since she's only got one arm at the moment — 'I'd be going round in circles all day if I tried to do it one-handed.'

'Can I hop in again?' I jest.

'Only in emergencies.' She laughs. 'Text Jomo to let him know we're coming.'

'I'm way ahead of you on that one.'

We make it to the top of the hill in time to catch the setting sun. Across the valley, smoke rises from the campfires in Camelot, and I picture bearded men squatted round boiling kettles. Clumps of snow remain tucked in the grass. They have a glassy look and will be joining the meltwater streams soon. We wait by the pillars of the unfinished temple, watching birds fly and the clouds drift through the sky.

Jomo comes out from behind the third pillar in due course, looking smart in his uniform. He opens his arms wide, cheesy grin on his face.

'Ropamatic and Priyasaurus,' he says.

'How come I'm the prehistoric one?' Priya asks.

'Because Ropa's the daddy – she's swimming in the green stuff.' Jomo reaches into the pockets of his white vestments and brings out a wad of cash, which he hands over to me.

'What's all this?' I ask, startled.

'Rob says that's your half from the sale of the milk float. He seemed pretty impressed with all this. Actually, I hope you don't take offence – as I know you don't do that stuff no more – but he says you can call him any time for a job.'

'Nae chance,' I say, splitting the bundle of cash three ways.

The big band of stress that had tightened around my chest releases and I can breathe again, stop worrying about having to leave HMS Hermiston and find new digs. This more than covers my rent arrears. I make to hand Priya and Jomo their share of it and they shake their heads in unison.

'I've already got a job that pays really well, thank you very much,' Priya says.

'And I've got a job that's not paying me at all, but I live at home – what do I need all that for?' says Jomo with a shrug.

'This was a team effort, guys. You've earned your cut,' I say, offering the money again. It's the principle.

'You can buy us dinner tonight, how about that?' Priya says.

'I'm all for that. There's a really cool ice-cream parlour on the Mile that I've been wanting to go to forever,' Jomo says, lighting up like a little kid.

'Clearly you and I have very different definitions of what constitutes dinner,' Priya replies drily. 'Go get changed out of that. We'll meet you at the bottom of the hill.'

'Don't leave without me,' Jomo says, dashing behind the pillar. He pokes his head out just before he heads back down to the library and adds, 'Oh, and Rooster Rob says you owe the Clan now, for looking after the kids.'

'I already figured,' I say as he vanishes through the crack.

Me and Priya are making our way down the path, past the empty stand where the old cannon used to be, when we spot Callander coming up the stairs. He puffs, out of breath, and uses the handrail for support. That is, until he sees us and straightens up. It costs him quite a bit of effort to reach us.

'Ladies,' Callander says in his old-fashioned way. He looks Priya over. 'What happened to you, Miss Kapoor?'

'I fell,' she replies.

'Hmm, and what about your face, Miss Moyo?'

'I fell too,' I reply.

'I should think both of you ought to be more careful in future.'

'Go on. Give it to him,' Priya says.

I open my backpack and take out the lab flask. The crystal scatters the light of the setting sun as I hand it over to Callander. He holds it close to his face and turns it round as though inspecting a precious antique. A grunt escapes his throat.

'This is a corrupt replica of the Gray's intromissioner, itself an ingenious remodelling of the simple Erlenmeyer flask. It was an experimental device used by healers during the Great War, to try and save troops who were too far gone for conventional treatments. The idea was to transfer the vital force from fit soldiers to their ailing comrades – using magical science, of course. But it was discontinued because the results for the patients were poor and the side effects for donors deemed unacceptable. But it should never have been allowed in the first place – the practice was abhorrent. So I'm concerned as to why you have this one. Does it have something to do with those missing children you came to me about, Miss Moyo?'

I bite my tongue, because I want to say, 'Yeah, the ones *you* refused to help,' but I hold my peace. Priya nods when Callander looks at her instead.

Callander throws the flask up into the air, but it doesn't fall. It stays hovering against the orange sky as he holds out his hands and slowly brings them together. The flask makes a high-pitched screeching sound – and then it implodes, just as Callander's hands clap together. The vile thing is now dust to be scattered in the wind. It will never be used to hurt anyone again.

'I heard news of a strange fire that raged through the night on Gorgie Farm,' Callander adds. 'They say firefighters couldn't put it out until everything was burnt to a cinder. Strange lights were seen in its depths and they found the curious remains of a lab within. Does this have anything to do with that? The Society will be looking into it, naturally,' Callander says, turning back to us gravely. 'A charred body was found there too. What do you ladies know of it?'

Priya opens her mouth, but I cut in quickly. 'Nothing whatsoever,' I reply.

'That's a lie, but it's the correct answer. Discretion is the better part of valour in this age we're living in. You've done well,' he says. 'Come with me, both of you. We have much to discuss.'

'Nah, maybe another time,' I say. Priya's eyebrows pop up in no small amount of astonishment, while Callander remains expressionless. 'We've already got plans for tonight after a tough few days. Come on, Priya, the ice cream's melting.'

Priya cringes and starts up her wheelchair, slowly setting off. I stand there for an extra second, with Callander glowering, before his face softens a fraction. He nods and puts his hands behind his back, swallowing his exasperation

'I expect you'll be in touch at your earliest possible convenience,' he says.

'That scarf you gave me – it keeps my neck real warm,' I say.

'That's what scarves are supposed to do. The hard part is keeping your head on your shoulders,' he replies, turning away and continuing towards the pillars.

Priya's still got the cringe written all over her face when I catch up with her, but her grimace transforms into a half-smile.

'You've got balls the size of kettlebells, I'll give you that,' she says.

'So do you,' I reply.

'You know, I was wondering – who on earth is this Tall Man, anyway?' Priya asks.

'I don't know, Siobhan must have been delirious at the end. She was thinking of her Midnight Milkman, I reckon. He was pretty tall.'

'But she'd already offed him, so . . .' she says.

'Screw it. I've had enough of all that. Let's go get ice cream, man. I want a whole tub of cookies and cream flavour to myself. With sprinkles . . . And hot fudge, no, make that a caramel topping. Or both, I'll have both.'

I don't wanna think about anything to do with this anyway. We won, Siobhan's dead and can't hurt any more kids, end of. I'm well zonked here and fed up with all this stress. I've got my life back and now I'm gonna have ice cream with my new bestie and my day one. After that, I'll go home and hang out with my two favourite girls and my super-cool vulpine companion.

My life's brilliant, if I do say so myself. I hope that it will stay that way for a while too.